At the age of eighteen, Alice Peterson had been awarded a tennis scholarship to America when she experienced pain in her right hand. It was rheumatoid arthritis and she hasn't picked up a tennis racket since. She has written two non-fiction books, a personal story called *A Will to Win*, which has been updated and republished as *Another Alice*, and a family memoir based on her grandmother's life in Rhodesia. Two novels followed, published by Black Swan. The theme of disability features in her fiction but there is nothing gloomy about Alice or her work. Rather, this gives her fiction the added dimension of true poignancy.

Also by Alice Peterson

Another Alice
You, Me and Him
Look the World in the Eye
M'Coben, Place of Ghosts

Alice Peterson

MONDAY TO FRIDAY MAN

Quercus

First published in Great Britain in 2011 by Quercus
This paperback edition published in 2012

Quercus
55 Baker Street
7th Floor, South Block
London W1U 8EW

A CIP catalogue record for this book
is available from the British Library

ISBN 978 1 78087 238 4

10 9 8 7 6 5 4 3 2

Typeset by Ellipsis Books Limited, Glasgow
Printed and bound in Great Britain by Clays Ltd, St Ives plc

To Bernice and Zek in memory of Alice

I

'You slot the capsule into the machine like so,' the shop assistant demonstrates, positioned in front of a deluxe coffee machine. Her red hair is pinned back into a tight ponytail that swishes from side to side. 'Press the cappuccino button and there you go!'

'Wonderful,' I say, as the gleaming machine gurgles, churns and froths the milk. This Italian coffee-maker was one of the wedding presents I had to return reluctantly.

For the finishing touches she sprinkles chocolate powder into the mug and hands it to me. I take a sip.

'Well, what do you think?' she asks.

And that's when I see him.

I stare into his face.

I knew that one of these days we would bump into one another.

After all we both live in Hammersmith.

I'm still not ready to face him.

My eye is drawn to the watch I gave him for his birthday two years ago. I remember putting it round his wrist, Ed leaning across to kiss me.

Now he can't even look me in the eye.

A fair-haired woman approaches with a piece of paper in her hand. 'Edward, darling, have we put the Le Creuset casserole dishes . . .' She stops, sensing the awkward atmosphere. 'On to our list?' she finishes, glancing at me and then back to him.

'We need to go,' is all he can say.

The glamorous woman whose groomed appearance gives the impression that she lives in a health spa waits to be introduced, but instead Ed takes her arm and firmly leads her out of the shop.

I exit the cookware department without my deluxe coffee machine and step numbly onto the escalator, clutching the handrail, tears stinging my eyes. I can't believe he's getting married! Six months and he's moved on. How could he?

I overhear hushed voices.

'Hang on . . . Gilly? Oh my God! *That was* Gilly?' Her powerful scent fills the air.

'Don't talk too loud,' he insists, before adding, 'we'll come back later.'

'You'd better not walk out on me,' she says, glancing over her shoulder.

I watch them leave the shop.

When it's safe to follow, I walk out of the double doors, catching a reflection of myself with froth decorating my top lip.

2

'This is Dorset FM playing you your favourite *hot* summer tunes,' the smooth-voiced radio presenter says, 'and here's another great track from a singer who needs no introduction.' Next I am belting out, 'Dancing on the Ceiling' by Lionel Richie as I drive into the open countryside.

Ruskin, my dog, barks in protest on the back seat, before sticking his nose out of the window again, enjoying the wind against his face.

'What's wrong, Rusk?' I call, glancing over my shoulder towards him. 'I have the voice of an angel!'

He barks again, clearly saying I haven't and that he's not too keen on my musical taste either. He's always been more of a Bach and Mozart man.

I pull over into the side of the road to let a tractor crawl past.

I think I needed to bump into Ed last weekend. I really do.

'Nearly there, sweetheart,' I promise Ruskin.

Following a friendly exchange between the tractor driver thanking me for waiting, and me thanking him for thanking me, I drive on.

I'm not going to dwell on it, I tell myself.

Ed looked handsome. Slim and tanned. I'd saved up for months to buy him that watch. I grip the steering wheel. 'Look, Ruskin, isn't it stunning? Look at the sheep and all this green space and blue sky! We are going to *love* it here!'

I'm convinced Ruskin and I should move out of London and make a new start in the country. I will miss London; I have so many happy memories. Dancing on Friday nights with my friends. Staying up until five in the morning and then enjoying lazy breakfasts as the sun rose. On Saturday nights Ed and I would usually go to a party or dinner and when we returned home, we'd carry on drinking cocktails and stick some music on and be silly. I loved those evenings. The museums are some of the best in the world . . . though it is true to say I don't make the most of them. Spitalfields and Camden markets on a Sunday. Ed introduced me to opera. I was never sure I was going to like it, but I found myself falling in love with my evenings at Covent Garden. It's where he proposed.

It is hard to imagine living somewhere else . . . except

recently . . . well, recently things have changed. For me London's lost its shine. Maybe that's because I'm single and many of my married friends have moved away. Only this morning did I receive yet another change-of-address card from an old school friend of mine, and on this card was a black-and-white illustration of a family waving goodbye as they ascended the sky in a hot air balloon, with the caption above, THE DIGBYS ARE TAKING OFF!

I drive past a thatched cottage, the front door open, letting in the sun. Now where in London would you be able to do this? Certainly not in Hammersmith, where I zigzag the pavements, avoiding one dodgy-looking person after another.

Late at night all I hear now are drunken voices outside my bedroom window and I wake the following morning to find shards of glass on the road. My car was broken into last week. Admittedly I was stupid enough to have left my gym kit on the back seat. The bastards took all of my CDs except for *The Best of Girls Aloud*.

I arrive in a sleepy market-town square and park right outside Hunters Estate Agents. As I unbuckle Ruskin from his seatbelt, I spot my *A–Z* squashed under the passenger seat, keeping company with an empty plastic water bottle, a heap of crumpled parking tickets and . . . what the hell's that? It's some old tangerine peel. I'll do a major tidy-up later.

Examining the parking sign, I discover with delight that I don't have to pay. In London I can barely utter my name without being charged, so that's another good reason to leave.

I open the door and walk into the middle of the room, Ruskin pulling me along at a pace towards a man sitting behind his desk.

'Gilly?' He stands up to shake my hand. 'Gilly with a G?' he adds cautiously with a wry smile.

I smile back, amazed by his memory. Dad used to say that I'd tell everyone I was different because my name was spelt with a 'G' and not a 'J'. I think the last time I met Richard was in Dad's kitchen. I must have been about ten; Richard would have been in his late teens. He had longish dark hair, was loud and confident. I remember thinking his cowboy boots were trendy. He'd come over for tea with his father.

I look at him now, guessing he must be in his mid-forties. I thought he'd be taller, but then everyone is big when you are still growing up. He's solid in build with a crushing handshake and . . . oh my God . . . such terrible dress sense now! Why is he wearing a glaring yellow tropical shirt with pineapples on it? He must be going through a midlife crisis.

'Good to see you again,' Richard says, 'it's been a long time. How's your dad?' Richard is my father's godson, and it was Dad who had suggested I see him if I really was keen on moving to the country. Richard's father,

7

Michael, and my dad met during their National Service and have kept in touch ever since. I remember Michael and my father reminiscing about getting up early in the morning to polish the toecaps of their boots until they shone like the sun, and constantly being shouted at by the sergeant. I had enjoyed listening to their stories.

'Please, take a seat,' he says, surveying me in my denim miniskirt, shades and pink Birkenstocks. I take off my sunglasses. Behind Richard's desk, mounted on the wall, is a large black-and-white framed photograph of an aerial view of Dorset. 'Cute dog,' he comments.

'Thanks.' I glow with pride. Ruskin is my rescue dog, five years old and a terrier of some kind with a tail like a palm tree, thick sturdy legs and a handsome head too large for his body. Children laugh when they see him but always want to stroke him. To my mind, he's the most loyal man in my life and I won't hear a word said against him.

After briefly exchanging news about each other's dads, Richard gets down to business. 'So you're looking to buy in this area?'

'That's right. I want an adventure,' I say boldly. There's no reason why I can't take off like the Digbys, I think to myself.

'I can't remember . . . do you have family here?'

'Yes, yes. My Aunt Pearl used to live in . . .' I narrow my eyes, trying to remember. 'Tolpuddle. That's it. Tolpuddle.' I remember, as a child, being sent off to Aunt Pearl's during the summer holidays with my twin, Nick.

We enjoyed it. She'd take us to lots of different beaches, and Nick and I climbed rocks and played ducks and drakes in the sea.

Richard crosses his arms. He has a strong square face, curly dark-brown hair and thick eyebrows.

'Anyway, I drove through some lovely villages this morning.' I decide not to tell him that some of these villages seemed half-dead, 'and saw a cottage for sale in . . . Poddlehampton, or was it Puddletown . . . Puddle-something anyway.'

'Piddlehinton.' He's trying not to smile. 'Would you like a coffee or tea?'

'Oh. A cappuccino please.'

'You're not at Foxtons.'

I blush. 'Instant's great, thanks.'

He heaves himself out of his chair, walks up a couple of steps, and then he's out of sight.

I look around the office restlessly before reaching down to stroke Ruskin, who's lying under my chair.

I gaze out of the window, telling myself not to think about bumping into Ed and his new wife-to-be any more. When I'd stared into his face all I could think was I used to wake up to that face each morning. I know his every line, the shape of his mouth, the story behind his faded scar on the left-hand side of his forehead. I look down at my hands. She wouldn't wear chipped nail varnish, or bite her nails. I wonder if Ed has told her the story behind his scar?

I am jolted from my thoughts by noise and cursing coming from the kitchen, and Richard asking me if I want milk and sugar. It sounds as if he's having a fight with the mugs and the kettle is about to explode. As I watch a doddery man shuffle past outside, pushing a trolley on wheels, a ripple of panic sets in. What am I going to do here? Would I find a job easily? I'd miss my father if I left London. He lives in our old run-down family home by Regent's Park. I don't think he wants me to move, but you can never quite tell with Dad. I know Anna doesn't want me to go. Like me she's single, and she and I are like sisters. I'd miss my twin, Nick, too. I'd especially miss his children. Still, they could all come and stay, couldn't they, in my idyllic country cottage with pale-pink climbing roses and a pretty front gate. I can see the girls now, running bare-foot around my lawn laughing and playing under the sprinkler. In the evenings we'd have fun picking rasp-berries from my garden.

I stroke Ruskin, thinking how much I'd also miss my Ravenscourt Park dog-walking friends. We've become an institution that meets every morning at eight o'clock, under the oak tree, come rain or shine.

God, I'd miss Susie too. Her daughter, Rose, is my goddaughter.

Then I think of Ed, again. 'Oh, my God, *that was* Gilly,' she'd said. I can't bump into her again.

'Gilly?' Richard hands me my coffee.

'I'm sorry.' I take the mug, thanking him. 'I was a world away.'

'Remind me, have you sold your London place yet?'

'No. It's all early days but . . .'

'What do you do, Gilly?'

'Good question.' I smile as I clear my throat. 'I work in my friend's antiques shop.'

'Right.'

'It's only temporary,' I rush to tell him. 'I used to work for this company that hired out locations for photo shoots, adverts, conferences, that kind of thing, but it went bust under new management. She was terrible, the boss . . .' I rub my hands together, realizing Richard doesn't need to hear all the details. 'Anyway, I'm just helping this friend out over the summer, until I move. Now, you said over the phone that you had a few houses within my budget?'

He shuffles some sheets together and a few fly onto the floor, which he doesn't bother to pick up. 'OK, let's start with this one.'

It's a thatched cottage. The kitchen has a black-and-white chequered floor and an ancient-looking cooker. 'It's on the main road to Dorchester,' Richard says.

Scanning the details, I search to say something positive, but . . . 'It looks *a little bit* pokey.'

'Too right! Awful place,' he agrees.

I watch him curiously as he produces another sheet, this one revealing a white cottage with a front garden and shutters over the windows.

'The thing is,' Richard begins, sensing I like it, 'it's down a steep hill and come the winter you'll be trapped if there's snow.'

'Is it a lively place?'

'Um, now what do you mean by lively?'

'Well, it would be nice to meet some people my age.' How about an attractive country gentleman who owns two golden Labradors, and who enjoys coastal walks and romantic meals by the fire? And dancing. Got anyone like that hiding in your filing cabinet?

Richard taps his fingers against the desk. 'I forget who lives there apart from the vicar and his wife. She, poor thing, has been laid up for months, fell into her wheelie bin and skidded down the hill.'

I can't help smiling at that.

He shows me another tiny cottage in a village that seems to consist solely of three houses and a postbox. The windows are the size of matchboxes and the curtains are drawn. I know I have a small budget, but come on!

'Right.' He pauses, looks tentative, but continues, 'Listen, are you sure you want to move?'

'Sorry?' I say, just as my mobile rings and Ruskin barks. Flustered, I reach for my handbag and rummage around in it, aware that Richard is watching me. All manner of things come out: diary, bronzing powder, Oyster card, lipstick, even Ruskin's poop-scoop bags. I'm sure mobiles conspire to hide the moment they call.

At last, you little devil. 'Sorry, what was that?' I switch it off.

He surveys my long dark-brown hair pinned back with a navy spotted scarf, my bangles and turquoise suede handbag; next he casts an eye down to my bare wedding finger. 'I'm not sure the countryside is a place for . . .'

'Single women?'

He strokes his chin, nods.

'I have thought about this,' I admit, 'but . . .'

'People will be suspicious of your motives in moving here.'

I look at him, puzzled.

'You won't get invited out much if that's what you think. No invitations winging their way through your door I'm afraid.'

I smile nervously. 'Why not?'

He leans in close towards me. 'Women will feel threatened.'

'No they won't. What do you mean?' I add.

'Believe me, it happens. They'll be scared you'll run off with their husbands. You're a good-looking girl,' he says, with a sparkle now in his eye.

'Running off with women's husbands is not my style, believe me. And if they wear pineapple shirts like yours, there's no chance,' I add, beginning to relax. 'I just need a change.'

'These villages are idyllic right now, but come winter no one will darken your doorstep,' he claims.

'Of course they will! I'll make sure friends visit me all the time.'

'What are you doing to do stuck down here? Play bridge?'

'I'll get a job. It'll be fun!'

'You haven't thought this through, have you?'

'I have! I want to be somewhere different. I want a garden for Ruskin and I want . . . I want a healthier life. Clean fresh air.'

'It smells of silage round here,' he laughs.

'Oh, don't be so stupid. I'll have a lovely garden where I can grow my own vegetables and fruit,' I insist. 'Raspberries, potatoes and . . . and . . . purple sprouting broccoli!'

'If you think you're lonely now . . .'

'Lonely! I'm not lonely.' I bend down to stroke Ruskin, curled up with his face resting on my feet.

'Why are you really moving?'

'What?' I daren't look up. His question takes my breath away.

'Gilly, someone once told me I should leave London only when I hated it, when I'd squeezed all the juice out of it. Stupidly I didn't take their advice and I miss it like mad. I'm not sure you've reached that stage yet.'

I picture Ed again and at last some courage fires up in my belly.

'Want to bet?'

He nods.

'I'm tired of the same old scenery. I've become immune to the wailing sirens and accidents that happen right under my nose. I hate paying the fucking congestion charge, Ruskin has no garden, just paving stones, hardly any of my friends still live in London and . . . and . . . the ones that do only invite me round for tea where I have to listen to their screaming children demanding ice cream in a cone not a bowl!'

I breathe again. My God, that felt good.

'I don't have a job, well, not a proper job right now,' I continue, like a pressure cooker letting off steam. 'I'm free and single so I have nothing to lose, right? So what if I'm single? What if I never meet anyone, Richard? If I just live my whole life in London and then get buried in Hammersmith too? I'm scared, I'm . . .'

He sits up. 'You're scared?'

'I'm so angry with myself.'

'Why?'

And then the strangest thing happens. I start to cry and Richard is handing me tissues and telling me to let it all out, his voice now soft, as though he's my therapist.

'I'm sorry,' I say eventually, wiping my eyes. 'I'm really all right . . .' I falter. 'Oh God, Richard,' I exclaim, knowing I can't fool him now, 'I'm so embarrassed! I haven't seen you in such a long time, and here I am breaking down in front of you.'

What must he think of me?

'You don't need to be sorry.' Richard smiles. 'Happens all the time.' I find myself smiling back at him. 'But tell me,' he asks gently, 'what is it?'

I sigh. 'I still love him,' I say.

Richard listens patiently as I fill him in on my four-year relationship with Ed and how it ended abruptly, only two weeks before our Christmas wedding. There was no explanation from him except for a scribbled note on the hall table that read, 'I can't do it. I can't marry you.'

'Do you sometimes feel like you're sitting on the sidelines, that you're watching everybody's life move on except your own?' I ask him.

'Often.'

I tell him that I'd bumped into Ed and his future wife in Selfridges.

'God, Richard, I'm stuck in a rut.' I wait for him to say something comforting. 'Tell me what I should do.'

'You need to stop feeling so sorry for yourself and get on with it.'

'What?' I say, taken aback by the sudden change of tone.

'I feel for you, Gilly, I really do. What this Ed did was unforgivable, but it's been six months. You need to move on.'

'I know,' I say, bottom lip quivering.

'Moving here isn't right. You're running away.'

I fiddle with the strap of my handbag. 'You're married aren't you, Richard?'

'Divorced. It's a lonely business. Believe me, I've felt like running away too.'

I glance at him, surprised by this sudden confession.

'If I were you, Gilly, I'd go back to London with my lovely dog and start having some fun again. What are you smiling about?' he asks me now.

'Going back home. London's dirty, so expensive and everyone's rude,' I add. 'You wouldn't believe it, but the other day I was told to fuck off by a drunk on my own doorstep who then proceeded to chuck his beer can at me.'

Richard smiles.

I tell him how Gloria, my neighbour, had asked me if I had a new lodger who'd forgotten his key.

'Oh my God!' he exclaims as he rolls up his glossy property magazine and thumps it against the table in triumph. 'I've got it,' he says, sounding like Professor Higgins. 'Get a lodger.'

'A lodger?'

He crosses his arms with satisfaction. 'Yes! I was only reading about it in the paper the other day and how everyone's renting out their spare room. Hang on, you've got a spare room, right?'

I nod. 'A very small one.'

'There you go then.'

'Oh, I don't know.' I need time to warm up to ideas.

'It's an easy way to make some money,' he tempts me.

I think about this. Since being made redundant from my last job my salary has plummeted. Mari, my dog-walking friend who owns the antiques business, can't afford to pay me much more than the going rate for working in a shop. Recently I've been making my own packed lunch to save some cash.

'I'm too old for a flatmate, I've done all that. I'm too set in my ways now.'

'Well, unset.'

Next thing I know he's ushering Ruskin and me out of the door. 'What are you doing?' I say in protest as he propels me out into the fresh air.

'Taking you out for lunch.'

'Hang on . . .'

'There's a good pub across the road. Clearly you need convincing,' he finishes.

3

I am scrolling through the job section of my newspaper when Mari staggers into the shop carrying a marble bust. She's just returned from a stock-buying trip in France. 'Look at this handsome fellow, Gilly!' She lowers him onto the sofa. Ruskin and Basil, Mari's Jack Russell, reluctantly make room. 'Isn't he gorgeous?'

He is, but where is he going to live for the next few months? The long oak table in the middle of the room is already piled high with treasures. 'Is there a lot?' I ask, following her outside.

'Less than last time, more than the time before.'

Soon I'm helping Mari unload the stock from her battered old white van, vases and lanterns littering the pavement. 'All they need is a glaze and rich fabric cushions,' Mari says, when she sees me raise an eyebrow at a set of rusting garden chairs.

★

Mari, short for Marigold, is one of my most flamboyant dog-walking friends. She's in her late forties with jet-black hair cut into a chic bob, and today she's wearing a lime-green jumpsuit. I first met her four years ago in Ravenscourt Park, standing under the shade of an oak tree near to the underground station. She was smoking a menthol cigarette in between hurling a ball for Basil to retrieve. Mari is divorced with no children. 'I never wanted them,' she told me on one of our walks. 'I only wanted a dog.'

Her shop, along the Pimlico Road, specializes in antique chandeliers, mirrors, lanterns and vases, and she's just been to various *brocantes* to find bargains. Mari has a great eye; she picks things up that most of us would walk straight past. With a bit of sprucing up, she can see that what is underneath the cobwebs, dead flies and dust is in fact a Georgian chandelier.

'Now this is interesting,' Mari tells me, both of us crouched down on the floor looking at a large, circular, silver light. 'I would think it was made in the twenties,' she guesses, 'and used by surgeons to perform operations. Some clever person had the idea of taking the design from the eighteenth-century peasant lights.'

'It's beautiful,' I say, imagining it in my own fantasy French rustic kitchen.

'What I love about antiques is they're dead people's stuff,' Mari states. 'Think of all the fabulous parties this light has witnessed,' she says, gesturing to one of her new chandeliers that looks as if it's come from the rubbish dump.

'Yes, yes, but when Bob gets his hands on it, it'll be perfect.' Robert Chamarette is Mari's glass and metal man, whom Mari loves almost as much as Basil. 'Think of all the servants that have polished her,' she continues, 'all the scratches and knocks she's had, and somehow she's found her way into my shop.'

'How much did it cost?'

'Oh, Gilly,' she tuts. 'It's not how much "it" cost. It's how much I can sell it for.'

Later that day, when Mari is out meeting a journalist who wants to hire some chandeliers for a *Hello!* photo shoot, I continue to scan the jobs section of my news-paper, but no jobs leap off the page. Maybe that's because I just can't face any more interviews? I think I'd rather endure root-canal treatment than be subjected to more rejections. I shut my eyes, remembering them . . .

Interview One: 'Gilly Brown, would you like to go in?' the glamorous receptionist asks me. This job is in the fashion business, working for a dress-design company, so I've gone out of my way to look the part, wearing a fitted dress with new gladiator-style ankle boots.

As I walk into the interview room, towards a stylish woman with blonde hair sitting behind her glass desk, I trip on the edging of the carpet, lose my balance and virtually fly towards her, finishing my grand entrance with a crash-landing into my seat. Straight away I know I haven't got the job, rather like when I took my driving test and bumped up and over the pavement within the first minute.

Interview Two: 'What are your strengths and weaknesses?' he asks. I've applied for a job in a bank.

'I'm very good with people, but *terrible* with figures,' I claim proudly. Why is he looking at me like that?

Interview Three: 'And you can work long hours, right?' This interview is for a hot-shot advertising company and to my amazement it's going really well.

'Absolutely,' I reply. 'I will put in one hundred and ten per cent. I won't let you down.' Under the desk I cross my fingers. I've always hated that one hundred and ten per cent expression, but judging from his beaming smile, he loves it.

He stands up and leans towards me. 'Are you hungry, Gilly?'

I glance at my watch. 'Well, come to think of it, I am a bit peckish,' I say, wondering where he's going to take me for a celebratory lunch to announce I've got the job.

'I meant hungry for success,' he says quietly.

I open my eyes and find myself laughing. Oh God. I failed so badly at the last fence. Needless to say I didn't get that job either and after a series of rejections I really lost my nerve and confidence, so when Mari asked me if I would like to replace her old assistant, I said yes immediately. I thought a temporary job could be the perfect opportunity to clear my head, earn some money, really think about what to do next and brush up on my interview skills. My friends and family had smiled when I told them I was working in an antiques shop. Anna, my best friend, who works in marketing, said she'd imagined people in the antiques industry to be short and bald with half-moon spectacles perched on the end of their noses and hunched shoulders from peering too closely at faded trademarks on porcelain.

But I like it here. Extraordinary customers come to Mari's shop, from all over the world. Only yesterday an Italian woman swept in, modelling a Vivienne Westwood outfit with a flowing designer scarf that she'd insist on dramatically throwing across her shoulders, so much so that it would get tangled up in the antiques. Repeatedly I had to extricate it carefully from a vase or lantern, praying the material wouldn't rip. When she attempted to walk downstairs in her killer heels, I suggested that she put on my Birkenstocks instead. You see, the shop is set on two levels. The ground floor has creaking floorboards, old kilim rugs designed to trip me up and treacherous stairs leading down to the basement. It smells *slightly* old and musty, and though everything is utterly higgledy-piggledy, it has a certain charm to it. I cannot afford to work here for too long though. The trouble is I've asked myself again and again what I would like to do next, but

I still don't know. I don't want to apply for just any old job; I want to find something that I feel passionate about.

Mari's real love is acting, and when people ask her what she does, she tells them proudly she's an actress. In her free time she auditions and performs in local theatre productions. 'I won't let my dream go,' she tells me. 'I don't want to die with a pinched, bitter face. You have to find something that makes you happy, Gilly.'

What is my dream?

Since leaving Manchester University with an English degree I've jumped from one job to another as if they were hot stepping stones. I smile, remembering one of my teachers saying I was like a little butterfly, never settling in one place for too long. 'When I grow up I'm going to be a farmer,' I'd say to my school friends one week. 'I want lots of horses and dogs.'

'A hairdresser,' was the next idea.

'Pop star.'

'Model.'

'Vet.'

My cv is a jumble sale of different roles, ranging from charity work to even (ironically) working for a career consultant to help others find their dream job. I could apply for another post in the locations industry; apart from the boss, I enjoyed working there for three years. My father said it was a world record. I made some contacts. I'm sure I could call them to see if they knew of any job opportunities coming up.

I gaze down at my paper. What's stopping me? Why do I feel something is missing?

'When you feel stuck in a rut,' Richard had said, over a ploughman's lunch, and sounding increasingly like an agony aunt, 'you need to do something different. Life can be like a padlock refusing to open. One small change in the combination can finally open the door.'

'Rusk, what am I going to do?' I stroke him, wishing he had the answer.

'Get a lodger,' I hear Richard pipe up again. I jot down my monthly expenses and fret as the list goes on and on. Maybe I should cancel my gym membership. I need to be going at least three times a week to make it worthwhile.

Richard's got a point. I should make the most of my home; after all I'm lucky that I'm even on the property ladder. Five years ago, when my mother's mother died, she left Nick and me enough money to put down a decent deposit on a house. My grandmother was an austere, distant figure in our lives; Dad always says she left us money in her will because she felt guilty for avoiding us when my disabled sister Megan was born.

I stare at the list again. This morning my credit card bill arrived. It's had one too many outings recently. I know I shouldn't have bought my Birkenstocks. Plus my gas and electricity bills have gone up.

There is no doubt that I need the rent. I pick up the phone.

★

'A lodger? Hang on,' Anna whispers, 'vile boss coming, will call back.'

Anna works for a marketing company that specializes mainly in sports and travel. Growing up, we went to the same school, formed our first pop band together with Nick called the Funky Monkeys, played and tobogganed in the snow, and Anna often came with our family when we took Megan to the seaside or the zoo.

Just as I'm about to tuck into my packed lunch, I hear the little tinkle on the door and shove my sandwiches back inside the box. A stooped old man enters, carrying a Boots plastic bag. He shuffles towards me and I quickly warn him not to trip up on the rug. 'Can I help?' I ask politely. He's wearing a collection of clothes that can only have come from a jumble sale.

'Um.' He lingers. 'Um. I'm looking, yes lovely things here, looking for er . . . er . . . a set of um . . .'

The phone rings and I'm wondering if I should pick it up. I notice the maroon socks inside his brown sandals. Oh, please hurry up.

'Er . . . yes, now, what I'm after is . . . um, a set of um, er, china platters.'

I try not to laugh. 'Oh, I'm so sorry, sir, but we only sell antiques, mainly lights and mirrors.' I gesture to the mirrors pressed against the wall. He looks lost and unsure what to do next. I guide him gently out of the shop and point him in the direction of Peter Jones.

I rush back, hearing the phone ring again. 'Mari's Antiques . . . oh, Anna, hi . . .'

'Sorry about earlier. Got to be quick. I've just been talking to one of the guys at work and he does this Monday to Friday thing. Google it,' she orders. She's about to hang up when she can't help saying, 'I'm so relieved you're not moving. I need you here. Us single girls, we need to stick together.'

I smile. 'I'd have missed you too.'

'Monday to Friday,' I type that evening, having just returned from a night out with Anna. We went to one of our favourite Greek restaurants near her flat in Clapham.

I love my evenings with Anna. We have known each other since childhood, and she is like a ray of sunshine, someone whom I always feel better for seeing. Currently she's single, though how long that will last who knows? Anna has no problem attracting men. She's fair with a spattering of freckles across her nose and cheeks, and men fall for her husky voice and infectious laugh. 'My problem is I become restless quickly,' she says. Anna claims she's had enough of men now, she positively *wants* to be single, but I know the real reason why she finds it hard to commit. She's always been in love with Paul, one of her colleagues at work. Nothing's happened between them because he's married. I haven't met him yet.

I click onto the Monday to Friday site now.

'By the way, how come you decided to find a lodger?' Anna had asked earlier tonight.

'I'm going to get over Ed,' I announced proudly. 'If he can move on, so can I.'

'About time!'

I tell her about Richard, and that while he was a useless estate agent, he'd made a lot of sense with this lodger idea.

'I could kiss the ground Richard walks on! Is he married?' she'd added.

A clean-shaven man called Miles pops up onto the screen with a beaming white-toothed smile, modelling a City suit. 'Monday to Friday works like a dream,' he says. 'No long commute to work, no traffic jams! Just a simple hop and a skip on the tube, and *voilà*! I'm in the office. Then, come the weekend, I go home for real. I couldn't recommend it more as it ticks all the boxes. It's a no-brainer!'

Steady on, Miles. He looks as if he's positively going to fly through the screen and land in my lap to convince me.

I scroll down to read some further testimonials from successful landlords and ladies.

'My Monday to Friday man is a professional and a pleasure to have around,' says Mandy. 'What's great is he doesn't have a lot of baggage, so my home still feels like my own.'

Now this is important because in my small two-bedroom house there isn't much space for anyone, let alone their baggage. One of my favourite hobbies is browsing shops and markets to find unusual things. Recently I found an abstract African sculpture of a bird in flight that I put in front of my fireplace.

There's a box which says, REGISTER NOW! With one simple click home-owners can be accepted into the system overnight. 'What do you think about that, Ruskin?' I ask him. He's lying on his back in his usual spot on the armchair, paws in the air. I go over to kiss him. 'Would you feel threatened by a stranger in the house, my little pumpkin pie?'

Returning to my computer, I wonder if I should register now or sleep on it. I'm not good at doing anything spontaneously. I err on the cautious side. When I drive, I will drive around the roundabout twice to make sure I am going in the right direction. Ed used to be driven mad by my indecisiveness. Dad says I will go to my grave flapping about one thing or another, like did I leave the iron on or forget to double-lock the front door.

'Gilly, just think about it,' I can hear Richard advising me again over our pub lunch. 'A guy can do any DIY around the house for you, fix the showerhead, change your plugs, unblock the drains, know where the stopcock is.'

'I can do all that, no problem!' I said hesitantly.

'OK, but you just never know who might turn up on your doorstep. Maybe, if you interviewed enough people, you could meet Mr Right.'

'I'm not looking for Mr Right.'

'Oh, Mrs Right then? You bat for the other team?'

I find myself laughing when Miles pops up once more, telling me that with just one touch of a key I am making a giant leap towards a richer and brighter future.

Go for it, Gilly. Think of the money. You need it.

I click on the REGISTER NOW button and hold my breath.

There. Done it. No hesitation. Richard would be proud of me.

'Can I ask you something?' I'd said to him, at this stage feeling he had quizzed me enough on my private life and it was now time to put him under the spotlight. Apart from Richard being my dad's godson I knew little more about him. 'Why are you an estate agent, because let's face it you're a pretty terrible one?'

He shrugged. 'I ask myself the same question every day.'

'And?'

'I still don't know the answer.'

'Are you happy?'

'Happy? That's a hard question. No,' he'd said with ease. 'It's simple for me to tell you what to do,' he confided, showing some vulnerability, 'but when it comes to our own lives, we make a right old mess of it, don't we?'

Life can be like a padlock refusing to open. Maybe Richard is also searching for that one thing to make him happy?

Perhaps we all are.

4

Ten days later

I type in my password BOBBY SHAFTOE. This is a folk song our family used to sing with my baby sister, Megan, on car journeys to the seaside.

Welcome, Gilly Brown, it says. I click on a box that leads me to my room's profile. **Your house in Hammersmith has had 28 VISITORS but O ENQUIRIES.**

I log off, incredulous. My house and me are like a wall-flower. No one wants to dance with us. What's going on? Surely there must be some administrative error on the system, but when I repeat the process I am told again that no one is interested. Zero enquiries.

I search the site for advice. *Sometimes lodgers' emails are accidentally sent to a Junk or Spam folder . . .*

Ah! I dive straight into my Spam folder, but nothing.

Maybe it's the recession? Perhaps I should lower my rent? I check to see if that shabby apartment just over Hammersmith Bridge has gone yet with its plastic sofa and mouldy curtains. It didn't look half as nice as my house *and* they were charging £100 more per month. It's right on the main road, I mean, who's going to . . .

I don't believe it.

The doorbell rings.

My neighbour, Gloria, single all her life by choice, just turned sixty, retired from the aromatherapy world (she used to be a masseuse), bursts in, silver hair wild, wearing a baggy purple T-shirt with black leggings. Every Saturday morning we go to the gym together. She's a lovely mix of nights out on the town with her friends, 'on the batter' as she calls it, and early nights in with a cup of hot chocolate listening to Radio Four.

She came into my life five years ago, when I had just brought Ruskin home to live with me. She knocked on my door to ask if I had a powercut. When I shone a torch in her face, she realized I was in the same situation, but she could also see I was anxious. I told her my puppy had disappeared.

We searched high and low. Was he locked in the downstairs loo? Had he slipped down the drainpipe? Was he under the sofa? He was nowhere! When Gloria found me lifting the lid off my teapot, she announced that I was officially mad.

She then beckoned me over, putting a finger to her lips. She had crouched down beside the sink. 'Come here, darling,' she whispered. Ruskin had slipped into the gap between the tumble drier and the washing machine. After gentle coaxing he came out, cobwebs stuck to his ears.

'I'm not sure I can look after him,' I said, my voice wobbling. Since I was a child I'd wanted a dog, begging Mum to let us have one, but she said she couldn't cope with a puppy and Megan. 'I'll be the one who has to walk it,' she'd said.

I promised myself that when I was older and had my own home, I'd get one. When I visited Battersea Dogs Home Ruskin was one of the first dogs I saw. He was fast asleep in his basket, curled up in the shape of a kidney bean. As I knelt down, he opened his eyes and walked towards me, placing a paw between the bars of the cage. The girl showing me round said he had never done that before and that's when I knew he was my boy.

'Maybe I've made a mistake,' I confessed to Gloria that night. The sense of responsibility overwhelmed me.

Gloria handed him to me, a bundle of fur. 'You're his mother now. He needs you.'

'Hi, treasure,' she says now, strutting into my sitting room and throwing her swimming kit onto my sofa. Ruskin bolts over to say hello, wagging his tail as she scoops him into her arms. 'Why aren't you ready?' she asks when she sees I'm still in my pyjamas.

'Sorry, I'm just coming.' I rush back to my desk. 'Like your flip-flops,' I mutter.

'Aren't they wonderful! They're so comfy, tone my pins and . . . well, they do everything for me but pay my bills quite frankly. What are you doing, ducks?'

'Changing my profile.'

Gloria pulls up a chair. 'No luck yet?'

'Not a squeak.'

'They ought to be snapping this place up. You should at least be getting a few bites by now.'

'They're not fish,' I laugh.

'Budge over,' she demands, 'let me take a look.'

Gloria scans my advertisement. 'It is the school holidays,' I remind her. 'London's pretty dead in August.'

Gloria reads out the description of No. 21. 'I live in Hammersmith, in a two-bedroom house on a quiet peaceful road.' She pushes me aside, clicks the 'edit your details' button. 'It's time for some serious artistic licence, Gilly.'

I look at my watch. 'What about our swimming?' Gloria and I swim three times a week; we call ourselves the Olympians. We're often overtaken in the slow lane but it doesn't worry us.

'Stick the kettle on,' she says.

Gloria describes our street as a lively place with a great sense of community.

'But they want somewhere quiet, don't they?'

'No! It's no bleeding wonder you've had zero response. This ad's as cold as a winter's day in Siberia.'

'Really? Is it?' I reread it, and have to agree that I wouldn't want to move in this very minute. It does sound pretty boring.

Gloria puckers her lips and gets stuck in now. 'Oh, look! Have you checked this out?' Gleefully she presses a button that takes us to a site that gives tips on what matters most to Monday to Fridayers.

'Monday to Fridayers like to socialize,' Gloria states. 'You see! They want some fun.' She then reads what I had written, 'There are a couple of pubs within walking distance.'

'There *are* a couple of pubs nearby,' I say.

'Oh, golly gosh. I can hardly contain my excitement.'

'Go on then. Say there are *superb* pubs all within walking distance,' I tell her. 'And numerous coffee bars, delicatessens and shops,' I say, enjoying this now, 'and a beautiful park on my doorstep.' Gloria and I have soon rewritten my advertisement, proudly alerting prospective Monday to Fridayers to the fact that I am only seconds away from the District Line and in prime position for all the motorways and airports. 'Excellent transport links,' Gloria types.

She glances at the next tip. *Some lodgers like to know a little about yourself so feel free to give as much information as you wish.*

She returns to my advertisement, reading off the screen, 'I like swimming, films, writing and reading.'

'Why not add that you play Bingo on a Wednesday night, charades on Thursday and you love to get about on your Freedom Pass. Listen, there's only room for one perky pensioner on this street and that's me.'

I laugh. 'OK. Say I'm a messed up 34-year-old, who needs the cash.'

She twitches her mouth, deep in thought before tapping into the keyboard, 'I'm thirty-two . . .'

'Gloria! It's not a dating site. None of the other ads say their age.'

'Exactly. You are going to stand out, rise like a Phoenix. OK. You enjoy parties, dancing . . . What's your favourite cocktail?'

'A White Lady.' Freshly squeezed lemon, gin and Cointreau. Ed and I used to make them all the time.

'Delicious,' she agrees, typing, when the whole ad disappears. 'No!' she wails. 'I did nothing, just pressed that button,' she defends herself as I move over and tap another key. All she's done is shrink it, I reassure her.

As we reach the end of our advert there's still something missing. 'I love dogs!' I exclaim. 'I have to say pets. The nation loves dogs!'

'That's my girl,' Gloria says in a way which makes me fear she's about to ruffle my hair and squeeze my cheeks.

If you want, you can add a photograph to your advert (of the house, not you!). Gloria looks at my photograph. It's a shot of my sitting room with the open fireplace, the

African sculpture, the invitations on the mantelpiece (I still can't get used to seeing only my name in the corner) the bookshelves crammed with novels and photographs of family and friends.

She gasps. 'It's your television, darling.' I turn to face my old-fashioned TV, the screen the size of an ant. She's right. There it is, sitting like a wart, putting off all potential Monday to Fridayers. Ed used to threaten to buy me a new one, but I was proud that I hadn't sold my soul to the plasma screen.

Gloria says, 'Get your coat on. We'll take Sadie out.'

Sadie is her electric purple car. 'I can't justify buying a TV,' I say, 'not right now. My credit card needs a rest.'

'Think of it as a loan.' As we reach the front door she turns to me. 'Before we go, I just want to say I'm glad you're not moving.'

'Oh, Gloria, so am I,' I say, touched.

'I mean, who's going to water my plants and feed my Guinness when I'm away?' Guinness is Gloria's black-and-white cat.

'And fix your computer?' Gloria always summons me over during a technical emergency, and I've just set her up on wireless broadband. 'I'd miss my fellow Olympian swimmer too. Let's just hope after all our hard work I find the perfect Monday to Friday man.'

'Gilly, by the time we've finished with your ad, the offers are going to come flooding through your letterbox,' she promises.

5

Later that evening, after Gloria and I have bought and installed a high-tech television screen the size of a tennis court in my sitting room (vulgar – am disgusted with myself) I race in my car to my brother's house in Richmond. I'm running late because I got delayed trying to change one of Gloria's spotlight bulbs in her kitchen. I curse my luck when I get stuck in traffic. Nancy, Nick's wife, has only one thing in common with my father. She's a stickler for punctuality.

Nancy opens the door in an elegant navy wraparound dress, legs waxed and tanned, her fair hair tumbling down slender shoulders. I burst into the hallway with a bottle of wine and a couple of presents I bought for the children.

'The kids are in bed. It's too late to read to them,' she says.

I always make up bedtime stories for them. 'Can I just run up and kiss them goodnight?'

'Go on.' She smiles tightly. 'Quick.' As I brush past her, there's a faint look of disapproval when she sees I haven't changed for the evening. Nancy believes in changing for dinner – it's important to add a new chapter to the day, she says.

'Don't worry,' she says when I gesture to my jeans, 'but what have you forgotten to do?' she asks with a smile and gentle nudge that hides a whip.

'Oh yes, sorry!' I slip off my shoes before rushing upstairs to kiss Hannah and Matilda goodnight.

Minutes later I join Nancy in the kitchen, the table immaculately laid with pressed linen napkins and white bone china. 'Is there anything I can do?' I ask, before adding that something smells delicious.

'No no, you sit down.' Nancy opens the fridge door, covered with photographs of the children and their artwork, and takes out a bottle of white wine. She pours us both a glass, telling me that the supper will be burnt if that brother of mine isn't home soon. Nick is a lawyer. He specializes in divorce. 'Is he always this late, Nancy?' I ask with concern.

'Always,' she replies. 'He lives in his bloody office.'

As Nancy fills me in on the dramas with Hannah's music teacher (Hannah is seven, Matilda four) my mind wanders to Megan, my own sister, and how I wish she were with me tonight. I often think about her. Would she have been like Nick and my father, a career-driven successful lawyer, or would she have been more like me? When I hear a key unlock, Nancy stiffens, glancing at her watch. Nick rushes in, shaking off his jacket, loosening his tie and dumping his briefcase on the kitchen table, apologizing to me for being late. Nancy picks up his case and orders him to hang up his jacket. 'You did get the milk, didn't you?'

His face says he forgot. 'Oh, Nicholas! We don't have enough for the children's breakfast now!'

Once he's apologized she allows him to kiss her on the cheek.

'It's just a Delia recipe,' Nancy smiles, as she serves perfect miniature onion tartlets for our starter. She then asks me how my love life is, as she always does. I try to deflect the question by praising the pastry, but Nancy doesn't let me get away with it. You see, she loved Ed and misses his presence round the dinner table. Ed got the measure of Nancy instantly; he was perceptive about people, which is why he's a good businessman. 'She's high maintenance,' he'd said. 'Insecure. Deep down that woman craves approval and recognition.'

Stop. Thinking. About. Him.

I tell Nancy that there's no one special on the scene at the moment. I add that I think attractive single men must hide underground. Though I do wonder who that young man was in the hat, walking his dog this morning. There was something interesting about him.

'Anyway,' Nick says, helping me change the subject, 'what else is going on?'

I am always shocked when I see my twin. Like me, he's tall with dark-brown hair, but he's aged in the last few years, and his pale skin reveals that he spends too much time at his computer.

'Well, I'm advertising for a Monday to Friday man,' I tell them.

'A what man?' Nancy asks.

I tell them both about the Monday to Friday scheme.

'I think that's very brave of the wife to let her husband loose in the week,' Nancy comments. 'I wouldn't let you do it, Nicholas.'

Nick smiles at me.

'Actually you live in the office, so it wouldn't make any difference,' she reflects.

When Nancy leaves the room to check up on the children, Nick leans towards me. 'I think it's a great idea,' he advises with a wry smile. 'At the rate she spends, we could do with letting out our spare room too.'

'Wow, this looks amazing!' I exclaim as Nancy places an exquisite slice of apricot flan in front of me with a neat scoop of vanilla ice cream on the side of the plate.

'Just a Nigella,' she says. 'Now, Gilly, you need to start thinking about your birthday.'

'November's months away,' I dismiss.

'Nancy needs a project,' Nick mutters quietly as she counts the months on her fingers. 'It's only three months,' she calculates, 'and if we're going to hire a marquee . . .'

'We're not,' I say, horrified by the thought. 'Nick, what are you going to do?'

'Nothing,' he says.

'Nothing?' I say, surprised. He usually enjoys a party.

'Maybe draw the curtains and hide under my duvet?' he suggests.

'Well that's typical,' Nancy complains. 'I'm married to a misery guts. And you're not much better either, Gilly,' she adds, refusing to let me off the hook when she sees me giggle.

'Sorry, Nancy, I probably will do something but . . .'

'Listen Gilly, I know thirty-five is a difficult age, a *sensitive* age. Don't get me wrong, I *so* felt that way too.'

'It's fine! I don't feel weird about it.'

'It must be hard being over thirty and single, especially in London,' Nancy continues.

I pick up my glass of wine and take a large sip, before excusing myself and going to the loo.

'Gilly has plenty of time to meet someone,' I overhear Nick say as I'm walking down the hallway, back towards the kitchen, 'and after what Ed did, she's bound to want to be careful.'

I stand behind the door.

'What *you* don't understand Nicholas . . .'

'Keep your voice down,' he warns her.

'. . . is that it's *hard* for women. Our biological clocks keep on ticking. If she leaves it too late . . .'

I rush upstairs. In the safety of Nick's study I sit down at his desk and breathe deeply. Don't let her get to you, Gilly. Sometimes I could murder him for marrying someone like Nancy.

When Nick first met her he couldn't wait to introduce Dad and me to this wonderful, pretty, courageous woman, 'who's somehow fallen for me,' he'd said laughing. It had been a whirlwind romance, Nick proposing after only two months. Before we met her, he warned us not to ask too much about Nancy's family. She had left behind an alcoholic father and a useless mother who lived off benefits, to make a better life for herself in London, he'd said proudly, but she doesn't like being reminded about it. They met at work. Nancy had been PA to one of the partners in Nick's law firm. I wasn't sure if I liked her, but I did admire her back then, as did my father. It was easy to see how Nick had fallen for Nancy too, with her long fair hair, wide mouth and deep blue eyes the colour of denim. She was pretty. I remember thinking she'd be the kind of woman every little girl dreams of turning into when she grows up.

I overhear Nancy and Nick continuing to bicker downstairs. If anything they are an advertisement for why not to marry, but I wouldn't be without their children. I love walking with the girls in the park at weekends and buying them ice creams. I smile, remembering Nick playing with them and calling, 'Last one to me has to eat Brussels sprouts for tea!'

I glance across to Nick's laptop. I wonder if I've had any response to my Monday to Friday advert? While I'm here? I press a few keys.

'Welcome, Gilly!' the site tells me.

'No need to welcome me,' I mutter, waiting for my Monday to Friday password to be accepted.

I stare at the screen. Am I imagining it?

I must shriek because next thing I know, Nick is in the room, taking me into his arms. 'I'm sorry, Gilly. Nancy can be so thoughtless.'

'No!' I pull away from him. 'It's fine. She's right,' I admit, 'my clock is ticking . . . But look, Nicky!'

Your house has had 55 VISITORS and 10 ENQUIRIES.

'Shh!' he says, though he smiles at my excitement.

One of the girls starts to cry.

'There there, darling,' Nick says to Matilda, who's sitting up in bed tearful at being woken up. He hands her the Cinderella flask. 'Ten enquiries,' he whispers, 'that's great!'

'Auntie Gilly!' Tilda cries and I press a finger to my lips, but nevertheless approach her bed to kiss her good-night again. She has a soft round face and smells of sleep.

'Where's Ruskin?' she asks. Tilda tells me she is going to marry him. 'He's in nod-nod land,' I whisper.

Hannah continues sleeping, sprawled diagonally across her mattress. Three years older, she loves playing the piano and cycling, though recently I've noticed how subdued she's been. Lately all she's wanted to do is watch television.

Both are pretty, with long honey-coloured hair, often braided into French plaits, and their limbs so beautifully formed. They are perfect to me in every way.

'By the way, Mum called this morning,' Nick tells me quietly, outside their bedroom.

'Good. I've been worried about her.' Our mother lives in Perth with Patrick, a wine merchant. She moved to Australia after Hannah was born. Nick was quite happy to see her go because he's never forgiven her. I felt differently, though I found it hard to say that I didn't want her to leave. Dad didn't seem surprised; he had known about Patrick some time before us.

'How was she?' I ask.

'Good. Happy,' he replies simply. He looks at his watch. 'Sorry, Gilly,' he says, heading back to his study. 'Work's awful at the moment, the company's letting so many people go and if I don't finish this case . . .'

'Nick, you're tired. Can't it wait till tomorrow?' I gently suggest, as I hear Nancy clearing up the supper downstairs.

He nods, exhausted. 'You're right. I'll be down in one sec,' he promises.

Alone, I join Nancy back in the kitchen, grabbing a drying-up cloth.

Lying in bed, unable to sleep, I think about Mum. Sometimes I miss her and wish things had turned out differently. Occasionally I find myself asking what would have happened if Dad could have forgiven her all those years ago when she had turned up on our doorstep. Or what might have been if I had decided to live with Mum, not Dad, when they divorced.

I think about tonight. When I was helping Nancy clear up the supper, she apologized if she had been insensitive, saying that at the end of the day all she wants is for me to be happy. 'Me too,' I'd said, thanking her. 'But, Nance, this time it's got to be right. I can't get hurt again.'

Like a horse and jockey in a showjumping contest, Nancy and I were doing so well until we collapsed at the last fence. Nancy said I mustn't forget the problems Mum had with Megan. 'I was reading the stats on women of a certain age, and the risk of having a child that's . . .'

'Nancy, I'd keep it!' And on that note I left.

I pick up the silver-framed photograph of Megan by my bedside. She had a round soft face similar to Matilda's, glowing skin and great big eyes that smiled. Nick doesn't like talking about her. He has chosen to shut off that part of his life, like closing a half-finished book and never going back. Yet I think of her often, especially at night.

Slowly I drift off to sleep.

6

December 1984

Nick and I are watching *Eastenders* with our babysitter Lisa, bowls of spaghetti on our laps. Normally we're not allowed to watch it. Dad took Mum to the hospital this morning. I heard this groan, followed by, 'Oh my God, it's happening!' I rushed out onto the landing to see what was going on. Nicholas didn't wake up.

'Mum?' I called out, scared.

'Back to your room!' Dad instructed. Seconds later he was at my bedside, reassuring me that Lisa would be coming over any moment to look after Nick and me and take us to school. 'Everything's going to be fine,' he said. I could tell that he was excited. When they left, I shut my eyes and dreamed about having a baby sister. I wanted to plait her hair and paint her nails.

I look over to Lisa, long legs curled up on the sofa.

She's nineteen and has golden-coloured hair, dead straight like a Roman road. Each night I pray for hair like hers, but in the morning I'm the same old Gilly with grey eyes which sometimes look dark blue. Mum tells me I'm lucky to have dark hair and magic eyes that change colour according to what I'm wearing. 'You're like a chameleon,' she says and then goes on to tell me I should never want to be anyone else, but be proud of who I am and walk to the beat of my own drum, whatever that means.

Lisa often babysits Nick and me. When we were much younger (we're nearly eight now) Mum and Dad used to go on 'date nights'. I would sit on Mum's bed and watch her get ready for the evening, powdering her nose and putting on lipstick. I used to go through her jewellery box and put on her high heels. They took it in turns to choose where to go. Mum likes weird food, called sushi. Dad eats curries. Mum loves ballet; Dad tells us he can't stand watching men in tights dance. 'Don't ever marry someone like your mother!' Dad advised my brother one evening after salsa dancing. 'She's now threatening flying lessons. I think she wants to kill me!'

Since Mum has been pregnant they don't go on their dates. I think Dad is secretly happy to stay at home. He likes having a bath when he gets back from the office. He pours himself a glass of something, I think it's whisky, and takes it upstairs and locks the bathroom door.

Before Mum was pregnant, Mum and Dad argued all the time. There was a lot of shouting. One time he told

49

her she was too old to have another child and she threw her glass of wine at him. He said something about not wanting to have a baby with problems. Nick and I often shared bedrooms after their fights.

Mum is old. She's forty-two. She married Dad when she was twenty-seven.

She and Dad have told us the story many times as to how we are miracle twins. I look over to my brother, watching the TV. I don't like the way Mum cuts our hair. We both have horrible fringes.

Seven years after they married they still had no children so they decided to adopt.

The week that they were due to sign the adoption papers she found out she was pregnant with twins. 'My seven years of bad luck had come to an end,' Mum told us.

After Nick and I were born Mum was too busy looking after us even to think about having another baby.

'You're pregnant?' Dad had said in the kitchen. Mum had summoned Nick and me into the room to hear the news too.

Dad poured himself a gin, drank it in one go. 'Nick, Gilly, I need to talk to your mother alone,' he said. We left the room, sloped upstairs, but remained seated on the top step, holding our breath.

'Please be happy,' we overheard Mum say.

'You promised me we were being careful, Beth. What do you expect me to do? Jump up and down with joy?'

'But, Will, when the baby comes you'll change, I know you will.'

'We agreed to stop at two.'

'I'm bored! The children are at school and . . .'

'Of all the underhand, selfish things you could have done . . .'

I asked my brother what 'underhand' meant. Nick whispered, 'It's not nice, Gilly. Naughty, I think.'

'I need this,' Mum went on.

'This isn't just about you!'

'Will! Wait!'

The front door slammed. We bolted down the bedroom landing and into Nick's room. We heard the engine revving. I looked out of the window, down at Dad's car driving off into the night. 'Do you want to sleep with me tonight?' Nick asked hopefully. 'You can have the top bunk?'

With child number three, Mum hasn't been feeling so well. She's been going to bed in the afternoons and often asks Lisa to come over at weekends to play with us. Lisa likes coming round because she fancies my dad. Sometimes Dad takes us on the double-decker bus to the Natural History Museum or to Madame Tussauds and we have a pizza afterwards, with lots of pepperoni.

Lisa clears the plates away. I stare at the telephone. All day long I had this funny feeling in my tummy that my headmistress, Mrs Ward, would call me into her office to tell me that Mum had died because she was so old.

A key turns in the door. Nick and I look at one another. Lisa puts on some lipstick and squirts something smelly onto her wrist.

Dad enters in his thick chunky jumper and scarf and sits down next to me. 'I'm so sorry, Nicky.' He shakes his head. 'You've got two bossy sisters now.'

'It's a girl!' I cry out, grabbing Dad's arm and hugging it.

'Yes, and she's beautiful and healthy, and your mother sends you both the biggest kiss.' His jumper smells of hospitals and washing powder.

'What are you going to call her?' Lisa asks, flicking a hand through her hair.

'Megan,' he says, 'we're going to call her Megan, after my mother.'

7

Ruskin and I rush through the gates of Ravenscourt Park and into an oasis of calm. Richard was right. Who needs the countryside when I have this on my doorstep? Sometimes it's dangerous to think the grass is greener on the other side.

I walk past the café, customers buying an early morning coffee, their dogs tied up at the gates. I follow the path that leads me into the open field and head for my circle of friends, who congregate in the distance, near to the entrance of the garden centre. There's Walter, holding Spike the Airedale tightly on a lead because Spike's too amorous when it comes to the other dogs, especially Hardy, the miniature schnauzer. Spike has to wear a muzzle now because he's got into the bad habit of having spats with dogs outside of our pack. There's Mari, my boss and the boss of this group too. I can hear her giving Walter a grilling, saying Spike's muzzle is on upside down.

'The straps are over his eyes for God's sake!' she shouts.

Today she's wearing a stylish denim apron over her clothes. She doesn't like getting filth and muddy pawmarks on her outfits. With the strength of an ox she hurls her chewed-up blue ball across the field for her Basil to retrieve. Basil has the speed of an Olympic medallist. By the time he's at the shop he's so tired that he and Ruskin sleep most of the day.

Since meeting Mari four years ago under the grand oak tree, like a magnet she's drawn Walter, Samantha, Brigitte, Ariel and me to this meeting ground. Sam is my age, and married with three children. Brigitte, half-French, is a food critic. Ariel, the youngest of our group, twenty-six, has a partner called Graham and like me has worked in a thousand different jobs, but his real passion is music. He's currently teaching contemporary music at a school in Hammersmith. He cycles to the park most days with Pugsy, his black pug, perched in the front basket. Walter is retired and in his seventies. He used to be a window cleaner.

As I approach the circle, we say hello and exchange news. Walter seems low today. 'I'm feeling out of sorts,' he confides to us all. 'My new TV isn't working. I have to kick it to get it going. It was expensive too.'

'That's not right,' we all tell him.

'Scandalous!' Brigitte exclaims.

'You need to go into the shop and speak direct to the manager,' Ariel advises.

He's dressed in skinny jeans and a white T-shirt, and I also notice he's changed his hair colour again. It's now short and blond, which accentuates his brown eyes. Ariel has one of those faces that can get away with a different image each month; I tell him with pride he's as versatile as Madonna.

I then mention my thirteen enquiries from prospective Monday to Fridayers. I had an extra three this morning.

'So you're not moving?' asks Sam, who's been away and needs to catch up on the news. Even in the summer she looks pale because her skin is so fair.

'I'm staying put.'

'Thank the fucking lord,' Ariel says. 'Pugsy would have missed you,' he adds, gesturing to an oblivious Pugsy sniffing something ominous in the grass.

'Oh good, we didn't want you to go,' says Sam, who has vibrant red hair, an infectious laugh and a figure that inspires me to go to the gym more. She's on a diet of looking after her family and working part-time as a secretary in an architect's firm. Sam owns Hardy, the miniature schnauzer whom Spike the Airedale has taken a fancy to.

'I'd have missed your pretty face,' says Walter. He has never been married but loves to flirt and since giving up window cleaning (the ladder got too heavy for him) he's now the resident dog walker in Hammersmith. At the moment he's not only looking after Spike but also a rescue dog called Gusto. He's rarely seen without his khaki rucksack on his back filled with every kind of dog accessory.

'I always thought it a dreadful idea to leave,' Brigitte adds with a heavy French accent.

Mari, hating to be left out, says, 'Me too. You can't live off a view.' I don't remind her that previously she'd thought it was a great idea, just as long as I didn't leave her until she'd found a replacement.

'So what's this about thirteen enquiries?' Sam asks. 'Who are they all from?'

I tell them about my interview with Roy Haddock that night and they laugh.

'I once knew a Mr Trout,' muses Walter.

'Roy,' Mari repeats. 'I'm not sure about the name. He sounds like a big fat man . . .'

'With a beer belly,' Sam finishes.

'Don't be such snobs,' someone says.

We turn to see before us a man wearing combats, T-shirt and a navy hat, dragging a Scottie dog on its lead. There's something familiar about him. I know! He's the man I saw the other day. He's tall, scruffy, hasn't shaved properly and looks about my age. In fact he looks as if he's just crawled out of bed, but his blue eyes are bright with curiosity. 'Sorry, have I interrupted something?' He surveys our group. 'Is this the official doggy hour?' He smiles and there is something appealing about his confidence. I can also tell Ariel is checking him out. 'Cute,' he whispers to me. 'Ask him if he's single, Gilly – go on, you need a bit of action.'

I stand on his foot. He yelps.

Guy glances at both of us. 'Are you all right?' he asks Ariel, who is still hopping up and down in pretend agony.

'Yes, yes, he's fine,' I say, ignoring Ariel's scowl.

Anyway, I tell Guy briefly about my plan to find a lodger, apologizing to Mari, who's heard it all before.

'The trouble with lodgers is you end up going out every night of the week just to avoid them,' he says.

'Well, the good thing is he's a Monday to Friday man,' I inform him.

'Monday to Friday? So what does he get up to at the weekend?'

'He buggers off,' Mari states, lighting up a menthol cigarette.

We don't introduce ourselves, but instead point out our dogs. That's Brigitte's dog Mousse, Hardy is Sam's, there's Basil named after Mari's favourite herb that she grows on her terrace. She adds that her tomatoes have been fabulous this year. That's Ruskin. And Pugsy's over there.

As I watch us all sussing out this man in his hat, I liken our circle to the school playground. We're never quite sure how we feel about newcomers. We become cosy, then all of a sudden along comes someone we haven't met before who unsettles the balance.

I tell this man that I've had thirteen enquiries and am interviewing my first one tonight.

'Thirteen?'

I wait for him to sound impressed. 'Unlucky for some,' he says.

After our walk, Mari, the dogs and I set off to work. On the Underground, heading to Sloane Square, Mari nudges me hard in the ribs. 'Look at them,' she gestures to the people sitting opposite us, with things stuffed in their ears.

'Shh,' I urge.

'They look half-dead!' Mari doesn't suffer fools gladly but she does suffer from a loud voice. 'No stimulation,' she tuts.

One of them stares at her.

Thankfully Mari shuts up and takes out her book. As the train rattles on, it occurs to me I'll need to give the house a good clean before Mr Haddock arrives tonight. I hope he's nice. Then my mind wanders back to the man in the hat again. I don't know why, but I have one of my strange premonitions that he is going to become an important person in my life. The next time I see him I'll ask if he wants to have a cup of coffee. I hope he joins our group again.

Mari and I step off the train. I pick up Ruskin, zap my Oyster card against the barrier and push us both through. 'What's your dog called?' I had asked him, when he didn't volunteer the name. Though he was friendly, there was something reserved in his manner too, which I found attractive.

'Trouble,' he'd said in that quietly spoken voice.

8

Roy is twenty minutes late. I mustn't drink any more, I say as I pour myself another glass of wine. I scan the sitting room, shoving Ruskin's dog comb and chewed-up toy rabbit into one of the cupboards. I hang up my summer coat, kicking the dog lead and bootjack out of the way. I look at myself in the mirror. I'm wearing my dark denim jeans with a black top and a leopard-print scarf holds back my hair.

I jolt when there is a knock at the door. Keep calm. Heart thumping, I put on my best smile.

I open the front door. 'Oh, Gloria.'

She skirts the sitting room, whispering, 'He's not here is he?'

'No!'

'Why don't I hide in the loo?'

I press a hand against her back and direct her out of the door.

'We need a code,' she says halfway across the road. 'If Mr Fish is weird open and close your shutters a few times.'

As I wait another ten minutes, the phone rings. It's Jonnie, this guy I met at my old job, asking if I want to meet up tonight. 'I can't,' I tell him, but suggest meeting up next week. 'Sure,' he says enthusiastically. I know he has a soft spot for me, I only wish I felt the same.

Soon my phone becomes a hotline. Dad calls, then Anna, asking if I want to grab a pizza and go to the movies.

'I can't,' I say. 'I'm about to meet Roy Haddock, my Monday to Friday man.'

'Roy Haddock,' she says thoughtfully. I can hear laughter in her voice.

'You never know Gilly, maybe Mr Roy Haddock is the man of your dreams,' she suggests.

'Oh, Anna!' I protest, but then think again . . .

'We met on the Monday to Friday site,' I say during the wedding speeches, clutching the microphone proudly.

I am standing next to Roy, who looks as handsome as James Bond. The marquee is set in the grounds of an English manor house, the ceiling lined with stars, the tables decorated with candles. I am wearing a simple but elegant ivory dress. 'After Edward,' I begin, 'I was convinced I'd never meet that special person again . . . not until Roy came along.'

Sighs. Admiration. Wonderment.

'If I'm completely honest,' I say, placing a hand on my heart. 'I was slightly put off by his name . . .'

Roy nudges me playfully.

'And his lateness.'

Friends and family laugh and clap as they cheer me on.

'But when I opened the door . . .'

'Hello!' A tall man stands by his metallic bicycle sporting a purple crash helmet and shorts that show off his muscled legs. He has hair the colour of a carrot. 'Sorry I'm late,' he says.

Wipe that disappointed look off your face and welcome him in, Gilly.

'All right if I leave the bike in the garden?'

'Sure,' I shrill.

'Good stuff.' He pushes it through the sitting room and Ruskin barks at this rude invasion. 'Hey, buster,' he says. 'What's this little cheeky chap called?'

Frantically I look up to Gloria's bedroom window but she's not there. Roy parks his bike against the crumbling wall in my garden.

'Bikes are a nightmare 'cos you can't leave them outside any more. No place is safe.'

'Don't you have a lock?' I suggest, thinking there was a perfectly good lamp post that he could have tied the bike up to.

'Yeah, but thieves just cut through the chains now, don't they.' At this point I panic about how long Roy is planning to stay. It would be very unlucky indeed if during the brief viewing of No. 21 a thief were lurking, ready to saw through his bicycle chain. Roy returns to the kitchen and picks up an apple from my wire fruit basket. He polishes it against his sweaty T-shirt as though it were a cricket ball.

I offer him a drink. He asks for a glass of water.

'Cheers. Nice place,' he remarks with a few nods. 'You lived here long then?'

'Four years, on and off.'

'Why do you want a lodger?' He winks at me.

I need to pay my council tax. 'I just thought it'd be a nice change,' I say brightly.

His T-shirt reveals him to be a Manchester United fan, and for a terrifying moment I imagine him switching channels from *How to Look Good Naked* to *Match of the Day*.

'Shall I show you round?'

'Great.' He leaps out of his seat. 'Show me the way.' When I walk on ahead of him I have this sneaking suspicion that he could be checking out my arse.

'It won't take long,' I joke. 'So, as you can see, this is the sitting room.'

'Nice,' he acknowledges.

Ruskin follows us as I show Roy the small loo on the ground floor followed by the bathroom on the upstairs landing. I stop dead. My washing is still hanging on the drying rail over the bath, rows of knickers on display. 'Sorry.' I blush. 'On we go,' I say, scuttling out of the room.

'Don't worry,' he winks. 'It's not the first time I've seen a pair of smalls.'

Oh God. 'What do you do, Roy?'

'I'm a teacher, maths and science. For my sins,' he adds.

Immediate alarm bells ring. Their hours aren't long enough. I don't want someone pitching up at five in the afternoon. Maybe all I want each month is a cheque through the front door – but no Roy attached to the payment.

'I got posted to this school in Ealing,' he continues, 'but my missus wasn't keen on moving and it's too far to commute from Devon.'

'Oh, I see.' But all I can see is Roy sitting on my sofa marking textbooks.

I take him up upstairs into the spare bedroom. It's a small room with a painting of a Spanish olive grove on the wall, shutters and a double bed with a spotty blue duvet cover.

He sits down on the bed. 'Comfy.' He smiles suggestively. I look away.

What am I going to do? I'm not going to show him my bedroom. He's a bit of a creep, isn't he? How can I say no? I might have to tell him that on the odd occasion he will have to share the bed with my father, and that my father suffers from bowel problems. Incontinence. My father will need the side closest to the bathroom. That ought to do it.

He jumps up, rubs his hands eagerly. 'So how's about tomorrow then?'

'Tomorrow!' I shriek.

'Yep. Whenever suits the lady of the house.'

'Oh, Roy, I'm not sure. You see the thing is . . .'

'I'm a really easy person to live with,' he interrupts, 'you'd hardly know I was here. All I want to do when I get back from work is put my trackie bums on and chill out, you know what it's like,' he says as he winks at me again. One wink breeds another. It's a disease.

At this critical emergency point my mobile vibrates in my pocket, alerting me that I have a new text message. I ask him if he'll excuse me for just one minute, quickly dashing out of the bedroom and downstairs. I have a message from Anna. 'How's Mr MTFM going? X' Will call her later. Right now I have to sort this out, I think, hearing Roy coming down the stairs.

'Come over NOW,' I text Gloria. 'Pretend u r interested in No. 21'. SEND.

Roy rejoins me and settles himself comfortably on my sofa when someone knocks at the door.

'Sorry, Roy, I was going to say, I have this other person interested in the room too, so . . .'

'Oh.' He springs up and chucks the magazine onto the floor. 'Sure. I'll get my bike.'

I feel guilty as I watch him wheel his chariot across my carpet but then again, could *you* live with someone who said trackie bums? No, I didn't think so. Ruskin doesn't want to either.

I open the front door and Gloria bursts in, dressed in her shapeless T-shirt, black leggings, flip-flops and silver hair tied back in an Alice band. She couldn't look less like a Monday to Fridayer if she tried.

I shake her hand. 'I'll be with you in a minute,' I say, mouthing, 'thank you.'

'What a charming house,' she enthuses, bustling in. 'I'll take it!'

Roy pushes his bike past us. 'Can you let me know as soon as you can?' he asks, giving Gloria a curt nod on his way out.

'Of course. Thanks so much for coming over.'

'No problem.' He mounts his bike and pedals off into the hinterlands of Hammersmith.

I turn to Gloria, relieved.

'Choosing a lodger and living with someone is like a marriage,' she insists. 'You rarely marry the first man you go on a date with, do you?'

Good point.

'Don't worry, Gilly. Only twelve more Roys to go.'

And on that note, we polish off the rest of the bottle of wine, order some Thai and watch *How to Look Good Naked*.

★

Later that night, in bed, I can't sleep.

Is Gloria right? Will I find the perfect Monday to Friday man? If so, why do I have such an uneasy feeling about allowing a stranger into my house?

9

'I have this uneasy feeling,' Mum says to the health visitor, when Nick, Anna and I return home from school. Megan is lying on her fleecy rug in the sitting room, toys scattered around her. Mum said Anna could come over for tea before we go off to Brownies together later on in the evening. I've just been made chief Elf and I'm taking my House Orderly test tonight; one of my main tasks is polishing a brass doorknob. I can't wait.

'She should be sitting up by now, surely?' Mum insists, as we clamber past Megan and the grown ups and into the kitchen.

'Mrs Brown, you're being an over-anxious mother,' she says. 'I see it all the time.'

'But Megan's seven months old.'

'I'm sure everything is fine. She's a happy little baby. Look at her.'

Mum doesn't say anything.

'Try not to worry,' the health visitor stresses as she puts on her coat.

'Gilly!' Mum calls up to my bedroom, after the health visitor has left. 'Can you come here!'

I emerge at the top of the stairs, pen in my mouth, brow furrowed in concentration.

'Please.' There's desperation in her tone.

Reluctantly I follow Mum into the sitting room and crouch down next to Megan, who looks up at me, smiling. Her dimpled legs look like doughy baguettes and she's wearing soft pink shoes, designed with felt piglets.

I stroke Megan's dark hair. Everything about my baby sister is big. She has a round face, the shape of a full moon, deep-blue eyes, chubby arms and legs, a mass of thick hair and a wide smile. Dad says she'll be a supermodel when she grows up.

'There's something wrong,' Mum says. 'I'm worried, Gilly.'

'Why?'

'Watch.'

Mum lifts Megan into her arms, holds her briefly, then places her gently back down on the rug. 'Did you notice anything?' Mum asks, staring at me.

'Like what? She's fine.' Impatient, I get up. 'Can I go now?'

But Mum asks me to watch again. Exactly the same thing happens. I shrug.

'Sorry – go, poppet,' she says distractedly. As I am about to leave the room I watch Mum picking Megan up again, rocking her in her arms and then putting her back down on the rug and watching carefully, as if Megan's about to do something different this time, but she doesn't. She just flops back down like she always does. I hover by the door.

'Go,' Mum says. 'I'm sure I'm just being silly.'

I nod.

'And Gilly?'

I wait.

'Don't mention this to your father, OK?'

It's Sunday morning. I was out last night, on a date. Anna set me up with one of her work colleagues called Harvey and we went to a new restaurant in Soho. The atmosphere was great, and unlike my last date, who'd turned up in a white top tucked into cord trousers, the overhang of his belly on display, Harvey had style. I am going to thank Anna for this one, I thought, as we flirted at the bar. There was chemistry, no doubt about it, but that was soon killed off when, at the end of the evening, he produced his calculator, saying I owed more because I'd eaten a pudding and he hadn't.

The telephone rings. Normally Mum calls me from Australia at this time of the day, but it's Susie. Along with Anna, Susie is one of my closest friends in London. She's married to Mark, who works in property, and they have two children: Rose, three years old and my goddaughter, and Oliver, who's four months old.

Susie was one of the first friends I made in student halls. We met in the communal kitchen area, where I was about to cook my boil-in-the-bag chicken and Susie was heating something up in the microwave. She had her back to me and was dressed in a miniskirt and knee-high boots. Her hair was short, almost cut in a boy's style, but when she turned I could see how much it suited her elfin features. The microwave pinged and out came a little white tray filled with brown mush. She peered down at it and we both laughed. 'Fancy a pizza?' she said.

She lives in Balham, has worked in insurance, but is now a full-time mum, but luckily has no intention of leaving London just yet.

'Gilly?' Susie says with hesitation.

I don't like the sound of this already. 'What's wrong?'

'I don't know how to tell you this.' She pauses. 'I was out last night . . .'

'And?'

'Oh God. I heard that Ed got married yesterday. I'm so sorry. Gilly? Are you there? Are you all right?'

Susie asks me what I'm doing today, telling me that she's meant to be seeing Mark's granny, but he can easily go on his own. 'She had an accident recently. She can't feel her feet but insists on driving, so what does she go and do? Drives into her porch and knocks the whole thing down.'

I can't help laughing nervously. 'Oh God, did she hurt herself?'

'No! Not a single scratch. Anyway, I don't have to go, if you want to come over.'

I tell her I'm meeting up with Nick and the children in the park.

'OK. Good. I just didn't want you to be on your own.'

'I'll be fine,' I assure her, stroking Rusk, curled up on my lap. 'Honestly, Susie, no one's died, I've still got so much,' I say, not wanting to scream that I'm so lonely and I *hate* it that he's married someone so quickly. Bastard. I curse my father for his stiff-upper-lip treatment. He didn't like it when Nick and I showed too much emotion; he'd send us to our bedrooms to calm down.

'Gilly, you don't have to be brave, not with me,' Susie says.

'I know,' I stammer. 'Yesterday?' I say out loud, thinking.

'Gilly?'

'Good.'

'Good?'

'It was raining.' I smile.

'Oh, Gilly. It was pouring,' she adds.

I put down the phone. Married yesterday? Ed hated rushing into things. Proposing, engagement and marriage all within a year was not his style. Maybe he met her when he was still with me? I shall never know.

73

The telephone rings. I pray it's not my brother cancelling me. I don't want to be alone today. It's Nick, telling me Hannah has caught some bug and Matilda has got lice. There's an epidemic at school.

'Keep still, Tilda!' I hear Nancy scream in the background.

'Come on, Ruskin,' I tell him. 'It's a shitty day, but we mustn't sit inside and mope about Ed. I deserve better than a coward who didn't have the courage to tell me face to face, don't I? Yes I do. Come on, let's hit the park.' Ruskin wags his tail as I get his lead and looks up at me with love in his eyes. 'It's just you and me today, just the two of us, my angel, and we are going to have a ball.'

As Ruskin and I enter the park the August sky threatens another thunderstorm. I walk past the playground area, water dripping off the swing seats.

Ruskin plunges happily through the muddy puddles.

In the distance I see someone wearing a hat, trainers and a cord jacket. It can only be him. My heart immediately lifts as I watch him chasing his dog round and round in circles. 'Trouble!' he calls desperately.

When I reach him Trouble and Ruskin do the usual sniffing of each other, though this time Ruskin takes it a step too far. At my age I shouldn't be embarrassed, but I find myself pushing Ruskin off Trouble's back. He laughs, saying they're playing piggyback. I ask him what he's doing out here on such a miserable afternoon.

'I could ask the same of you,' he says before replying, 'I'm trying to train Trouble, but she's not interested, as you can see.'

I come into my element, remembering puppy-training school all those years ago. 'Plenty of treats because bribery works, and I only have to mention the word chicken or squirrels and he's by my side. Watch.' I demonstrate and he seems impressed when Ruskin bolts over to me, ears alert.

'The other day, I didn't catch your name,' I say.

'Guy. How do you do.' He shakes my hand.

'Gilly,' I say, 'with a "G". Careful!' I squeal, grabbing Ruskin's collar and pulling him close towards me. 'Get Trouble! You need to watch out for that man,' I warn him.

'Where?'

'Eleven o'clock, eleven o'clock!'

Guy turns and locates a man with a grey beard and a figure like Santa Claus, walking combatively round the edge of the park dressed in what looks like a bulletproof jacket and camouflage trousers. Behind him is a large black-and-white dog on a lead that looks more like a prison chain.

'Thanks for the tip,' Guy whispers, Trouble safe beside him. 'Is that a dog or a wolf?'

I laugh. 'Most of the dogs are nice,' I reassure him, 'it's the owners you need to worry about.'

'I can see that. I wouldn't like to meet him in a dark alleyway.'

'How old is Trouble?'

'Nine months. She's not mine.'

'Oh?'

'My girlfriend's.'

'Right.' Why did I imagine he'd be single? No one's single except for Harvey with his calculator . . . and me.

'She's travelling at the moment.'

'Really? For work?'

'Holiday,' he says awkwardly, adjusting his hat. 'Long story. Anyway,' he continues, 'my life's not worth living if any harm comes to Trouble while she's away.'

I smile, telling him about my first experience with Ruskin and how paranoid I'd been about letting him off the lead when he was a puppy. The moment I did, he'd headed straight for the pond where a little girl was feeding the pigeons. Ruskin had jumped up at the girl with auburn curls, grabbed the bread from her podgy fingers, her mother screamed at me, I blew my whistle, the little girl wailed, Ruskin merrily chomped on the bread . . . and then Ed intervened.

'Ed?' asks Guy, enjoying the story.

'An old boyfriend. He was my . . .' No. I reject the idea of telling Guy the miserable tale, which ends in him getting married yesterday. 'Long story,' I smile.

It starts to pour with rain and Guy and I sprint across the park and out of the gates.

At the zebra crossing we stall, a car driver beeps his horn. 'Do you fancy a drink?' we ask at the same time, rain slashing against our clothes.

'Yes,' we both reply. 'Come on,' Guy says, and we clutch onto one another, running down the pavement with our dogs, laughing as we dodge the puddles.

That evening I drive Ruskin over to see my father with a couple of homemade lasagnes for his freezer. Dad still lives by Regents Park, in our old house along Fitzroy Road. When Mum left us all those years ago, he didn't remarry.

When I arrive, Dad fixes us both a strong drink, smiling as he says his biggest relationship since our mother has been with the gin bottle.

I sit at the kitchen table as Dad cooks us scrambled eggs. Being here always reminds me of my childhood. In this room I see Dad, all those years ago, cooking eggs for Nick and me on a Sunday night. I was assigned to toast duty, Nick had to lay the table and Dad was in charge of the cooking. I also remember us both getting on with our homework at this table.

I can hear Mum telling us the news about Megan that fateful day when she'd returned from the doctor's clinic. I sat in this chair, facing the garden window. I recall Dad being so strong for all of us that night.

I look at him now. His hair is grey, his pale skin as fragile as tracing paper, but there is and always has been a distinction in the way he holds himself, dresses and talks. He is a proud man. At home, rarely do I see Dad without a tie on; I've never seen him in a pair of shorts. I remember him only once dressed in a pair of blue swimming trunks, paddling in the sea with Megan on his shoulders. Mum, Nick and I poked fun at his white legs, but he was still one of the most handsome men on the beach. Mum said the first time she met our father a thousand lights went on in her head.

Dad has been a wonderful father to Nick and me, but he's always found it hard to express how he feels. When Mum left, something died in our family. Nick and I were eleven and scared, but Dad seemed almost clinical in his ability to carry on.

We had to 'brace up' because we had no choice. But behind closed doors I'm sure he wondered how he was going to cope. Would she ever come back? After losing Megan I think he grieved in private and wished Mum was by his side.

Over our scrambled eggs I tell Dad about Edward getting married.

He takes my hand. In the past few years he has shown more affection, as if he understands now there is no weakness in being vulnerable.

'Oh Dad,' I sigh, when he keeps his hand clutched around mine. 'I just want to be happy again.'

'You will be. I know it's little consolation right now,'

he begins, 'but in time you will meet someone else, Gilly.'

I tell him about my date with Harvey.

'You will meet someone else,' he repeats, 'maybe not Harvey,' he adds with a dry smile, 'but someone clever enough not to let you go.'

I I

Summer 1985

Dad, Nick and I are sitting round the kitchen table when Mum tells us the news.

It turns out Mum wasn't being silly.

She had just taken Megan to see a paediatrician, praying she was an over-anxious parent, but he told her that Megan had 'spinal muscular atrophy'.

Megan has no strength in her muscles, which is why she can't sit up. She's not going to be able to lead a normal life, run around like Nick and me. She is nothing more than a ragdoll.

I burst into tears.

'What can she do?' Nick says, a question I'm not brave enough to ask.

I can't imagine not being able to toboggan in the snow, collect conkers, bicycle into town and ice-skate with friends. It isn't fair that Megan will never be able to do all these things that Nick and I do.

'Well, she can enjoy being with us,' Mum replies. 'She can understand every word we say, so we mustn't treat her any differently and . . .'

'Beth,' Dad interrupts.

'She'll go to a special school when she's older,' Mum continues. 'She'll need lots of love and attention and we . . .'

'Beth, this is no use. Tell them,' Dad insists. The colour in Mum's cheeks vanishes. She shakes her head. 'Not now,' she says.

'Tell them,' he repeats, this time more softly. 'Or I will.'

A silence descends across the room. I clutch Nick's hand.

'Well . . . The doctor, he said, he told us . . .' But Mum can't go on. She rushes out of the room and upstairs.

Nick and I turn to Dad.

What can be worse than what Mum has already told us?

12

Just enquiring if your spare room is still available? Your place has probably been snapped up by now but if it hasn't, give me a call. I urgently need a place by the beginning of September. All the best, Jack Baker.

'When I had a lodger I used to spend all the rent money eating out,' Guy says, as we are on our fifth circuit of the park.

It's late August and over the past month meeting Guy has become as regular as drinking coffee each morning. Unobtrusively he has entered my life. We don't call each other because we haven't exchanged telephone numbers. I don't know where he lives; just that at the end of our walk he turns left at the zebra crossing and I turn right. I don't even know his surname. He is simply Guy, my dog-walking friend.

During August dog walkers dwindle in numbers

because schools have broken up and families are on their summer holidays. I've missed Sam and Brigitte, but Mari, Ariel and Walter are rarely away from their posts.

Guy, now a fully accepted member of our club, joins us in our discussions about politics, films, the funny man who always comes into Mari's shop asking for platters, the dogs' latest diets and grooming styles, and of course the weather.

Guy has discovered a lot about me. He knows my sister Megan died and that my mother lives in Australia with her second husband, Patrick. The last time I saw her was when she flew home last Christmas to help with the wedding preparations. Do I miss her? Guy asked. Yes. When Ed left me, I saw the mother I'd loved as a child when she held me in her arms. I didn't want her to go home.

I told him Mum lives in Perth and has inherited a second family from Patrick, who has two grown-up sons. 'Why don't you visit her out there?' Guy suggested.

'I'm happy she's built a new life for herself,' I said, 'but I rely on her coming here to Nick and me . . . and to Dad. I don't want to meet another family,' I'd confessed. 'One is enough.'

I have learnt that Guy left advertising and now runs his own landscape design company, 'which means I'm a glorified gardener,' he claimed modestly.

'My friends think it's daft too,' he said when he saw I was smiling, 'me wielding my hedge cutter.'

He has a sister, Rachel, who lives in the country. She's a teacher and is engaged to a man twelve years older than her. I've talked to him about his girlfriend, Flora, and now understand their relationship isn't quite so straight-forward, in that she isn't exactly on holiday; she bought a ticket to see the world and isn't coming home until November. Flora is an artist and professional photographer. She freelances for some of the mainstream news-papers, but her dream is to have her own art gallery.

Why is she travelling on her own? Isn't she lonely?

'I asked her to marry me,' Guy explained, 'she said yes but that she needed time out to travel before she did the whole "settling down" thing, that she had to get it out of her system. It wasn't quite the reaction I'd hoped for when I was down on bended knee.' There was hurt and wounded pride behind his smile.

'Ed and I were engaged. He left me, two weeks before the wedding.'

Guy readjusted his hat. 'Oh my God, I'm so sorry.'

'It was some time ago now,' I nodded, 'but you're right. It was awful.' I found myself telling him about it.

'I'm so sorry, Gilly,' he repeated again.

'Me too. I had to return all my presents. I've always wanted a waffle-maker.'

He looked at me curiously, then smiled saying he was surprised I'd put a waffle-maker onto my list in the first place.

It's strange how easy it is to talk to someone I haven't

known for long. I've told Guy things about my family that I didn't even tell Edward. 'It's like stripping in front of strangers at the gym,' I told him, 'the less well I know someone the easier it is to show them my cellulite.'

Both Mari and Ariel sense something is going on between Guy and me. 'Gilly,' Ariel says, 'any fool can see the way your eyes light up when he's around.'

In the shop Mari quizzes me about Flora. 'There's no way I'd want to come between them,' I tell her. Anna also asks me if I'm sure that there isn't any attraction because I mention Guy on a daily basis, but I deny it, saying it is possible for men and women to be friends. 'He's not my type,' I assure her. However, what I do know is true is that I've come to be disappointed if he's not in the park; my morning just doesn't have that same kick-start if I don't see him.

'I used to lodge with a man called Carl,' Guy says. 'That worked really well because every now and then we'd bump into one another on the stairs, but that was about it. The older I get, the worse I am at small talk. I just want to open my front door, relax and not talk to anyone.'

'Lucky Flora. She must find your company thrilling.'

He shrugs. 'Maybe I'm too old for lodgers.'

'I'm beginning to think I am too. You should have seen some of the people that turned up on my doorstep.'

'Go on . . .'

The story of Roy Haddock and his trackie bums comes first.

Guy laughs, saying that I can't live with a fish anyway.

'Exactly. And anyone who thinks they can lounge around in their trackie bums has to be either devastatingly handsome or funny, or both,' I insist.

Next was Catherine the American, who worked in recruitment and fired questions at me like a tennis-ball machine. I nicknamed her Ms Clipboard. Could she leave her 'toiletries' in my restroom? What 'facilities' were near by? Did I have white labels to stick onto our preserves? Was my canine vaccinated?

'They're perfectly reasonable questions,' Guy assesses with amusement. 'Terrible accent by the way,' he adds.

'If I work late can I stay on for the weekend?' Richard the consultant had asked.

'Doesn't he understand the concept of a Monday to Fridayer?' Guy asks.

'Exactly,' I say, delighted Guy understands my plight. 'I should have directed him back to the website to refresh himself on the definition.'

'Can I bring Freddie?' asked Jonathan, the surveyor.

'Freddie?'

'My corn snake.'

I told Jonathan that the viewing was over.

Guy shakes his head, clearly seeing my predicament.

'I've just been dumped so can I move in permanently?' asked Sam the headhunter.

'Alexander, whose request was so urgent, never turned up.'

'Can you halve the rent?' asked Tim, the City banker.

'Wanker!' Guy exclaims at the top of his voice, just as we walk past Rita, the ex-Mayor of Hammersmith, who feeds the squirrels from her red shiny scooter that is parked close to the memorial statue. Rita quite rightly tells him he needs to wash his mouth out with soap and water and I tell her I agree. His language is shocking.

As we complete another circuit, I tell Guy I need to be much more savvy about my questions when it comes to interviewing Jack Baker tonight. I have drawn up a list of house rules, advice given to me on the telephone by my mother's spinster sister, Aunt Pearl. Aunt Pearl is a veteran landlady who has had more than fifty lodgers in her lifetime, including a conman supposedly called Clint, who turned up on her doorstep wearing a beige mackintosh and carrying a red rose. 'I fell for his charm and good looks, Gilly. Don't you go making that mistake,' she had warned me.

'Do you think it's really sad to set a rota for the kitchen?' I ask Guy. This was Aunt Pearl's advice. Aunt Pearl now lives in Edinburgh, with her new boyfriend. 'Companion,' she'd corrected me. 'I'm too old for a boyfriend.' She also told me that if I had an old TV I should stick it in the spare room, keeps them out of the way.

'I should get a reference too, shouldn't I?'

'Definitely.'

'I need to know that each month my rent will be paid, not start noticing that things in the house are going walkies.'

'That is a good idea . . .'

I cut him off. 'Aunt Pearl told me that she once caught one of her lodgers in the act of stealing her hedgehog trinket from the dining room. Can you imagine?'

'No. Why would anyone want a hedgehog trinket?'

Come to think of it, the portrait of the nude over my bed is valuable too. My father and I chose it together after I had graduated from Manchester with a 2:1 in English. When the gallery owner was telling me I'd made a wise investment Dad clamped an arm around my shoulder and said, 'She's a great girl, she deserves it.' Dad rarely shows emotion, so when he does I can recall it vividly, every word and touch.

I make a mental note to insure my painting against theft.

'How's Flora?' I ask, as we stall at the zebra crossing. 'Any news?'

'We spoke yesterday – it was her birthday.' He pauses. 'She's having such a good time, I sometimes wonder if she'll ever come back and marry me.'

'Bobby Shaftoe's gone to sea,' I recount nostalgically, 'Silver buckles on his knee. He'll come back and marry me, Bonny Bobby Shaftoe.'

Guy looks bemused.

'It was Megan's favourite song: we used to sing it with her on long car journeys,' I explain.

'Do you think about her?' Guy asks gently.

'Sometimes,' I confess.

Her memory is like a pebble in my shoe. There are some days when I know it's there but I can live with it. Other times it's so sharp that it digs and cuts into my skin, my foot bleeds and I can't walk on. I have to stop because I'm crying unexpectedly.

Tears fill my eyes.

'I'm sorry,' he says again. 'She must have been special.'

'She was. It's stupid really, when it happened such a long time ago.'

'You haven't really told me how she died.'

Traffic rushes past, our dogs are pulling on their leads and a police car's siren blasts.

'Tell me another time,' Guy suggests, touching my arm.

I nod, feeling the warmth of his hand. 'Flora will come back, Guy. She'd be mad not to.'

Guy turns left; I turn right.

13

December 1985

'Happy birthday dear Megan, happy birthday to you!' we sing as Mum walks into the sitting room with a chocolate cake lit with one pink candle.

Megan, one today, sits in her high chair made of foam, moulded to her shape to support her spine. I'm glad her birthday is close to Christmas because her purple dress covers the splints on her legs; her cardigan covers the splints on her arms. As she sits in her chair, I make myself believe she is normal, that she'll go on to have lots more birthdays, like Nick and me.

I cut the cake and Mum tells me to make a wish. Normally I wish to be a famous author like Enid Blyton. Today I wish that Megan will live forever.

We take it in turns opening her presents: animal mobiles for her bedroom, sparkling hairclips and nursery rhyme books. Megan points to the 'Bobby Shaftoe' page, insisting, 'That one!' and Aunt Pearl, Mum's sister who lives in Dorset, reads it to her. Aunt Pearl isn't married. She has long dark hair dyed with plum-coloured streaks and she wears gypsy dresses with high-heeled boots. Nick and I love staying with Aunt Pearl during the holidays because she has a dog called Snoop and she lives in a pretty thatched cottage with a large garden that we can play in. My bedroom looks out at horses in a field, and I tell myself that when I grow up I will live in a country cottage too, just like this one. Aunt Pearl always has funny lodgers staying in her house The last time we stayed we met a Japanese man called Luke, who taught Nick and me origami at her kitchen table. Her current lodger is an opera singer, and Aunt Pearl says she wakes up to the most beautiful voice.

I saw Aunt Pearl handing our mother an envelope earlier. It was from Granny. 'Megan needs our mother's support, not her bloody money,' Mum said angrily when she took out a fifty-pound note. 'Why doesn't she visit us? Is she ashamed?'

We play games and it seems unfair that my baby sister can only watch, but each time I look at her, she's smiling. I decide Megan is the real miracle in our family.

Over the following year we're happy. At mealtimes we sit down together to home-made fish pies. We talk to Megan about our day and ask her what she has done in playgroup.

Megan becomes the reason why my father starts to come home early from work. He strides into the kitchen and scoops Megan up from her chair before taking her upstairs for her bath. Sometimes I help him. We pile crocodiles, sharks and ducks into the bubbling foam and Dad rolls up his shirtsleeves to support Megan's head and lean her back gently into the water. After her bath she has to be wrapped in heated towels and dressed immediately.

Megan goes to bed at the same time every evening and I hear the sound of Mum's footsteps in the middle of the night heading towards her room, where she will gently turn her over in bed. In the morning Mum lays her down on the sheepskin rug and has to remove all the mucus from her mouth with a suction machine, which is placed over her mouth and nose. She tells me that it doesn't hurt, that I must remember that it is this machine keeping Megan with us. Everything in the house is sterilized. Mum is always cleaning obsessively.

At weekends we get out of London. Before Megan was born Nick and I would meet up with school friends, but now we go on day trips, and during the summer we all bundle into Dad's car and drive to the coast. His car is hot and smells of curry, but I love escaping from the city to explore. Mum wraps Megan in so many layers, saying she looks like an Egyptian mummy. 'Too hot,' Megan sometimes protests, but Mum explains to us that it is vital she doesn't catch a cold.

Driving to the beach, we play games and sing songs. There's always music in the house or in the car when Megan is around. My little sister has the voice of an angel. The doctor explained to us that because she doesn't have to concentrate on movement her brain tells her not to bother with anything but her voice. She is far more advanced in speech than Nick and I were at her age. Before she's two she knows all the rhymes and songs she's learnt at her playgroup off by heart. 'Bobby Shaftoe' is still her favourite. She has a poster of him in her bedroom.

'How does it go?' we ask her each time, sardines squashed in the back of the car.

> *'Bobby Shaftoe's gone to sea,*
> *Silver buckles on his knee:*
> *He'll come back and marry me . . .'*

Then we all join in, 'Bonny Bobby Shaftoe!'

Sometimes we visit Aunt Pearl and she takes us all to the seaside. Nick and I clamber up rocks and play ducks and drakes in the sea. We paddle and collect fossils. Dad picks up Megan and runs along the sand, lifting her high into the air, the wind blowing in her face. Mum and Aunt Pearl run alongside screaming, 'Don't drop her!' One time Anna came with us, and it was so hot that Dad put on his pale-blue swimming trunks and we all laughed at his white legs.

Dad kisses Mum in public. Sometimes they hold hands.

On Sundays Mum and Dad take us to church, and Megan enjoys singing the hymns. When I kneel down to pray, I pray that the doctor got it all wrong. Yet I know her time is running out.

In a week she will be two. Mum is going to bake a cake and we've bought her a red velvet pinafore dress for her party.

'She won't live beyond the age of two,' Dad had told us that day, after Mum had rushed out of the kitchen.

That means we have just seven more days left with her.

She is slipping away from us, like sand slipping through our fingers.

14

As I wait for Jack Baker to arrive, I sift through my mail. Bank statement . . . ugh . . . letter from Hammersmith and Fulham Council . . . boring. Ah, now this looks more promising. Rarely do I see a handwritten envelope. I open it eagerly, hoping it's a party invitation, praying it's not a wedding invite, or another change of address card.

'The Heron clan Are Moving TO UIST!'

Another friend bites the dust.

On thick printed card is an illustration of a mother and father heron holding hands with their two baby herons as they head off into the sunset.

Jessica, my old sixth-form college friend and her husband Thomas are moving to North Uist, a tiny island in the Hebrides. Thomas is going to learn about the fishing industry and Jess's plan is to set up a bed and breakfast business. Jess had talked about the move for some time. She was desperate to leave London after having the children.

'Gilly,' Jessica scribbles on the card, 'please come and visit soon. We'll miss you.'

As I mount the Heron clan change of address card on the mantelpiece the telephone rings. Maybe this will be Jack cancelling? Suddenly I don't feel like showing anyone round the house.

'Look out of the window,' Gloria demands.

I look out and catch Gloria, from her bedroom, frantically pointing to the road, but I can't make out what she's mouthing. Then I glance to my left. Parked outside my front gate is a convertible black BMW. I see the profile of a tall man looking at the numbers on the doors, trying to locate No. 21.

Ruskin barks, sensing that something extraordinary is about to happen, and follows me to the door. Flustered, I pick him up and take him back to his basket in the kitchen, firmly shutting the door behind him. He can be a nuisance when it comes to showing people round the house, nipping interviewees' ankles. I remain resolute to ask Jack my questions, so have the list ready in my pocket. I rush back to look through the peephole. He's tall, very tall, fairish hair. He's coming closer, black leather jacket flung over his shoulder. Thank you, God! I can definitely live with this man! He's divine. I'm still looking through the peephole when there is a confident knock that makes me stagger backwards. I'm losing my balance. My heel is trapped in something. It's the bootjack.

I am about to fall.

Oh fuck.

'Hello?' he says.

I'm lying across my doormat and my head hurts. I'm bruised. I think I've broken something.

'Hello?' he calls again. 'Is that Gilly Brown? It's Jack. Jack Baker. The Monday to Friday man.'

'Hi!' I screech, spreadeagled on the floor. 'Hang on!' Have I twisted my ankle – or worse? I look down and my ankle is puffing up before my very eyes. 'Be with you in one sec!' I shuffle on my bottom towards the coats hanging on the pegs. I grab the hem of my dog-walking anorak and attempt to heave myself up with it. Instead, a few of Ruskin's poop-scoop bags fall out of the pockets.

'Hello?' Jack calls again. Ruskin barks furiously, head pressed against the glass door of the kitchen. 'Gilly?' He opens the letterbox now and sees me. 'Crikey, are you OK?'

I attempt to pull myself up again. 'Fine,' I shrill before collapsing back onto the floor. 'Actually no, Jack, I'm not great. I've had an accident, nothing major!'

'Can I help?'

'Um. No. Perhaps come back in five minutes?' I suggest before I hear her voice.

'Hi, I'm Gloria from across the road.'

'Jack. Jack Baker,' he says smoothly. 'I've come to view the spare room. Something's very wrong I'm afraid,' he says. 'She's on the floor.'

'Oh dearie me,' Gloria replies, turning the key in the lock.

Mortified, wishing I could die, better still just disappear in a puff of smoke, I sit in a collapsed heap waiting for them to come inside. 'Darling,' she cries out, flying towards me in her purple crocs. 'What on earth happened, ducks?'

Jack takes one arm, Gloria the other, and they heave me into a standing position. I whimper as I put my bad foot down. 'I can't walk.'

'Oh, sugarplum fairies!' Gloria says, and Jack and I catch each other's eye and smile. He has a smile that draws me to him immediately. I take in his white shirt loosely unbuttoned, his light-brown hair with soft tufts of blonde, coloured from the sun, his blue eyes the colour of Matilda's nursery paintings of a sky. He has a young, fresh face. Oh no. Maybe I can't live with him. I don't want him to see me first thing in the morning. I'm done for.

'What should we do?' I overhear Jack say to Gloria, jolting me back to reality. 'Gilly? Can you walk?'

I move but scream in agony.

'Right,' Gloria says calmly to Jack. 'I think she should go to A & E.'

'Fine,' he agrees.

And before I know it, Jack has lifted me into his arms, is strapping me into the passenger seat of his convertible, and soon we're racing down the Fulham Palace Road, heading for Charing Cross Hospital Accident and Emergency.

15

When I arrive at the park, I see my doggy crowd in the distance, under the oak tree. It's like déjà vu. There's Mari wildly throwing Basil's spongy blue ball across the grass, which he pelts over to retrieve. Back and forth he goes, his speed as fast as a furious ping-pong match. Ariel's just arrived and is parking his bike against the tree. He's dyed his hair back to brown and is wearing a stylish cord jacket, jeans and Converse trainers. He tips out a newly groomed Pugsy from the front basket before giving everyone a good-morning kiss. My heart lifts when I see Sam. There's something reassuring about seeing everyone return after the summer holidays. There's an autumnal chill in the air, the copper leaves are falling, no children are in sight and routine is restored. The only person who isn't here today is Brigitte.

When Ariel asks why I am hobbling like an old lady I explain that I have a badly sprained ankle. Walter, Sam and Ariel listen patiently as I exaggerate my fall, poor Mari having to hear it for the second time. In my account I don't crash down onto the floor, my heel wedged in the bootjack. No, no. I fall over with finesse. I find myself looking over Mari's shoulder.

'He's over there.' She rolls her eyes at Sam.

'Who?' I feign ignorance.

'Hat man,' Mari says.

'I was looking at that strange dog,' I pretend, 'I can't make out what it is.'

'Gilly Brown, you liar!' says Ariel, hands on hips.

'You and Guy?' Sam turns to me. 'What have I missed?'

'Nothing,' I say.

What they don't understand is that the reason I get on so well with Guy is precisely because there is no agenda. He's engaged. I can be myself because I'm not trying to impress him.

'Something's not right with his girlfriend,' I hear Mari telling Sam and Ariel again. She won't let it go.

There's nothing wrong with his relationship with Flora, that's just Mari making a drama out of nothing. Typical actress.

I change the subject, telling them I have a Monday to Friday man who's moving in to No. 21 tonight.

'Is he hot?' Ariel asks.

'Very.' I smile.

'Tonight! That's quick!' Mari exclaims. 'Did you ask him your questions?'

When Jack and I had returned from A & E that night, he'd picked up the list that was on the doormat, by the offending bootjack. 'Ask Jack if he has a criminal record,' he read out with amusement in his eyes. He guided me over to the sofa and helped me sit down. Blushing, I asked for the list back.

'I don't have a criminal record,' he said, 'though there was this one time when I stole a roast potato from my brother's plate and every now and then I do cheat at racing demon.'

Great. Handsome *and* a sense of humour, I thought. Jack could lounge about in his trackie bums any time. He glanced at the list again.

'We really don't need to go through it,' I objected in vain.

'Find out if Jack cooks and if he does, set a rota for meal times. Discuss.'

He paused, stroking his chin. ' "*Discuss*". Sounds like a school exam. Well, I can just about rustle up eggs and bacon on a Sunday morning, but seeing as I'm only here Monday to Friday, the kitchen remains all yours.'

'Where do you live?' I asked.

'Make sure Jack doesn't have BO,' he read. He erupted into laughter so loud that I thought the walls around us might shake.

'Come close,' Jack had gestured.

Our eyes met again. He's trouble, I thought. 'It's fine.

You don't smell.' He did though. He smelled of expensive aftershave.

'Make sure he likes dogs,' he continued which reminded me that I needed to call Gloria. After my fall, she had taken Ruskin back home with her.

'He sounds fun,' Sam claims, impressed. 'How old is he?'

'Thirty.'

'Thirty,' sighs Walter wistfully. 'Makes me wish I was young again. You young these days, tie yourself down to just one shell in the sand . . .'

Uh-oh, he's off, we all think, exchanging glances.

Mari shakes her head, irritated. 'I'd watch out for this one,' she says as though she can see something sinister through her crystal ball. 'I never trust people who are too forward.'

'He'll be great,' I reassure myself. 'And it was good of him to take me to A & E, to give up his evening.'

'Exactly,' Sam agrees. 'My husband would have shoved me into a cab.'

Guy finally approaches asking what we're all talking about and it's not long before Basil mounts Trouble's back. 'Now that's forward,' I point out to Mari, and she shrugs as she lights up another cigarette.

'What does Jack do, Gilly?' Guy asks as we separate from the group. Mari told me she wanted to get to the shop early today because Bob, her metal and glass man, was calling round.

'He works in television. Produces *Stargazer*.'

Stargazer is a singing contest that propels unknowns to stardom. I love it. It's one of my guilty pleasures.

'So what else? Has he got a family?' Guy asks.

'Don't think so.'

'Married? Single?'

'I don't know. Single, I think.' I don't tell Guy about our flirting.

Ruskin sees a squirrel, chases it unsuccessfully. I ask Guy if we can sit down on the bench as my foot is sore. For the next few minutes we watch people walk by, sitting comfortably in silence, until Guy says, 'I wonder why he doesn't have a friend he can stay with.'

'You can't stay with friends for that long Guy – the odd night, yes, but not months.'

'Where does he live?'

I'm about to answer, but then can't remember what Jack said. 'He did tell me,' I say. 'Must be the painkillers, I can't remember.'

'Oh well, doesn't matter.'

'I'll find out tonight.'

'Sure.'

'Why are you looking at me like that?' I always know Guy is anxious when he adjusts his hat.

'Gilly, did you get a reference?' He smiles, but beneath that smile he means every word.

I shift in my seat.

'I need a base until the show's over in December,' Jack

had said, giving me the list back, 'but if you're still unsure, I can get you a reference.'

Reference? With an angelic choirboy face like that, who needs one?

'And just remember, if you hate me and think I smell, I'll be gone by Christmas anyway,' Jack vowed.

'Maybe you should know a bit more about him before he moves in?' Guy suggests. I must frown because he adds, 'A few of my friends have had bad experiences, that's all.'

Faintly ruffled, I say in Jack's defence, 'He's not weird, has no pet snake and I like him.'

He turns to me. 'Sorry, I'm being insensitive. I'm sure he's a nice guy.'

Relieved, I tell him I'm ready to walk on. 'What's even better,' I say, 'is he doesn't have much clutter.'

I smile, remembering what Richard had said. He has an annoying habit of popping into my head. 'Men have a lot less clutter too. I had this lodger once, Melanie someone. Nightmare. She'd put all these bloody fruit-shaped soaps and candles round the bath.'

'Jack said all he'd be bringing home tonight was one rucksack.'

'Big enough to put his carving knives in?' Guy says with a cheeky grin, but when he sees my face he apologizes immediately.

As Ruskin and I walk to the tube station, I tell myself firmly that I will not be put off by Guy's doubts. Besides,

I need the cash and I've wasted enough time. I can't face any more interviews; the search is off. When I see Jack tonight we'll have a chance to get to know each other. Did he tell me where he lived? I'll ask him. Tonight.

16

'*That's right, you're watching* Stargazer, *the show that could make your dream come true! We've had thousands of auditions all across the UK and now we've whittled it down to just fifteen lucky contestants, but tonight one of these will be going home disappointed, their dream of stardom shattered.*'

Susie, Anna and I sit glued to my enormous television watching the sing-off between single mum Lori and sixteen-year-old Steven. Lori goes home. She cries, but through her tears she says she's doing it for her kids and the crowd cheer.

Jack should be coming home soon.

I confess to the girls I'm nervous, that it's like a first date in that I want to skip all the formalities and get to the comfortable part when I can be myself. I tell them about the chemistry I'd felt that first night. What if I were imagining it?

'I'm sure you weren't,' says Anna. 'Chemistry's either there or it isn't.'

'You seriously fancy him, don't you?' Susie asks.

I nod. 'I probably should have lived with a woman, much simpler,' I smile, glancing repeatedly at the front door.

'He may not be back for ages,' Susie says, urging me to relax. But I can't. I find myself shoving a copy of *The Week* over a glossy magazine. Anna shakes her head and lifts it up, revealing *Heat* magazine underneath.

'What's she doing now?' Anna asks Susie as I toss a random CD into the cupboard. In the run-up to Jack's arrival I have been throwing away or hiding anything that hints of a lonely life before, for example the chicken Kiev for one in my freezer. A few flowery drying-up cloths have also been hidden and will make their flowery reappearance when Jack leaves after Christmas.

Soon Anna and Susie are helping me rifle through my CD collection. '*The Best of Carly Simon*?' Anna suggests.

'Cupboard,' I say.

'Enrique Englesias?' Anna continues.

'Cupboard!' we all shout.

'I love him, though,' Susie admits.

'Me too,' I add.

'No.' Anna confiscates it.

Next, the three of us are rummaging through my DVD collection and the girls confiscate *Terms of Endearment*, *Mamma Mia!*, *Footloose* and . . .

'*Ladies in Lavender*?' Anna sighs, holding up the box. I burst out laughing.

'Why don't you suggest a cosy night in with Jack watching it,' Susie mentions.

Why didn't I check the bathroom either? I was so intent on making Jack's bedroom perfect that I forgot all about the little things. From the mirrored cupboards over the sink we gather boxes of tampax and a box of unopened condoms.

'Who knows? They might come in handy,' Anna suggests.

I chuck each item over to Anna, Anna chucks to Susie, and Susie shoves the various embarrassments into a sponge bag. Anna holds up a tube of thrush cream. 'Oh, thank God,' I say, grabbing it from her. 'And I don't think Jack needs to see this first thing in the morning?' Susie suggests, chucking my bikini-line kit into the bag. 'Not that I need it right now.' I smile at both of them.

'Nor me,' adds Anna.

'Well, I certainly don't,' finishes Susie.

Next I show the girls Jack's room. New life has now been breathed into this space. There are flowers on the dressing table, a jug of water with a glass by his bedside and clean sheets on his double bed. I've washed and ironed the blue-spotted duvet cover and I've taken down the Spanish olive grove painting, replacing it with an abstract print of New York which I thought was more Jack's style. I walk over to the curtains and draw them. 'Why don't you pop a chocolate on his pillow too,' suggests Anna.

'And a "Do not disturb" label on the door handle?' Susie adds. 'I want to live here. When can I move in?'

We hear a taxi pulling up outside No. 21 and scarper out of his room and downstairs like naughty teenagers. We hear a gate clanging and the rustle of leaves. In a fury of activity we plant ourselves back on the sofa. I adjust my hair, apply lipstick, cross my legs, then uncross them. Susie grabs a magazine, it's the television guide, and flicks through it. We laugh nervously.

'Say something!' I demand of Anna. 'Tell a funny joke!'

Anna stares at us. 'You two are pathetic,' she states. 'By the way sweetheart, you've got lipstick,' she gestures to my mouth, 'on your front tooth.'

'I hope he won't be too late,' Susie says an hour later. 'I need to get back.' She calls Mark to check up on the children.

'Here he is!' I call, beckoning them over to my desk. I have logged onto *Facebook*.

'OK,' Anna concedes, looking at his image on the screen. 'He's beautiful.'

There he is, sitting on a lawn modelling an open shirt and jeans. We read his profile. Jack Baker is interested in:

Women

'Good start,' Susie says with a vigorous nod.

Status: Single

'Why?' Anna asks.

Favourite activities: Making TV shows, making love

'That's what's wrong with him,' Anna proclaims. 'He's full of himself!'

'I'd be if I looked like that,' Susie insists.

Favourite TV show: Stargazer *(because it's mine)*

Favourite books: Do magazines count? (Stuff *and* Nuts)

Jack has a colossal four hundred and eighty-nine friends, mainly glamorous, pouting women, many with Russian-sounding names. 'It's fairly shallow, isn't it?' Anna remarks.

'Do you want tickets to his show or not?' Susie berates her.

'I mean, who out of those friends is going to jump in front of a double-decker bus to save his life?' Anna continues. 'She certainly isn't,' she says, pointing to Theresa Hampton-Williams, who looks like a *Vogue* model. 'I doubt she'd even break a nail for you. Oh, Gilly, I know I had to ask you something. Are you free next Tuesday?'

'Next Tuesday,' I mutter, opening one of my drawers to try to find my diary. Anna glances at a framed photograph of Ed and me, hidden underneath a mass of paperwork. It's the only photograph I have left of him. I couldn't quite throw the last one away.

'Does Jack know anything about you by the way?' she asks as I shut the drawer.

'Nothing.'

'They were too busy flirting,' Susie adds.

Anna picks up a photograph on my desk. 'Oh my God, I remember that holiday!' she says. It's a picture of the three of us in Ibiza. We're standing outside our apartment, wearing dresses that show off our tans. We can have only been about twenty-two. It was at the beginning of the evening (more flattering) and the three of us were about to go dancing on a hot summer's night.

The girls leave at 10.30, disappointed, and I leave Jack a note before heading to bed. That's another thing about hitting your mid-thirties. You become more sensible about going home at a civilized hour. Anna has an important breakfast meeting tomorrow with her vile boss; Susie can't stay up too late because she needs to be up early to feed baby Olly, and I . . . well I like my goosedown duvet.

I turn the light off.

Lying in the darkness I find myself thinking of Ed. Do I miss him or simply miss his presence? What I find so hard about our relationship was that it was like a great book, yet at the end, for no reason, the author went off the boil.

The story started so well in the park that day, when the mother and daughter were screaming at me because

Ruskin had pinched the little girl's bread. Ed had been reading his *Financial Times* on the bench and had come to my rescue, gently talking to the girl, telling her there was no need to be scared of dogs, that Ruskin was just a greedy monkey. I took a back seat and watched as he waved a magic wand over the crisis and peace and calm were restored. That's what I loved about Ed; just by being there he made me feel safe.

My first impressions were that he took pride in his appearance and he had an authority about him, rather like my father. Kicked out of home when he was seventeen because he didn't like his new stepmother, Ed was determined never to have to crawl back to his dad and beg for money. When I met him he ran his own company, selling advertising space on the internet. He'd made a fortune.

'How can I thank you?' I said when we were alone, sitting down next to him.

He closed his newspaper. 'You can buy me a coffee,' he suggested. Our coffee extended to lunch, which then extended to him taking me out to dinner. He whisked me off to a restaurant in Mayfair which his cousin ran, where we were given complementary champagne. We talked until the staff had to tell us it was time to leave. In the taxi on the way home, he reached for my hand and placed it in his. 'I'm going to marry you,' he predicted.

When we arrived at No. 21 he ordered the driver to go round the block. 'I've scared you, haven't I?' he said, noticing how quiet I'd been since he had almost proposed. When the taxi driver pulled up outside my house for the third time, Ed ignored the driver's impatient sighs. 'Come back to my place,' he said.

I wrote my telephone number on the back of his hand. 'Let's do this properly,' I said with a smile as I stepped out of the taxi.

I look across to his side of the bed, now empty. When Ed and I first started going out he used to sleep over here for half the week, and I'd camp at his house for the other half. We'd had our own drawers to put things in and laughed, saying it'd be so much easier if we just moved in together for good. But we didn't want to, not until we were married, partly because there was little point when we only lived round the corner from one another.

Being single is hard. Friends say it's good to be independent, and I agree, to a point, but what Nancy said is also true: that being single and over thirty in London is a lonely business. It is true that lots of women decide not to marry or thrive on being single and enjoying their careers, and I admire that. But for me, it's not what I want. While friends are settling down, I feel as if I've missed the last bus home. Being single makes me feel like a boat without an oar. Sometimes I do feel adrift.

When Ed and I first started going out neither of us could wait to go to bed. Often we'd talk and make love until the light began to creep in through the curtains, and we could hear the early-morning London traffic, people returning home after night shifts, the recycling bags being collected. Towards the end of our relationship we didn't have sex so often, but I thought that that was normal, like any other relationship. I do remember, however, one holiday in Spain, me trying to drag him out of the villa, as all he wanted to do was sleep and read his book. Had we become too comfortable with one another?

I used to ask Ed what he wanted out of life. He'd always tell me he didn't even like to think about the next day, let alone the future, that he was much more a 'live for the moment guy'. 'What does that mean for us?' I'd asked once, letting my insecurity creep into my voice.

After Megan's death and my parents' divorce, I yearned for some stability, though I couldn't bring myself to tell him this.

I am jolted from my thoughts when I hear a key in the lock. Jack's talking as he comes up the stairs. 'I'll be back this weekend,' he's saying on the landing just outside the bathroom. 'We can talk about it then. Yes, lots of love.'

Who's he talking to at this time of night? Next I hear the sound of footsteps outside my bedroom. Should I call out casually, 'Evening!' No, Gilly, I laugh at myself. I don't think so. He might think I'm inviting him into my bedroom.

Now I hear him crashing around in the bathroom. I smile, thinking about Anna, Susie and I hiding all the unmentionables. I shut my eyes.

A tap is now running, he must be brushing his teeth. Minutes later he walks towards my bedroom. I think of Guy. This is the part in a horror film when he enters my room brandishing a carving knife with a mad cackling laugh.

Then I hear his door shut.

And I breathe again.

That night I dream that Jack Baker is in my kitchen. He has long hair down to his knees and eats like a caveman, gripping a wooden spoon. When I am closer to him, I see that he is eating my porridge.

17

The following morning, after my bad porridge dream, I wake up bursting for the loo.

Go, a voice tells me. Just go. It's no big deal. You've got to bump into him at some point.

I hear vague noises coming from his bedroom.

I slip the duvet off me, open the door and, like a detective, glance to the left and to the right. Jack's door is closed. I look ahead. The coast is clear. In my oversized T-shirt and baggy striped pyjamas I tiptoe down the hallway, down two steps and into the bathroom, shutting the door swiftly behind me. Now, this is when I wish I had a lock, for what I am about to do is unforgivable. I turn on the tap full blast, and just to make sure Jack knows the room is in use, that there's absolutely no doubt about it, I turn on the shower. Then I rush to the loo, slam the loo seat down and go. Ah, thank God!

After a lightning-quick shower I open the bathroom

door and sprint back along the landing, and am so close to reaching my destination, until . . .

'Hi there,' he says in his dressing gown. 'Bathroom free?'

I pull the towel closely around me. 'Yes, all yours!' I squeak, scampering back into my bedroom.

When I hear the sound of running water I find myself smiling as I imagine Jack, naked in my shower, water running down his broad tanned back.

As I'm getting dressed for work, I decide to wear the new black dress I bought (with Jack's rent) which shows off my cleavage. As I stick my pyjamas under the pillow, I decide I might upgrade them with next month's rent. Maybe I'll buy myself a skimpy silk nightie too.

Applying lipstick, I hear him whispering on the landing. I lean into the door to try to catch what he's saying.

'Yeah, I'm off. Thank God it's Friday . . . I've been locked in the edit suite . . . She's nice, hardly seen her though.'

He must be talking about me.

He laughs. 'Any plans for the weekend by the way?'

'Got to go,' he says, when I walk out of my bedroom. He slips his BlackBerry into his pocket. We both head downstairs, Jack behind me. 'Is the room all right, the mattress comfortable?' I ask, as if I am running a bed and breakfast business.

'Very comfortable.'

'You have everything you want?'

'It's fine. Thanks for the flowers too.'

Our conversation is an ocean apart from how we reacted to one another the first time we met, and it occurs to me that Jack might be as apprehensive as I am.

'How's the foot?' he asks, followed by, 'I hope I didn't wake you last night?'

'No.' I pretend, still thinking about him naked in my shower.

We need to hit this politeness thing hard on the head. I shift from one foot to the other until Jack says hesitantly. 'Well, I'm off! Great to see you.'

'You too,' I reply with a dopey smile.

'See you on Monday then.'

'Absolutely!'

And he's gone.

Surreptitiously I push open Jack's bedroom door. It's dark, the curtains are still drawn but already it has a different smell. I glance over to his unmade bed. On the bedside table is a crumpled packet of cigarettes and some loose change. The top shelf of his chest of drawers is open and I spy a pair of Calvin Klein pants lurking under his dressing chair, which makes me smile about the knickers left in the bathroom incident.

I walk over to the wardrobe, and like a police officer searching for evidence I swing open the doors and see a line of shirts and a leather jacket. Just clothes, things you'd expect to see in a wardrobe. What did I expect or want to see? Disgusted and shocked at myself I leave the room.

I make a coffee, despondent that I am no further on in discovering anything more about Jack Baker. I don't even know where he lives. 'Oh Ruskin, why does it matter, anyway?' I ask him.

'Hi again,' Jack says, and I must jump so much because milk sloshes everywhere: onto the floor, under the table, down my brand-new black dress.

'Oh, sorry!' Jack grins. 'I didn't mean to give you such a shock.'

'Not to worry!' I turn to the sink to grab a dishcloth. Oh dear God, Gilly, stop talking with exclamation marks. I'm also mortified that he caught me out talking to my dog.

'I hope that's not a favourite dress?'

I point to it. 'What? This old thing!'

Ruskin sniffs Jack's jeans and looks up at him suspiciously, wondering who this person is invading his breakfast routine.

'Did you forget something?' I ask, composing myself.

'My script.' Jack pulls an 'aren't I stupid' face before heading back upstairs to his room, his telephone ringing again. He's turning my house into an office. 'Hi, sweetie,' I overhear him say.

I rush to mop the milk from under the table, wondering who his 'sweetie' is. I am on all-fours with Ruskin beside me, when he bends down and says, 'That was the office. They don't need me until later. How about some bacon and eggs? You got time?'

I nod, before forgetting where I am, and crash my head against the table. How am I ever going to relax around this man? Perhaps Roy chilling out in his trackie bums would have been a better and safer option.

As I watch Jack cook (even the way he fries the bacon and cracks the eggs into the bowl in one neat action is sexy), he fills me in on the *Stargazer* gossip. One of the contestants has threatened to pull out due to negative attention from the press. Jack reaches for his leather jacket, hung on the back of my chair, and in the process brushes my shoulder. From his jacket pocket he produces a pack of cigarettes and a flash silver lighter. I must frown without realizing because he says, 'Sorry, I forgot your house was non-smoking, I'll go outside.'

He opens the French doors leading out into the garden, taking his mug of black coffee with him.

As I watch him light up, for a split second I see my mother in a mouldy blue dressing gown standing in the kitchen. I see her flicking the ash into the sink as she stands gazing out of the window. 'Dreadful habit,' I tick him off, but Jack even looks sexy smoking. All he needs is his Martini, shaken not stirred, to go with it.

He rolls his eyes. 'You sound like my mother.'

I smile, noticing a bundle of clothes in a bag by the kitchen door.

'You're welcome to use the machine here if you want.'

'Don't worry, I'll take it home.'

'Where's home again?'

'Bath.'

'Right.' I don't know why, but I'm surprised he lives in Bath. I think of Bath as a place to visit for the day by coach.

'Do you live on your own?'

He nods. 'I split up from my girlfriend . . .'

Hallelujah! In excitement I knock a knife onto the floor.

'. . . about a year ago now. Christ, time flies.'

'I'm sorry,' I say, trying to look it.

'Past history. What are you up to this weekend?' he asks brightly.

'Oh . . .' I pause. 'Um, a couple of parties . . .'

Ruskin barks, as if to say, 'Liar, liar, pants on fire.'

'Cool.'

'Why don't you live in London?' I ask.

Jack stubs out his cigarette. 'Sorry, Gilly, would love to chat but I need to make a move.'

'Yes, right, me too,' I say. 'I need to take you for a walkies, don't I? Don't worry. Not you, Jack.'

He smiles. 'Have a great weekend.' He picks up his laundry bag and heads off.

Just as I am about to go upstairs to put on a new dress I spot his script on the sitting-room chair. I grab it and bolt out of the door. Jack is striding down the road, car keys in his hand, heading towards his BMW on the other side of the street.

'You left this,' I say breathlessly, as he zaps a button to unlock the front door.

He takes the script. 'God, I'm an idiot. Thanks.'

'You need a full-time assistant.'

'Are you offering?' He winks at me, a hint of mischief back in his voice. Now I didn't like Roy winking at me (poor old Roy), but somehow Jack can be forgiven. I think I could forgive Jack for quite a lot of things, even for leaving the loo seat up.

'Only if it's well paid,' I say back.

As Jack drives off, I walk home smiling to myself, already eager for Monday to come round. There's something about him. I can't put my finger on it, except that all I know is I'm looking forward to getting to know Jack Baker.

18

My wild dream of Jack and I skipping off into the sunset like the Heron clan is interrupted with a 'Hello'. Guy stands by my side with a coffee, modelling a different hat today, this one like a French beret, and he's wearing black-checked trousers that make him look like a chef. Most men couldn't get away with this outfit, but somehow it works on Guy. 'Want to do a circuit?' he suggests as if we were in the gym.

'So how's it going with Jack?' Guy asks, sharing his coffee with me. 'Have you seen him yet?'

This time I am glad to be able to report the news that I have seen him, this very morning, and I now know that he lives in Bath.

Guy looks surprised.

'I know. I can't picture him there either,' I say.

'Bath is a fabulous place,' says Mari, catching us up.

'One of my friends moved there. Beautiful architecture and I love the theatre.' She peers more closely at Guy. 'What are you wearing?'

'Trousers,' he says as his mobile rings.

When Guy disappears to take the call Mari huffs and puffs that his international phone bills must cost the earth. 'By the way, Blaize is flying in from the States.'

'Blake?'

'Blaize,' she corrects me, 'Blaize Hunter King.'

Who the hell is he?

'Come on, Gilly, I've told you about him. He's one of the best-known interior design agents in the States, buys stuff for all his celebrity clients.'

'Right, sounds great.'

'It's serious money. He's dropping by tomorrow morning, called me late last night. Serious money, Gilly,' she repeats. 'We need to roll out the red carpet, OK?' She peers more closely at Guy. 'Why is Hatman dressed in his pyjamas?'

'I love the way Flora asks after Trouble before me,' Guy says, putting his mobile back into his pocket.

'How is she?'

'Fine. Have you ever had this urge to travel?'

'No, not really. It would be great to be adventurous and backpack my way across Tibet, but . . . I love hotels,' I admit.

'I'd rather sleep outside under the stars,' Guy says.

'I'd rather look at the stars drinking champagne from my terrace.'

Guy is strangely quiet. 'Are you all right?' I ask. 'Do you miss her?'

'Yes . . . oh, Trouble, don't eat that!' he despairs when he sees her with what looks like half a Yorkshire pudding in her mouth. We liken the park to a buffet. 'I do miss her, but I've got to get on with it,' he says. 'Flora funded me for three years while I did my horticultural course, so it's my turn to support her.'

'I see, so this travelling is her time.'

He nods. 'Exactly. She's only away for another couple of months.'

'Listen, don't shoot me down . . .'

Guy pretends to shoot me.

'But why don't you join her for a week? I could look after Trouble.'

He shakes his head. 'Thanks, Gilly, that's so nice of you, but she has to do this for herself.'

We reach the zebra crossing. 'Right,' he says before adjusting his cap. 'I'd better go.'

'See you Monday,' I call over my shoulder as I head off to work.

Ruskin and I walk briskly towards the tube station when I hear 'Gilly!' I turn to see Guy catching me up. 'I was just thinking . . .' He hesitates. 'What are you up to at the weekend?'

'Um, just pottering,' I tell him.

I know Guy well enough now not to care about sounding boring or lacking invitations on my mantelpiece. There's no doubt my social life isn't quite what it used to be. Things have slowed down. The wheels have stopped turning.

I smile. 'How about you?'

'I need to buy a suit for my sister's wedding.' He twists his hat round, something I've noticed he does when he's thinking. 'I don't suppose . . .'

'Um?'

'Well, I'm a bad shopper and you're pottering, whatever that means, so . . .'

'You want me to help you?'

'Yes.' He laughs. 'Yes, please.'

We exchange telephone numbers. Guy and I are getting to be serious friends. Our friendship has progressed to a whole new level, which is beginning to move beyond the world of Ravenscourt Park. We have moved from Grade Two piano to Grade Three. Chords are becoming a little more complicated now.

'Great,' we both say when numbers are tapped in. I tell him I'm working tomorrow morning, so why not meet me at Mari's shop and we can take it from there?

We cross the zebra crossing, Guy turns left and I turn right, reassuring myself that it's a sad world if a boy and girl can't meet up at the weekend without any question marks hanging over their friendship.

*

'How's it going in the funny chandelier shop?' Nick asks me that evening, after work. We're eating out in a crowded Spanish tapas bar near to his office in the City.

'It's great,' I reply, 'giving me time to think about what I really want to do.'

'Which is?'

'I have *no* idea.'

We both laugh. 'Don't ask silly questions, Nicky,' I add.

'You should be doing something creative, you've got a great imagination. I remember you reading those stories to Megan.' He orders another beer. 'She loved them.'

I look at him, surprised. Nick never talks about her. Rarely does he even mention her name. 'I enjoyed them too,' he goes on. 'Can't remember what the hell they were about . . .'

'Mickey the Magic Monkey,' I remind him.

When I read to Megan, Nick would also sit at the end of the bed in his rocket pyjamas and listen attentively.

'Or you should teach,' he says, 'you're a natural with children.' I nod, so happy that it's just the two of us tonight, with no distractions.

His BlackBerry vibrates. 'It's Nancy,' he says, looking at the screen.

I spoke too soon.

He picks up. 'I'll be home soon, Nance. I'm out with

Gilly. No, I won't be late.' He rolls his eyes at me. 'Don't wait up.'

When he switches off, and the waiter clears our plates, I ask him if I can give him some advice.

'Be kinder to her,' I say.

He rubs his forehead hard.

'Seriously, I know she's difficult . . .'

'Difficult?' he interrupts me. 'Try spoilt and demanding. Oh God, let's not talk about it.'

Nick never wants to talk about his marriage, but during this last year I can't help but notice how withdrawn he's become. I don't see Nancy and Nick working together as a team any more. I don't like the atmosphere in their house either; it doesn't feel like a happy home. Dad says the same too. I wish Nick would confide in our father, but Dad finds it hard talking about anything personal too. Between us all, we're useless. We need our mother.

'Nick,' I say tentatively, 'Nancy drives me mad sometimes.' I pause. 'But I think she's lonely. Bored. You're never there.'

'I have to work, Gilly!'

'I know, I know you do,' I say, trying to calm him down, 'all I'm saying is she probably misses you, and maybe if you could talk more . . .'

'She's changed,' he says more quietly now. 'I don't know who she is any more.'

I reach out for his hand, rub it. 'She's your wife and you have two lovely daughters.'

'Let's change the subject,' he says tightly, withdrawing his hand.

'You get more like Dad every day, Nick. Be careful,' I warn him.

19

1986

Nick and I return from school. I can't wait to tell Mum that Anna, Nick and I raised seventeen pounds in the playground this week, selling chocolate butterfly cakes so that Megan can travel to Germany to be cured by sheep cells. We cooked the cakes last weekend. Anna and I laughed when Nick put on Mum's flowery apron.

Mum was told by one of her friends in Megan's special needs group that there is a professor in Germany who thinks he can help us. This sheep cells treatment is expensive, thousands of pounds. Some of the older children at school are doing sponsored runs and canoeing races. Mum is so proud, saying we're all going to be in the papers and on television, telling Megan's story. Dad is quiet. He's always at work.

Later that night Nick and I hide in our bedroom, just to get away from the shouting.

'You don't understand,' Mum shouts. 'We have to do something!'

'Beth, we can't afford it,' Dad says. 'We'd have to remortgage the house, the . . .'

'You can't put a price on Megan!'

'I'm not – how can you think that? I love her too.'

'Show it then. Oh, that's right, you can't.'

'Please,' he urges, 'be realistic. What do we know about this treatment? You're so vulnerable . . .'

'What does vulnerable mean?' I whisper to Nick, scared of the noise.

He doesn't hear me. His hands are over his ears.

'I'm not . . .'

'Let me finish . . .'

'We have to take a risk . . .'

'You are vulnerable,' he repeats slowly, 'and ready to believe anyone who says they can help. Is it really a viable option?'

Nick and I hide under the covers when she screams, 'You're not at work now!'

'Keep it down, Beth!' Dad begs. 'The children.'

'Act like a father, not a lawyer! What choice do we have? There are no other bloody options! I can't sit here and watch her die! Maybe you can, but I can't!' We hear the clatter of glass; something has been smashed. 'Nick and Gilly support me . . .'

'They're children! It's difficult for them to understand,' he shouts. 'Beth, please,' he says more calmly, 'think about it. You're giving them false hope, it's not fair.'

'No. We have to find the money and if you won't help me, I'll do it on my own.'

The door slams.

Nick says that when he grows up he's going to make lots of money so he can move away, as far away as possible, and forget all about Mum and Dad. 'They're always shouting! I hate them,' he says darkly.

He promises to take me with him. Under the duvet, we lock hands and promise to be best friends forever.

20

'You're doing what?' Mari says, as we both do a quick scan of the shop to make sure it's looking ready for Blaize's arrival. She told me that Blaize had once knocked into one of her lanterns in the basement, and then cursed loudly because he'd scratched one of his new crocodile-skin boots.

'Taking Guy shopping,' I repeat.

'Just the two of you?'

'Uh-huh.'

Mari is unable to keep it in. 'Gilly, do you fancy Guy?'

'No! God, no,' I add.

'I don't blame you,' she confides, as if I've said yes. 'He's funny and good-looking, in an unconventional way.'

'I don't. Anyway, he's engaged,' I remind her.

'I know, but you can still fancy the man. I've just noticed there's this nice chemistry between you. You two connect. I do wonder about his girlfriend too.'

'What do you mean?'

'Well, why would she disappear off the face of the earth the moment he proposes?'

'Everyone's different, Mari. You didn't even live with your husband.'

'That's why it worked so well, my darling. The moment Percy moved into my apartment . . . curtains,' she says.

'I don't go for men in hats, Mari.'

'Fine, I believe you,' she smiles.

No. He's not my type at all.

I really don't fancy him.

I find myself smiling.

When Blaize Hunter King enters the shop, dressed in a pristine white shirt, tailored trousers, leather boots and his dark hair slicked back with gel, I nearly drop the French rococo lamp base on the floor. Mari and Blaize's dramatic air kiss is promptly interrupted by about four of his mobile telephones ringing at the same time.

He takes out the first, flicks the lid open dramatically. 'Oh, Madonna, darling, can I put you on hold . . .' He searches for the next phone.

'Madonna?' I repeat. 'He's putting *Madonna* on hold?'

Mari tells me to stop looking so shocked. 'This is Blaize Hunter King, one of the best-known interior designers to the stars,' she reinforces proudly again, 'and he does what the hell he likes.'

When she introduces me as her new assistant I almost curtsy as I say, 'How do you do?'

'Very cute,' he says, eyeing me up and down in my black dress, my hair swept up with a gold clip.

Soon Blaize has both Mari and I taking off our shoes and clambering over piles of stock to reach the perfect verdigris lantern for Madonna's home in New York. Mari is clever the way she knows exactly what light would look good in a certain setting. 'No, Gilly, not that one, the other one!' she orders me. I laugh, saying it's like a game of Twister in here.

'Oh, Mari, it's divine,' Blaize sighs, before pointing to one of the chandeliers in the window. 'Madge would love that. How much?'

'Five and a half thousand,' I say, adrenalin flowing.

'A steal! Take a picture, will you,' he demands, clicking his fingers at me. Mari warned me he'd do this, so I am ready with the camera.

Two hours and fifty pictures later, I am exhausted. I've been on my hands and knees in the basement searching for the right rustic lantern to go in Madonna's French chateau, up ladders to unhook mirrors for Pierce Brosnan's place in Aspen, and rushing into our local deli to buy Mari espressos and Blaize organic detox juices. I completely forget Guy is meeting me here until the doorbell tinkles and he enters the shop. 'Mari, darling, how much do I owe?' Blaize asks, brandishing his American Express card in one hand.

'Guy! Come and meet Blaize,' I say breathlessly, brushing the dust off my dress. I catch Guy looking around the shop in awe, with precious objects teetering on tables and shelves, an accident waiting to happen. Blaize has bought four lanterns, two lamp bases, one mirror and the chandelier in the window.

'Surely Mari can give me a small bonus?' I whisper to Guy as we head off to the shops.

Our search to find a suit for his sister Rachel's wedding begins along the Fulham Road. Rachel is getting married in a fortnight and she has instructed him that he *has* to look traditional, so I decide to take him to Ed's favourite shop, run by a stylish balding man called Adrian. Ed used to compare Adrian's head to a shiny white snooker ball. It's a small, intimate shop that sells beautifully tailored suits, shirts and silk ties, right down to designer boxer shorts and cufflinks. I buy my father the same maroon cashmere socks every year for Christmas. Maybe I'll buy him a different colour next time.

'Gilly, come in.' Adrian welcomes me as if I were a long-lost friend, before assessing this new man beside me, so different from Ed.

He then asks if we need his help, so I tell him to make Guy look fit for his sister's wedding.

'You, my friend, shall go to the ball,' Adrian says to Guy with a dazzling smile, his gold tooth shining.

*

Adrian presses different-coloured shirts against Guy's chest and I enjoy telling Guy what does and doesn't suit him, though he remains deathly quiet, as if he's in a torture cell.

As I hunt through the rails of clothes, Adrian taps me on the shoulder. 'I was very sorry to hear about Edward,' he says.

'Thanks.' I touch his shoulder affectionately. 'How did you know?'

'News travels fast. Really, Gilly, the swine. She's not a patch on you,' he adds before whispering, 'I like your new man. Good on you, girl.'

'Oh, Adrian, he's just a friend,' I whisper.

'That's what they always say!'

'Do you ever see him?' I can't help asking.

'Um.' He purses his lips. 'He was in the other day, but let's just say, after what he did to you, sweetheart, I'm very cross with him!'

I select an electric-blue coloured shirt and for the finishing touches I approach Guy with a silk spotted tie, though he looks at me as if I were about to feed him a cockroach. 'Come on, this won't hurt,' I assure him as I lift up his shirt collar. 'Why do you hate dressing up so much? What are you going to wear at your own wedding?'

'Don't know. We want to keep it low key.'

'That's a surprise.' I smile as I confide to Guy that everyone has hang-ups. I have an aversion to marquees and tights. Marquees make me feel giddy; tights make me feel itchy. 'I hated the thick woolly ones I had to wear at school.'

Finally Guy relaxes, telling me I'm a professional when it comes to putting on ties.

'I used to help my brother, Nick. He's so badly co-ordinated, always got it in a knot or did it the wrong way. There.' I stand back and look at Guy, now my work of art. Then I cast an eye to his woolly hat.

He backs away.

'It's like me wearing a wedding dress with trainers!' I protest, marching towards him.

'No, Gilly.'

'Take it off! Flora will thank me.'

He laughs, keeping one firm hand on his hat. 'No.'

'Can I help?' Adrian asks, bemused.

I cross my arms and stare at Guy. 'He won't take off his hat.'

Adrian surveys Guy, one hand on his hip. 'I think it would look better without,' he agrees.

'I come with my hat. Take me or leave me.'

'Right, I'm going then.' I walk away and exchange a secret smile with Adrian.

'Gilly!' Guy calls.

I turn.

There is something achingly vulnerable about seeing Guy without his hat on.

'I haven't had the chance to dye it yet,' he says gesturing to the grey at the side. His dark hair is wild, unkempt;

he looks as if he's been on a long coastal walk in blustering wind. Self-consciously he runs a hand through it.

I brush a loose strand of cotton off his shoulder and turn his face to mine, noticing for the first time the colour of his eyes. They're blue, not vivid like Jack's but a soft gentle colour.

'Better,' comments Adrian. 'Much better.'

'You look handsome,' I tell him.

'You're very privileged you know, I don't take my hat off for any old person,' Guy says.

As we clutch our shopping bags (I bought a pair of black ankle boots that I've always hankered for – thank you, Monday to Friday Jack), Guy turns to me, saying that it's my turn next; he'll do whatever I want.

'OK.' I think. I look at my watch, it's close to four o'clock. 'Let's pick up the dogs and then I'd like to visit someone.'

'Who?'

'You'll see.'

I lead Guy into St Mark's Church, large and impressive, on the edge of Regent's Park.

'On Sundays we used to come here,' I tell him. 'Megan called it her church because she could see it from her bedroom.' I point to a small window in the south transept. It's modern and in the centre is an engraved monkey. 'This is Megan's,' I say.

'It's beautiful.'

'I wrote these stories for her, called *Mickey, the Magic Monkey*, and Mickey took Megan everywhere in her dreams. He'd dress her up like a princess and take her to palaces and parties and fly her on magic carpets to places far and wide, like Egypt and India . . .' I stop. 'That's why Mickey is here, in this window, right where he should be.'

'May I?' Guy picks up a candle and lights it. 'Hey, Megan,' he says in a hushed tone, 'it's Guy here. I hope Mickey's looking after you and you're having fun. In the meantime, I want to tell you what's going on down here. Well, I've met your big sister, Gilly, and she's lovely.' He turns to me and grins. 'She's just been helping me buy a suit. She's very bossy, you know, telling me to take my hat off.'

I nudge him. 'Honestly, Megan, if you'd seen him with his hat on, you'd have done the same,' I say quietly.

'Anyway,' Guy resumes, 'we met in the park, dog walking. She's got this cute little dog called Ruskin and my dog's called Trouble. I know! Isn't it a ridiculous name, that's what I said to my girlfriend too. Well, Gilly and I are about to take the dogs for a walk up Primrose Hill, and when we get to the top we'll wave to you, OK, so you'd better be looking out for us! Anyway, in case you're worried about Gilly, she's doing fine. I'm looking out for her, just as Mickey is looking out for you.'

★

Guy and I make our way up the hill. It's early evening; the sun beginning to set. When we reach the top, a few stray tourists are examining the information site.

We wave to Megan, just as we'd promised. 'It must have been hard,' Guy says, 'losing her when she was so little.'

I nod.

'How did you cope?'

'We didn't.' I pause. 'We knew she was going to die, but you can never be prepared for it, never. There was no structure any more, that's what was so hard, the shape of our days . . . it just vanished. When Megan was around a lot had changed and it was hard for Mum looking after a child completely dependent on her. Our entire lifestyle, where we went on holiday, what we did at weekends, it all revolved around Megan, but I loved the security of knowing Sunday was a church and zoo day.' I look ahead. 'When she died, Nicholas and I prayed Mum would get out of bed, let alone do something with us at the weekends. Dad buried himself in his work, didn't want to admit the family was falling apart. We might have had four walls around us, Guy, but they were made of nothing.' Tearful, I stop, aware that I may have said too much, but am touched to see he's listening to me, so patiently. I never really talked to Ed about Megan. He would tell me it was in the past.

'What was your Sunday? Tell me about your family,' I ask as we walk back down the hill.

'My Sunday? Well, it was Dad's one free day on the farm so we'd have a Sunday roast, and if we were really good, we'd have spotted dick and custard for pudding.'

Back at No. 21 I ask Guy to stay on for supper, tempting him with the fresh squid that I'd bought from the fishmonger in Primrose Hill.

'Lucky we're not kissing anyone tonight,' Guy says, raising an eyebrow when I'm chopping the third garlic clove for the mayonnaise.

As the squid sizzles in the pan, Guy opens a bottle of wine and sets the table. This is what I miss, I realize. Being with someone. Today has flown by because I've been absorbed in his company and completely at peace.

Perhaps this is where Ed and I went wrong. We began to spend too much time apart.

Ed's internet business was expanding. He set up an office in Singapore, which meant he was always away. I believed him when he told me his distance was due to stress at work, but maybe, in reality he was in turmoil, wrestling about whether he was making the right choice. Why didn't I see these signs?

I particularly recall one time when Ed had returned from a work trip. He had clambered into bed, exhausted. When I put my magazine down and reached over to touch him, he kissed me perfunctorily on the cheek, saying he was tired.

I should have questioned him more. Why didn't I? I

remembered Mum telling me that her engagement to Dad was the happiest time of her life, though that didn't exactly end up like a fairytale, mind you. Maybe I thought I was in love with him because I was desperate to create what my mother and father hadn't had i.e. a happy future, but if I am honest I've never been passionately in love with any of my boyfriends, not even Edward. I enjoyed being with him but I'm beginning to see how I was hanging on to what our relationship was like at the beginning, not wanting to see that we'd run our course. I stand at the French doors watching Guy survey the garden. The evening light catches his face.

Perhaps I've never been in love at all. What is love? I only caught glimpses of it in my parents' marriage. I captured much more hatred.

'Tell me more about your family,' I ask Guy as we eat our squid. 'Are your parents still together?'

'No, my father's dead. He died when I was twenty-three.'

Guy pours me another glass of wine.

'Were you close?'

'Very.'

I lean towards him. 'Was he like you?'

'No.' Guy smiles, as if the idea is far-fetched. 'Dad was a farmer to start with. I didn't even like living on a farm when I was a boy,' he admits. 'It smelled of manure and death and decay.'

I continue to listen to Guy talking about his family. I love the way he talks. He speaks quietly, yet his voice tells the story with a liveliness and endearing honesty.

'Dad was interesting, though. His true love was pictures, and when he retired from the farm he went to college and learned how to restore paintings. He wished he'd done that right from the beginning.'

'Why didn't he?'

'He had no confidence, just thought being a farmer was all he could do, like my grandfather. Not that being a farmer isn't a good job,' he's quick to add, 'and it's hard work. If he wasn't sleeping, he was working. He didn't go to school, had no education or qualifications because his mother kept him at home. He was the youngest of eight . . .'

'Eight! Are you Roman Catholic?'

'Lapsed,' he smiles. 'Anyway, Dad's mum wouldn't let him go. I think she must have been unhinged by this stage. I mean, you would be after giving birth to eight children, wouldn't you? So in the end Dad taught himself to read and write from home, but he had no experience in the outside world. He inherited his father's farm and that was that. If you're told that's all you're good for, that's what you believe.'

'Did he resent his mother?'

'Oh yes. That's why he used to tell me to get good qualifications so I could have the freedom to do something I loved. That's why I got out of advertising in the end. My heart wasn't in it. I became bored, stuck in a rut,' he says, just as I'd said to Richard.

'You needed a change?'

'Exactly. I'd loved gardening since I was a little boy, and something was telling me to do it. I remember being so nervous about ringing the woman running the course. I kept on worrying about how Flora and I would manage without a second income, and did I really want to go back to school again? I nearly put the phone down, but I'm so glad I made that call. Isn't it weird how one call can change your life?'

I nod. 'You found something that makes you happy. Your father would be really proud.'

He shrugs. 'I don't earn as much money,' he says, 'but yes, I'm happy. Most of the time,' he adds. 'Hey, what's wrong?'

I wipe my eyes on the sleeve of my jumper. 'I know I'm lucky, Guy. I'm young . . . ish,' I say, 'have lovely friends, my own home . . .'

'With a hot lodger,' Guy reminds me.

'Seriously hot,' I add. 'I have my loyal Ruskin.' Ruskin is under the table, lying at my feet. 'I'm healthy. There are people much worse off than me.'

'So why are you sad, Gilly?'

'I haven't found my something yet.'

Guy leans over to me and wipes a tear from my eye with his thumb. Without thinking, I take his hand and hold it gently, and our fingers link. Abruptly we free our hands and I sense Guy is asking himself the same question: what happened just then?

'Let's go out,' he says, to break the tension. 'I'll take you for a drive.'

'Have you noticed there's no horizon in London?' Guy comments as we drive over Lambeth Bridge. 'Sometimes, when I'm tired and can't sleep, I drive round here. I love the Embankment at night, with the bridges all lit up. It reminds me why Flora and I still live here.'

'When's she back?'

'About five weeks now.'

'How did you meet?'

'At a tennis charity thing. She was wearing this cute pleated skirt and I couldn't take my eyes off her.'

'Off her legs you mean.'

'Off *her*. Well, OK, she did have great legs. My partner blamed me for not concentrating.' He smiles. 'Anyway, after we were thrashed I asked her out.'

'Then what happened?'

'We had a couple of great months together . . . then she asked me to go to New York. She wanted me to meet a few of her friends who lived out there.'

'And?' I sense there is more to this story.

'I was in the office, about to book the flight and all I can remember thinking is if I hit the confirm button, Flora and I will probably end up marrying. I can't explain it, but it wasn't just a holiday. I pressed the key and then ran around the office like a madman.'

I laugh, picturing him.

'I still think about it,' he says.

'About what?'

'What would have happened if I hadn't gone to New York. I'm not sure we'd be together. Oh, I don't know,' he says quickly afterwards, perhaps fearing he came across as disloyal, 'maybe we would.'

'Well, I'm looking forward to meeting her.'

As I look at the river lit up at night, I wonder if I am really looking forward to meeting Flora. We say so many things that we don't mean, the truth hidden beneath the layers of what we ought to say. The thing is, when Flora returns inevitably my friendship with Guy will change.

I look over to him and he smiles, asking me what I'm thinking about. I'm thinking about him lighting a candle today and the way he had talked to my sister. Today has been a one-off day that I shall always remember and treasure. A bit of gold found at the bottom of the ocean. I'm thinking that out of the blue, through Ruskin and the park, I've met someone unusual and special.

'What a lovely day I've had,' I say, 'Thank you.'

21

'Evening,' Jack greets me as my head is in the fridge, trying to work out what to eat tonight. 'Hi, Ruskin.' Jack strokes Ruskin, but my boy isn't quite sure who he is yet. Often I find him in Jack's bedroom, sniffing around or having the audacity to sit on his bed to mark his own territory.

Jack has been living with me for three weeks now, but so far we have been like ships passing in the night. However, I am getting more used to his presence. In the morning I can smell his aftershave in the bathroom and fresh coffee coming from the kitchen. I know we're becoming less self-conscious about living together in that our bedroom doors aren't quite so firmly shut any more and I don't run all the taps in the bathroom before I'm about to go to the loo.

Late at night when I'm in bed I find the sound of Jack's key turning in the lock comforting. I imagine him knocking on my bedroom door and lying beside me, taking my face into his hands and kissing me. During the quiet moments in the shop, I find myself fantasizing about him, hoping our collisions on the landing or under the kitchen table are going to develop into something more 18-rated.

'Did you have a good weekend?' I ask him, shoving the remains of a quiche that needs to be eaten into the oven.

'Weekend? That seems like years ago.' He helps himself to a can of beer and joins me in the sitting room. I grab the television guide to see what's on. 'So, what did you get up to?' I ask him.

'Nothing much.'

'Nothing will come of nothing. Speak again,' I demand, before explaining that my boss, Mari has got the part of Goneril in *King Lear* and we've been running through her lines together, so I've reread the play.

He grins. 'One of my mate's children had a birthday party,' he says, rolling his eyes.

'It gets slightly boring, doesn't it, when friends have children. Don't get me wrong, I love them but . . .'

'I know exactly what you mean,' he says.

When Susie had told me she was pregnant with Rose, of course I was happy for her, but there is no doubt I also knew our friendship would change.

'I once went to this party,' I carry on, enjoying the fact that Jack's single and understands, 'and was sandwiched between two mothers talking about where they were going to send their children to school. The only thing they asked me was if I could pass the horse-radish sauce.'

Jack laughs. 'Why were you sitting next to two women in the first place?'

'There's always a shortage of men,' I say. 'Do you ever get stranded at parties where people flip open their mobiles and show you pictures of little Oscar and wee Nathaniel?'

'So boring,' Jack agrees.

'I tell you what else can be annoying,' I continue now with great gusto, 'You're telling friends a story and you're about to get to the *really* juicy part and then little Olly has to go and drop his Mr Whippy ice cream down his jumper . . .'

'Or throw your car keys into the pond,' Jack adds.

'I know I'll be the same if I ever have children,' I admit reluctantly. 'Ruskin's on my mobile *and* my screen-saver.'

'Dogs are much simpler. I'd like a Ruskin,' he says, scooping Rusk into his arms and tickling his belly. Ruskin wriggles away and jumps down.

'What else did you do?' I ask.

'Um, I went to the movies Saturday night.'

'What did you see?'

'I can't remember, it was so bad.'

Drawing information out of Jack isn't easy. 'Aren't you going to eat anything?' I ask when I hear the oven timer beep. I take my quiche out. 'You must be starving,' I call from the kitchen. 'Do you want some of this?'

I join him back in the sitting room, grab the controls and turn on the television.

'Hang on! I love *The Tudors*,' Jack says, asking me to go back to the previous programme, where there is heavy breathing, bouncing bosoms and moaning. Shrieks of ecstasy now come from the television as Henry VIII beds Anne Boleyn. Jack glances across at me.

'How was your day?' I ask over the heavy panting.

'Difficult. So, the theme for next week is love songs, right?' Jack says, without averting his eyes from the screen, 'and the judges are arguing about who's having what song.'

Come on, Henry. Get on with it.

Anne Boleyn screams in ecstasy and the scene is finally over. Never before have I been so relieved to see credits on the screen.

I throw Jack the controls and tell him to choose what to watch next. Jack zips through the channels at a mighty pace, racing past gardening and house programmes, cop and hospital dramas.

Next channel is a woman with enormous bosoms talking about her vaginal problems and why she's considering reconstructive surgery. 'Move on!' I demand.

'Hang on.'

'Oh, come on. You're doing this on purpose!' I laugh.

There's now a close-up of her . . . er . . . vagina . . .

and I don't know where to look. I stare at Jack, who is enjoying this. Forget about PG; there should be, NFL: NOT FOR LODGERS.

I return my attention to the television and there is now a full-blown picture of her you-know-what on the screen. 'During sexual arousal, and particularly the stimulation of the clitoris, the walls of the vagina self-lubricate,' says the presenter.

'Come off it!' I exclaim. 'Why does she need to show the whole world what her you-know-what looks like?'

'Vagina? Loosen up, Gilly. Anyone would think you hadn't seen one before.'

'I'd rather watch football.'

I take my plate into the kitchen.

'You can come back, I've turned it off!' Jack joins me in the kitchen. 'What are you up to tonight?' he asks.

'I think I need an early one, hectic weekend,' I pretend, taking some ice cream out of the freezer. 'Want some?' I ask. 'It's mint choc chip.'

Jack takes the pot away from me, his face only inches away from mine. His closeness makes me feel like a school-girl with a crush. 'I want to take you,' he says, 'out for a drink.'

I hesitate, though can't understand why. Here is Jack, the most attractive man I have come across in many months, asking me out. What is there to think about?

'One quick drink, that's all I'm asking,' he says,

grabbing his leather jacket and heading towards the front door.

The thing is, it's never one quick drink though is it?

I show Jack the delights of Hammersmith. We have a drink at a couple of the local pubs, and Jack is intent on paying each time, producing crisp banknotes from his leather wallet with a smooth, 'Let me, Gilly, my shout.'

At one pub there's a local quiz night, at another it's a comedy evening, then we head to a smart bar near Hammersmith Broadway, where someone's hosting a Chicago-themed fortieth birthday party in the private room upstairs. We enjoy watching women arrive wearing fishnet tights and feathers in their hair and then men wearing sequined jackets and trilby hats.

I discover Jack is even more charming than I'd imagined, and surprisingly easy to talk to. He tells me he didn't go to university, but got his first work experience job at nineteen as a runner on a haunted house programme. 'I always thought I was way too good to be running around making tea, but you can never be too proud,' Jack said. Then he worked for the BBC in the basement of Television Centre in the tape despatch department. Every programme that needed a clip for their show, Jack Baker had to locate it. It was his job to find tape BBC15609, that was some ancient clip from *Noel's House Party* that everyone had forgotten about until it was resurrected. 'I was on my hands and knees trying to find these great big solid black things coated in dust,' he says.

Jack endured this job for eight months in an airless building, but each morning he'd press his cv on desks in the vain hope that someone would see his promise at tape-locating and coffee and tea-making. But Jack wasn't complaining when he told me any of this. There was complete acceptance that this is what it takes to make it in the television world. He now gets cross with young twenty-somethings who swan in having done media studies at university and think life owes them a living.

Jack's first break was working on a dating programme that flew him all around the world to exotic places like Thailand, Turkey and Greece. The show was being made for a major commercial channel, and as a producer one of his main jobs was making sure the contestants had signed their release forms.

'I know it sounds easy being on a beach, but you try racing round in sweltering heat trying to get through to some Greek guy who's swimming out to sea to sign a consent form,' Jack had impressed upon me.

At the final pub Jack and I play a game of pool and drink another beer. I tell him about my old job. 'It was a shame that the new boss was so terrible,' I confide. 'All she cared about was filling in the job sheets and ticking the boxes. She didn't care about the clients. If we hired out locations for adverts or something she'd bustle in on set, and piss off the cameramen. They couldn't work with her, so we lost a lot of jobs and she let me go.'

I find myself telling him about Mari's shop and all the different customers, starting with Blaize Hunter King.

'I don't often see the celebs, but their agents who decorate their homes,' I explain. 'We also get a lot of rich Russians and Americans. Today this American lady comes in, right, and points to one of the mirrors, saying, "Oh my God, I love this, but what a shame it's broken in the middle."

'"But it's an antique," Mari replies. "That's what you're paying for."'

Jack is right in front of me now, positioning the cue on the table and I can't help myself from tapping his beautiful bottom just as he's about to hit the ball. The ball swerves, misses the pocket. 'Ah, what a shame,' I say, talking closely into his ear. 'You were doing so well.'

'One more game, and no cheating this time,' Jack says over his shoulder, as he excuses himself to go to the loo. When he's out of sight I brush my hair and flick open my powder compact to look at myself in the toy-sized mirror. I snap the lid shut. Jack is my Monday to Friday man, nothing more. Could be awkward. Quickly I splash my wrist with perfume.

We play one more game of pool before leaving the pub, only to find someone throwing up by the garbage bins and two men swearing at each other, ready for a fight. One of the drunks approaches me. 'All right, love?'

he leers into my face, before checking me out. Jack steers me away from him, placing a protective hand against the small of my back. I like him touching me. He doesn't take his hand away for some time.

Jack and I walk home. Hammersmith Broadway is lit up, twinkling lights in trees. Music booms out of clubs, women totter out in heels; the pavements are alive with smokers lighting up.

We take some shortcuts down narrower roads and alleyways. I show him the coffee shop and the butcher's where I buy my steaks. We walk past a children's shop, the windows decorated with balloons and coloured cupcakes that cost about a pound a bite. Then I show him the lap-dancing club, a famous landmark in Hammersmith. 'It's great round here,' Jack concludes.

'I nearly left London,' I tell him. 'I was thinking about moving to the country.'

'Really?' he asks. 'You're too young to retire to the country.'

I'm about to say thirty-four isn't that young, when a car pulls over to our side of the road; a man winds down the window and spits, before driving on. Then we walk past a bright yellow sign that reveals a fatal car crash at 18:00 hours yesterday, a pedestrian killed in a hit-and-run accident, appealing for witnesses.

'There you go,' I gesture to him. 'That's why I wanted to go.'

'Oh come on, Gilly. I know it's awful but . . .'

'I don't like walking on my own at night round here either.'

'It's hardly *Miami Vice*.'

I shrug. 'It's not worth taking the risk though, is it?'

Jack shakes his head. 'You're only young once. Life's not worth living if you never take any risks, Gilly.'

'I'm not scared,' I correct him, though I can't quite put him straight on my age. I like being thirty-two. I don't like being thirty-four, it's too close on the edge to thirty-five. 'I'm sensible. I also won't walk in a field with cows.'

'You only get cows in the country,' he reminds me. 'Anyway, what's wrong with cows?' He smiles. 'What have they ever done to you?'

Back at home, Jack and I drink coffee on the sofa.

'Do you like living on your own?' I ask him, realizing how much I'd enjoyed coming home this evening and not locking the door behind me.

'I don't mind. I'm surrounded by people at work,' he shrugs, 'so I like my own space.'

'You haven't met anyone since your last girlfriend?'

'Nope.'

'Really?'

'I know it's hard to believe.' He smiles.

He crosses one leg over another, runs a hand through his hair. 'Meeting people is a lottery,' he claims. 'It can lead to a lot of trouble.'

I clutch my mug of coffee, take a sip. 'Trouble? Tell me more.'

'No thanks.'

'I nearly got married you know.'

'What happened? Did he do a runner?'

'Yep.'

'Oh, Gilly, I'm sorry. Oh God, it was a joke, oh fuck, I . . .'

I tell him not to be sorry, that I'm bored of feeling miserable about it.

'I'm sure the "m" word isn't all it's cracked up to be. 'Maybe you had a narrow escape.'

'Maybe.'

'I think I'll be a bachelor for the rest of my life. Much simpler.'

I punch his arm playfully. 'There are not nearly enough decent men around, so don't you dare go depriving us of another.'

He smiles.

'So where do you live in Bath?'

'In the town.'

'Why don't you live in London? Isn't most of your work here?'

'Not really, I never know where my next contract will be. My last job was in Indonesia for five weeks. Mum wasn't too keen on that . . .'

'Your mum? Why?'

'She's a worrier, thinks these places aren't safe and that

I'll catch some bug like dengue fever or something. You know what mums are like, always worrying.'

'Mine doesn't have a clue what I'm up to half the time.'

He doesn't ask why.

'She lives in Australia,' I explain.

'Oh right,' Jack nods without asking any further questions.

'I think you should move here,' I tell him.

'Not everyone wants to live in London, Gilly.' He gets up to leave.

I follow Jack into the kitchen. 'Sorry. I'm being nosy.'

'I went to university in Bath and loved it there. I don't have the time to move right now so I travel to London for work. That's all you need to know about me.'

'I'll shut up right now.' I pretend to zip up my lips. 'Are you tired?' It's past midnight.

'No, not really.'

We make ourselves another drink and then move back to the sofa, switching lanes from personal to general; we talk about our political views, does Jack vote? Yes he does. So do I. Does he approve of Barack Obama? Yes he does, so do I. We have so much in common. What does he think of the recent banking troubles? I tell him it's lucky I don't have any money to lose. He agrees. We share our pet hate phrases. Jack's is 'with all due respect'. Mine is 'I love him to bits.' We talk about inventions. Who were those clever people who invented the paperclip and the elastic band? What genius decided it was a good idea to whisk egg whites and then add sugar to make meringues? Jack tells me that he's worried that now he's hit thirty the ageing process will settle in and make itself more at home. 'I'm vain,' he admits. 'They say thirty-three, thirty-four is the problem age, when you just can't pass for being a 27-year-old any more.'

'Nancy tells me the trick to looking young is keeping a neutral expression at all times.'

'Nancy?'

'My sister-in-law. She's got no wrinkles. I think she's had botox.'

'You don't need botox, Gilly. You're perfect the way you are.'

'Oh please!' I push him away. Tell him you're nearly thirty-five. Go on. See if he thinks you're so perfect then.

'I mean it.'

I turn back to him, my heart singing with his compliment. He looks into my eyes. 'Have you got any brothers or sisters?' I ask, my heart pumping with adrenalin.

'You're perfect except you ask too many questions,' he says.

I hold his gaze. 'You're perfect . . . except you avoid answering them.'

He raises an eyebrow. 'It's never good to give too much away on the first night, Gilly. That's a golden rule.'

When the time finally comes to go to bed, we say goodnight on the landing. I kiss him on one side of the cheek. He kisses me on the other.

'Sweet dreams,' he whispers into my ear, before he goes to his bedroom and reluctantly I go to mine.

In the middle of the night I wake up. I can't remember, but did Jack say he went to university in Bath, or am I imagining it? Didn't he say at the pub that he hadn't gone to university? That he got his first job at nineteen as a runner?

I don't sleep very well that night.

22

It's Sunday and Guy and I are browsing in a secondhand bookshop after a dog walk in Richmond Park. It was glorious out today: the October sun warming our backs and faces, the grass glistening with dew, and a deer stood right in front of us, as if we weren't even there.

I know my time with Guy is borrowed because Flora is back in a month's time. I ask myself if I would mind knowing that my boyfriend was spending time with another woman while I was out of the country. Of course I would, even if he swore blind there was nothing in it. I know I shouldn't become too attached to him; yet I enjoy his friendship. Being with Guy is as comforting as listening to the sound of rain when wrapped up safe and sound indoors. It also helps that he never knew Ed. I'm not reminded of my past when I'm with him.

I love this bookshop. It smells of leather and coffee beans, but what I particularly love about it is, like the chandeliers in Mari's shop, each book has a history and has to be handled with as much care as a fragile piece of glass. I enjoy opening the covers and reading the inscriptions in the front, as much of a story as the tale inside. Old editions of Emily Brontë's *Wuthering Heights* are signed for loved ones, touching messages in ink with neat dates by the side.

'I wish we did that now,' I whisper to Guy, holding a copy of Daphne du Maurier's *Rebecca* and showing him the inscription: 'To my darling Boot, with my love, Muffin'.

'Boot?' Guy raises an eyebrow.

'It's nice, intimate, just between them. I've never had a nickname, have you?'

He shakes his head.

'Ed called me Gilly or honey.' Equally I didn't have a special name for him.

I clutch the copy of *Rebecca*, telling Guy my father had read the story to Nicholas and me. I remember loving this particular mystery and being intrigued by the characters, especially the sinister Mrs Danvers. Even Nicholas, who frowned when given hard rectangular-shaped presents, was drawn into the story.

Back at home I make us some lunch: omelettes and a salad. 'How's it going with Jack?' he asks as I beat the eggs in a bowl.

'Great. We went out last week.'

'Out?'

'Just for drinks.' My mobile rings.

'Where is it?' I ask Guy. Together we follow the sound of the ringing; I catch Guy looking under the mess on my desk, and then glancing at the photograph of Megan. Eventually I find my telephone wedged between the sofa cushions, but whoever it was has long since rung off. I have one missed call from Anna, so I quickly call her back. Last night I went out for drinks with a few of her work friends, including the married Paul, whom Anna has been in love with for a long time. It was the first time I'd met him and I was careful not to say, 'Anna's told me so much about you.' No, I was cool, and asked him questions without scrutinizing the poor man. He'd told me briefly that he was in the process of getting a divorce. He's forty-six and has one son called Benjamin, seven years old. Paul had a gentle quality about him. He was quiet, but interesting, and I discovered that outside work his passion was motor racing. That surprised me.

'I'm with Guy,' I tell her, when she asks me what I'm doing. I catch him scanning the books on my shelf.

'Again?' she asks.

'Come over,' I suggest. He's now picking up a photograph of Ruskin and me.

'Too hungover. Paul . . . he stayed the night,' she whispers excitedly.

'Oh my God!' I shriek. 'More! Tell me more!' Guy looks across at me.

Anna cruelly tells me she can't, that Paul is in the bathroom, but she promises to phone later.

I go back to the kitchen, to finish making the salad, and fill Guy in about Anna, but he's keen to return to the subject of Jack. 'What's he like? Can I do anything, by the way?'

'He's lovely. No, nothing. Diet Coke or normal?'

'Normal.'

'He's easy to live with too.'

'He must have *one* bad habit,' he says as he cracks open his can.

'No. Well, he does leaves his teabags in the sink, but that's about it.' Guy detects I want to say more. 'And?'

I smile. 'He thinks I'm thirty-two.'

'How come?'

I tell him Gloria made up my age.

'Well, you're only thirty-four.'

'Nearly five. I wish Gloria hadn't mentioned my age in the advert.'

'Just tell him, it's no big deal. Gilly! You're blushing. You like him, don't you.'

'Guy!'

'Come on.'

'OK, I'm attracted to him,' I admit now. 'I know he's my lodger, I probably shouldn't but he's . . . God, he's so *sexy*.' I stop. 'I'm sure nothing will happen.'

'Why not?'

'He's too young.'

'No he's not.'

I confess the real reason. 'I'm out of practice! Honestly, you should see me around him. I can't relax. I know this sounds stupid . . .'

'Go on.'

I tell him how I'd hesitated when Jack had asked me out for one quick drink. 'It's like I'm nervous of getting hurt again, of being a stupid idiot. I'm putting up this barrier. I don't want to, but there's something about him too, that I'm not quite sure about . . . No . . .' I think out loud, deciding not to make a big deal of the Bath university comment. 'I'm being paranoid.'

'About what?'

'No. Nothing.'

'Gilly, maybe you're over-analysing everything,' he suggests. 'I think you need to stop thinking so hard and have some fun.'

'I like the sound of that.' I raise my can of Coke to his. 'To having fun,' I say.

Over lunch Guy and I continue to justify our friendship because we know our friends and my dog-walking circle are beginning to talk about us. Anna says I mention Guy on a daily basis.

The thing is, I told her, we're sailing in a similar boat right now in that neither of us has a family; we're single or on our own for different reasons but alone all the same. Anna understands this more than anyone because she and I feel the same about our married friends. We still adore each other, but at this moment in time we're like a road forking off into two directions. It's natural that I don't see friends like Susie as much as I used to.

Guy tells me many of his friends with families have moved to the country, determined to have a better quality of life, but sometimes he doesn't feel like driving out of London at weekends, nor does he feel like fractured conversations.

'When I speak to Susie, it's "Rose! You don't poke your brother in the eye!" '

Guy laughs.

'Or, "Show me your boobies!" Matilda says when I'm trying to read her a bedtime story. "Boobies" is her favourite word at the moment. She's my niece,' I add.

He raises an eyebrow at that. 'Her idea sounds much more fun,' he says.

After coffee I beckon Guy over to my desk in the corner of the sitting room. It's an antique desk that belonged to my father's mother. I reach down to the bottom drawer and produce a batch of paper. Guy takes the top sheet, 'Mickey the Magic Monkey,' he reads. 'Ah, now these are your Megan stories, aren't they?'

I nod. I wrote them when I was thirteen. They're not finished, I tell him, just rough drafts.

I tell Guy I used to love reading when I was little.

I'd shut myself away in my bedroom. 'I did it to escape, to enter a much nicer world than home. Later on, I loved Daphne du Maurier's novels. I used to drop my pennies into the wishing well at church and pray to be like her. She was so wild and imaginative and had endless affairs with women and men. Fascinating,' I say, my heart beating fast. 'One of these days I'd like to try writing a novel.'

'What's stopping you?'

'Stopping me?'

'Yes.' He looks at me as if a light has suddenly switched on. 'From writing?'

'I don't know.'

'Seems to me you're too scared to push yourself out there, to be rejected.'

I examine him, wondering how he seems to know so much about me. 'I don't know, Guy, it's hard to make a living out of writing. Maybe if I had more time . . .'

'Time? Gilly, you have all the time you need!'

I tell him Nicholas had said the same thing too.

'Your brother's right. If you want something in life, you have to go out there and get it.'

I tell him that Ed used to say, 'You don't have the discipline, Gilly. I can't see you sticking at it. Keep it as a hobby, honey.'

Guy looks cross. 'Well, that's a bit patronizing.' He turns me round to face him. 'You need to have more faith in yourself,' he demands. 'People love to put you down. Prove them wrong.'

When Guy and Trouble leave, I sit down at my desk and open the bottom drawer, the drawer that hides my ambition, and decide it's time to give myself a chance.

Early evening, just as I am deep in concentration, the doorbell rings. I peer out of the window to see if I should pretend I'm out. I don't want to open the door to a Jehovah's Witness or someone trying to sell me rip-off dusters and drying-up cloths.

I smile when I see him.

'I've got something for you.' Guy holds out a present. It's wrapped in brown parcel paper, hard and rectangular-shaped.

'Open it,' he says.

Inside is an old leather book which smells of the second-hand bookshop.

I open the first page.

"To Gilly with a G,' I read, 'maybe this is your something. Get writing. Love, Guy.'

I look at him, my eyes watering.

'It's just a blank book,' he says sheepishly, when he sees how much this means to me.

When Guy has left for the second time, I sit down at my desk and open his book, rereading the message. I think about Guy going back to the bookshop and buying the book for me. It makes me feel warm inside.

For the first time in months I do feel happy.

Perhaps I have turned a corner. I have reached a new chapter at last.

The memory of Edward is slowly beginning to fade.

23

1987

'Ladybirds mean good luck,' I say, as I dress Megan for bed in her ladybird-embroidered nightie. Her room is small and bare, with a sheepskin rug and a single bed raised on blocks, so that her feet are tilted upright at night. I tuck her up, then lift down a nursery book, but Megan shakes her head at me.

'Want a Gilly story,' she demands. 'Make up a story.'

My mind goes as blank as it does when Mum tells me I must write a thank-you letter to Granny, who always buys me presents that I don't want, like napkin rings.

'Please, Gilly,' she goes on.

'OK.' Tentatively I sit at the edge of her bed and Megan waits for me to begin. I shut my eyes and transport myself to a land of make-believe. I cough before I start, 'One lovely summer's evening, a magic monkey comes to

Megan's window and invites her on a trip to Planet Z. Her family tell her she can go, so she puts on her favourite travelling sunglasses, – they are bright pink with glitter, – and she climbs onto the monkey's back. He tells her his name is Mickey and that he has especially picked her out from the rest of the world because she's such a good girl.' I smile, beginning to enjoy this place I am imagining. 'So Megan and Mickey fly through outer space, all the way to Planet Z. Now on Planet Z everything is silver and sparkles like diamonds. The trees are silver, the lakes are silver, and even the people on Planet Z are silver.'

I look over to Megan, her eyes shut, but she says, 'More.'

'When they arrive, Mickey tells everyone how beautifully Megan can sing, so she sings her "Bobby Shaftoe" song for all the shiny silver people. There are animals too, all shiny and silver. They clap and jump in the air with excitement, waving their silver balloons and making silver sparks with their hands. After her song, she bows and then the animals give her a silver milkshake.'

Megan is asleep. I kiss her gently on the cheek. 'It's getting late, so Megan waves goodbye and jumps onto Mickey's back. They follow the silver star back home, where Megan goes to bed and dreams of everything that's silver and glitters.'

24

As I stride into the park, there's a reason why I want to sing at the top of my voice, 'The Hills are Alive with the Sound of Music', and it's not just because it's Friday.

Who cares that it's raining! I knew there was attraction the moment I met Jack. My mobile rings. Today I don't struggle to find it in my handbag, a sure sign that today is going to be a good day. It's Susie, sounding stressed, asking me if I can babysit tonight. Their sitter cancelled at the last minute. When I say yes, she calms down.

'You sound in a good mood,' she says.

Excitedly I tell her about Jack.

Last night I took him to my local Indian restaurant because there was nothing on the television and neither of us felt like cooking. As we were waiting for our curries, Jack slid an envelope across the table towards me.

'What's this?' I asked.

'It's to say thanks for making me feel so welcome . . . and for washing my shirts,' he added with a smile.

I've managed to persuade Jack not to take his washing home at the weekends, that I can add it to my load, that it's all part of the Monday to Friday service.

'What else is in the Monday to Friday service?' he'd asked with that mischievous look in his eye.

'What a flirt!' Susie laughs before ordering Rose not to hit his brother with her cereal spoon.

'You don't have to thank me,' I said to Jack, promptly taking the envelope.

'I know . . . but I want to.'

Inside was a pair of dazzling silver VIP tickets to his show the following week, Thursday night. He told me I could bring a friend.

'I'll be there!' Susie says breathlessly. 'Rose, do you want time out?'

I now hear Olly crying.

'Listen, I'll call you later, OK?' I say, thinking Rose should just be given time out, not be asked if she wants it.

'No, quick, tell me more.'

'Then I thought I could take you out for dinner?' Jack suggested.

I smile, remembering how I had tried so hard to create that look that implied I had a heavy packed schedule but somehow I might just be able to squeeze in another social engagement. Forget it. I couldn't play it cool, not when it came to tickets to *Stargazer* or to Jack . . .

'I'd love to! Where will you take me?'

'It's a secret.' Jack raised his glass to mine. 'It's a date then?'

'It's a date.'

'I want that ticket, Gilly. I need a night off,' Susie finishes, before promptly hanging up.

Mari is standing under the oak tree wearing a wax jacket, thick knitted scarf, purple laceup boots and dark lipstick, water dripping off her cheeks. Normally she'd be cursing the dogs for getting mud on her trousers, but ever since Blaize visited she's been in a better mood. 'He's asked you out?' she asks, lighting up, before screeching, '*Basil!*' as if she were Sybil in *Fawlty Towers*. Basil is busy rolling in something he shouldn't be. Ruskin sniffs the very same spot and decides he wants to roll in it too.

'Who's asked you out, Gilly?' Sam says, catching us up, with Hardy running behind.

Walter approaches us in his khaki rain hat and wearing some new waterproof trousers. 'TK Maxx,' he says when Mari comments on them, 'ten pounds. It's grey out today, isn't it,' he continues. 'I've heard it's going to be like this all over the weekend too.' Walter often likes to be the bearer of bad news.

Guy joins us with a bright pink umbrella that we all stare at. 'Flora's,' he explains. 'Couldn't find mine. What's going on?'

You can never keep a secret in this park.

I tell them about Jack. They gather round me, the oak tree sheltering us from the rain, and they listen to me as if I am reporting hot news off the press.

'What are you going to wear?' Sam asks. 'Oh, Hardy, don't roll in that!'

Good point, I think. What shall I wear?

'Stop!' Ariel interrupts, parking his bike against the tree. 'Who's going on a hot date?' he asks, tipping out a soaking Pugsy from the front basket.

'Gilly's going out with her Monday to Friday man,' Sam fills him in.

'Ah! The hot Jack Baker. You lucky bitch,' he adds. 'So what are you going to wear, Gilly?'

'Morning!' Brigitte says to us all, approaching our circle.

'*Bonjour*, Brigitte,' Ariel replies.

She tells us she's brought some cooking apples from her mother's tree. 'I thought we could make delicious *tarte tatin* in this terrible cold weather.'

'He's given her tickets to *Stargazer*. I'm so jealous!' Sam continues as we all peer into Brigitte's bag to look at the apples.

'*Non, non*, not the bruised ones at the bottom,' Brigitte points out.

'I love that show,' Ariel confesses, 'Little Hal's going to win.'

I notice Guy is quiet. I nudge him. 'I decided to take your advice and have some fun.' He smiles, saying he needs to talk to me, before Sam insists on more details about Jack.

Basil has lost his chewed-up ball and Guy helps Mari find it. They search the muddy grass, Mari cursing Basil. 'I'm not sure she should be *dating* this man,' I overhear her saying worriedly to Guy. 'We don't know anything about him.' Mari doesn't suffer fools but she does suffer from a loud voice. 'You know what happened to Gilly, don't you? You know about Ed, and her mother disappearing off?'

'She's a big girl, Mari,' I hear Guy reply.

'Shh!' Ariel urges them, before turning to me and ordering me not to pay any attention.

Sam notices that I've heard what they said too. 'Where's he taking you after the show?' she asks, attempting to distract me. She rubs her hands together to keep them warm. I tell her he's taking me out for dinner, but won't tell me where: it's going to be a surprise.

'So romantic,' sighs Sam. 'Sometimes I wish I wasn't married.'

'You have fun, Gillyflower,' Ariel says to me. 'You deserve it.'

'I stepped out once with my lodger,' says Walter. 'We used to walk along the docks. She was beautiful. French, mind you, so we didn't understand a word each other said.'

'I need to talk to you,' Guy says when I approach him with two cups of coffee. The others have left the park, put off by the rain, but it's still only 8.30 in the morning, so Guy and I decide to walk one more circuit.

'Sounds serious.'

'I've just found out that I've got this job in Kent.'

'Oh, right. When are you going?'

'Monday, after the weekend.'

'That's good isn't it?' I suggest, wondering why he's looking worried. 'How long are you going for?'

'Two, maybe three weeks.'

'Three weeks!' I exclaim, followed by a calmer, 'three weeks?' The disappointment takes me by surprise. I'm used to seeing Guy every day. I don't want him to go away for three weeks.

We walk our circuit and as we approach the exit gates of the park, we move impossibly slowly, like learner walkers. 'Walter's going to look after Trouble,' he says.

'I could have done that.'

'I know, but I think you've got enough going on, like your date next week.' He nudges me.

'It's not a date,' I'm quick to tell him, not feeling quite so zingy as I'd felt earlier this morning.

When we reach the zebra crossing we stall. Three weeks is still screaming in my head. Twenty-one days of not seeing Guy.

'Are you around over the weekend?' I ask, not wanting to say goodbye just yet.

He shakes his head. 'I've got to work, prepare for Monday.'

I can't hold it in any longer. 'I'm going to miss you,' I say.

'No you won't,' he replies with that dry smile. 'While I'm away, you've got Jack to play with. Listen, I'd better go.' Briefly Guy kisses my cheek and turns left at the zebra crossing. 'Gilly?' he calls over his shoulder.

I stop. Turn.

'I'll miss you too,' he says.

As Guy leaves, someone taps me from behind and I swing round. 'I thought you'd gone,' I say to Ariel.

'I'm taking Pugsy to the vet. He's got a bit of hay fever. Now listen, you're not to worry about Mari, OK? You know what she's like.'

I'm still watching Guy leave. Ariel follows my gaze. 'I think he's a little jealous,' he states, as if he's just worked it out. 'I was watching him earlier, when you were talking about Jack.'

'He's not jealous!' I find myself laughing.

'The thing about Mari,' he continues, 'is that she doesn't want to see you get hurt again. None of us do,' he says.

'I know. And thank you, but I have to live my life, I have to move on.'

He nods. 'Pugsy says have some fun with Jack, don't you Pugs?' He snorts.

I smile as I watch Ariel cycle away with Pugsy perched in the front basket.

He's right.

Let's see where it goes.

*

Nick calls me that evening, warning me that Nancy is insisting once more that I mark my thirty-fifth birthday now only next month.

'What are *you* going to do?' I ask him.

'She's taking me away, to some smart hotel in the country with a jacuzzi. She wants to throw a party for you. Just let her do it,' he pleads, knowing it will make his life easier.

'Fine. A dinner party would be lovely,' I concede. 'I'll call her.'

Shall I invite Jack?

Maybe see how our evening goes first.

Gilly Brown. Soon-to-be-thirty-five.

Oh, how I hate birthdays.

25

December 1987

Megan is three today. The paediatrician said she wouldn't live beyond the age of two, but he doesn't know everything. Something is wrong now, though Megan shouldn't be crying on her birthday.

'Is she dying?' I ask Mum.

She can't be because Anna and I and all our neighbours have raised the money to take her to Germany. Next week Mum is taking Megan on an aeroplane to see a specialist who is going to make her better. She can't die now.

'No!' Megan cries, when Mum tries to make her swallow a pill with water. Mum asks me to help get my sister dressed. 'Don't want to put clothes on,' she shouts. I'm not used to her being cross. She's never like this.

Mum doesn't look me in the eye when she tells me Megan is going to be fine.

'Is she in pain?' I ask, scared.

She pretends she doesn't hear me.

We're in Megan's bedroom and Father Matthew, a tall, stooped wise man, is with us, saying a prayer. Megan hasn't cried as much since he arrived. Mum called him after breakfast, saying she was worried. Megan wouldn't let Mum dress her, so instead Mum gave her a bath and wrapped her in a blanket before asking Dad to ring the doctor.

On the television there are weather warnings telling us not to drive unless our journey is essential. Snow is falling, great big silvery white flakes settling on the ground. School is cancelled for the day; Nick and I are pleased we can stay at home. Dad can't get into work. He's downstairs, ringing the surgery, arguing with someone. 'It's an emergency,' he's saying. 'No, we can't bring her in.'

Father Matthew leaves Megan's side and says something quietly to Mum. I hate grown-ups sometimes. They never tell you what's really going on. Mum is nodding. 'What does Megan love doing most?' Father Matthew asks Nick and me.

'Being outside,' I reply.

'Going up Primrose Hill,' Nicholas adds.

Father Matthew looks out of the window. 'Then you must wrap her up warmly and take her,' he says.

Megan, Mum, Nick, Dad and I are outside in our moon boots and thick coats, the snow glistening in the trees and on the rooftops, snowflakes melting into our clothes. There is something magical about snow. It's soft and fluffy and I love the sound of it crunching beneath my boots. Mum hands Megan over to Dad and he cradles her in his arms. We look like an ordinary family on a day out, but it's only when I see Dad crying that I know something is badly wrong. I rush to kiss Megan; Nick kisses her after me, clutching her small hand into his own. She's quiet, but when I look into her eyes, I see into her soul. Megan has a beautiful soul that holds no anger, only love. When her fingers grip mine I sense she is trying to say goodbye and thanking me for my stories. She seems to be at peace, or maybe I am just hoping she is. If only I could ask her.

We go for a short walk up Primrose Hill and then return home. Children are tobogganing and building snowmen, but we are in our own world, just being with Megan.

She died later that morning with all of us by her bedside.

A part of each one of us went with her that day.

Later that night, I sit with Mum, her eyes red, and ask her if everything will be all right. 'Megan will be in heaven now and she'll be able to walk,' I tell her, but she looks through me, as if I'm not here. Finally she says we'll all pull through, but I know from the look in her eye that she doesn't believe that.

Mum has lost the person she loved the most.

Nothing will be the same again.

26

Susie and I are whisked through the crowds and into the *Stargazer* studios. We don't have to queue with our special VIP tickets. We drink champagne at the exclusive bar before being shown to our seats. 'I could get used to this,' I whisper to her.

When the judges walk onto the stage it's like a pantomime, everyone booing and cheering Hunter Jones, loved and loathed in equal measure. As I'm clapping, my mind turns to Guy. 'I don't like reality TV,' he'd said during one of our circuits. 'These shows buff up the mediocrity.'

'Oh don't be such a snob,' I'd replied.

Tonight Kylie Minogue is the celebrity guest. Susie and I, at one point, are only metres away from her. Jack had told me proudly earlier in the week that he'd clinched tickets for one of the best nights.

After the show, Susie has to head home to her children

and husband, but as for me . . . well, Jack, and I are enjoying drinks in one of London's most famous skyscrapers. I can't believe I've never been here before.

'Oh my God, this is incredible!' I say, standing with Jack on the top floor of the Centre Point tower, gazing at views looking out right across London.

In the nightlight the views are even better.

'Gilly, someone once told me I should leave London only when I hated it, when I'd squeezed all the juice out of it,' Richard had said to me. 'Stupidly I didn't take their advice and I miss it like crazy. I'm not sure you've reached that stage yet.'

As I glance across at Jack, looking so handsome, suddenly I feel lucky to be alive and living in London. Jack brushes my hand and we smile at one another, almost in recognition that this is just the beginning of our evening. My time's not done here, Richard. Not by a mile.

Back at No. 21, the karaoke machine is up and running. 'OK, so what are you going to sing for us tonight, Gilly Brown?' Jack asks, imitating Hunter Jones.

'Well, Hunter, I'm going to sing, especially for you . . .' I blow him a kiss, 'a song by my heroine, Whitney Houston.'

Jack grins. 'If you could stand on the star, please.'

I step forward onto the imaginary star.

'When you're ready, darling,' Jack says, crossing his arms.

When I belt out 'Saving all my love for you', Jack attempts not to laugh.

'Thank you, Gilly,' he says at the end. 'That was hideous, but strangely memorable.' He sits back, observes me. 'How much does winning mean to you?'

'Everything. I'll be *devastated* if you don't put me through.'

'How much does it mean to you?' he asks again.

'The whole wide world.' I pretend to cry.

'I'm putting you through, kid.' He winks at me.

Soon Jack and I are dressing up and picking themes. It's Abba, and I perform, 'The Winner Takes it All', and then it's homage to Frank Sinatra and Jack sings 'I've Got you under my Skin'. Watching him sing, I picture Jack Baker riding a motorbike in a hot country, me on the back, clutching onto him, resting my head against those broad shoulders. My dream is to be a girlfriend in a hot climate. And of course he has the voice of an angel. I'm beginning to wonder if there's anything Jack Baker can't do.

'You're not what we're looking for,' I tell him when he reaches the end, before I then go on to perform (badly) Madonna's 'Get into the Groove' in legwarmers, red lipstick and bangles.

Next we raid the fridge, hungry after our dressing-up games.

★

'I'm tired,' I say, though make no attempt to move off the sofa.

'No you're not.' Jack smiles suggestively. 'You're going to dance with me.'

'Am I? You're so sure of yourself, aren't you.'

'All the time.' He pulls me to my feet.

Jack holds me, swings me back, reels me in, twists and turns me so much that soon I am giddy with laughter and happiness.

We dance well into the early hours of the morning.

I collapse into bed, make-up still on.

I can't sleep. I thought he was going to kiss me. When we danced he held me so close, I felt the heat of his hands against my back. Maybe I should have kissed him, except I'd have preferred it if he had made the first move. I'm sure he wanted to kiss me.

'Night,' he'd said outside my bedroom.

'Night,' I replied.

'Sleep well.'

'You too.' Pause. 'Thanks for tonight, Jack, for the show, for everything.'

He was looking at me again with that charming smile. 'My pleasure,' he said, before going to his room.

It's no use. I can't sleep. Perhaps it's for the best. Jack is my Monday to Friday man after all, so why go and spoil it all with a one-night stand. Think of the awkwardness tomorrow morning. I don't want to interview any more Roys either. We were absolutely right to keep our hands to ourselves.

I stumble out of bed and head for the bathroom, open the door . . .

'Oh God! Sorry!'

There he is, lean and bare-chested, beautiful Jack, going to the loo. I shut the door and race to the downstairs loo, hearing him laugh.

I badly need a glass of water. As I open the glass doors leading into the kitchen, I press a finger to my lips to warn Ruskin to be quiet. 'It's only me, sweetheart.' I jump when I feel a pair of arms around my waist. Ruskin barks now.

'You scared me!' I say, wondering exactly what Jack's doing, but whatever it is, it's exciting. Ruskin continues to bark at the late-night intrusion, jumping up against his stripy-blue pyjama bottoms with jealousy.

'It's three in the morning, Gilly,' he murmurs. 'Down, Ruskin!'

'I know. But I can't sleep.'

'Nor can I,' he says. Pause. 'I've been thinking about you.'

Oh my God. 'D'you want a cup of tea or something?'

He shakes his head. 'Come to bed.'

Come to *bed*?

He takes my hand, guides me out of the kitchen, leaving a cross Ruskin glaring at us through the door.

I turn to him, nervous of what he's going to do next. 'No one's turned me down for a cup of tea before,' he grins.

Before I have time to say anything, Jack takes me by the hand and leads me upstairs. When we reach the landing, he turns to me and asks, 'My bedroom or yours?'

Later, in bed, after glorious spine-tingling sex, Jack reaches over for his pack of cigarettes.

'Oh,' I say, without thinking. 'Do you mind? It's just . . . well, it makes the room, you know, *smell*,' I whisper. Oh, listen to yourself, Gilly. Talk about ruining the moment. You've just had sex with a gorgeous man so you should be in a giving mood and not talking about room odours. 'Go on, of course you can have one. Sorry, I'm a boring old bat sometimes.'

He puts the pack down and kisses me. 'You weren't very boring just now. Anyway, I happen to rather like this boring old bat lying next to me.'

I laugh, grabbing his arm and resting it over my stomach. 'I'm funny about smoking. You see, when my mother was . . .' But Jack's not interested in hearing my childhood stories. Instead he climbs on top of me, and grabs my arse as he whispers into my ear, 'You're right. I shouldn't smoke, it's filthy.'

'Disgusting,' I add, kissing him.

'I'll do exactly as I'm told, just as long as you keep the talk dirty,' he adds.

And I laugh, abandoning myself to Jack Baker all over again.

27

1988

I help Nick put on his tie. He brushes the back of my hair, the part I can't reach, and says my hair is static, like electricity. We help each other pack our satchels and games bags. Mum always forgets to put the right things in. My sports teacher was cross when I turned up to swimming class without my goggles and costume. I had to wear my vest and knickers.

Dressed and ready for school we walk downstairs to the kitchen. Mum stands at the sink in a cloud of smoke. Nick looks cross.

Mum's forgotten it's a school day.

There's a hole in our lives and it's Megan. She follows us to bed, to sleep, to school and back, to the supper table; even in the car there's a hole where she used to sit.

Mum stares at the photograph on the window ledge of Megan sitting in her blue-checked chair in the kitchen. Dad says Mum needs to get rid of her things in the house – her pram, chair, splints for her legs, her special little leather boots; Megan's clothes are still hung in the wardrobe. I don't know what to say to Mum most of the time. I'm scared of saying the wrong thing so instead I hug her.

Mum's wearing her blue dressing gown, which looks too big on her now, and she drifts around the house in horrible dirty cream slippers. She asks us to sit down and eat some breakfast before school. Nick and I look at the messy table. I pick up a tin of spaghetti with bite-size frankfurters swimming around in the sauce. It smells. I open the bin and nearly choke. It stinks of rotten cabbages. I shove the tin inside and then slam the lid shut, noticing even Nick stagger back, curling his lips in horror. I look at Mum and then back to him. He shrugs his shoulders. Our house used to be clean all the time, Mum scrubbing everything obsessively. Now I can't even invite Anna round. I'm embarrassed by the mess.

We don't know what to do. Dad's away. He's working in New York. I wish he'd come home.

Mum starts to clear yesterday's supper plates off the table. She says we're wasting away, but it's only because the food she puts in front of us is worse than school dinners. I try to force it down, telling myself to think of the starving children across the world that I see on the news, their stomachs swollen and their legs so thin. I must not complain. I'm not cross with her. Dad tells us that in time things will go back to normal, that right now Nick and I have to be patient.

Nick sulkily asks Mum if she's remembered to make our packed lunches. 'Of course,' she replies vacantly as she fishes out some squishy bread rolls from the breadbin. I don't tell her I can see mould on them. 'What do you want in your rolls?' she asks with dead eyes.

'Cheese and ham,' he replies.

'Can I have that too?'

Mum opens the fridge, blows smoke into it. I don't like her smoking. It makes my uniform smell; the whole house smell.

'We've run out of cheese. Oh dear, no ham either.' She picks out a few jars, examining the labels on them. 'You can have honey, OK?'

'I hate honey,' states Nick.

'Honey's fine,' I say, staring at my brother.

Mum spreads the honey into the rolls, slaps the two halves together and shoves them into plastic bags. She used to make us cucumber and tuna sandwiches cut neatly into four squares. She puts an apple into each sandwich box and a digestive biscuit, and clamps the lids shut. She looks at her watch, tells us we just have time for breakfast if she runs us to the bus stop in the car. We used to walk all the time, with Megan. If my sister could see us now, she'd be angry, saying that we don't sing or have fun any more.

I pick up the cereal box and tip some flakes into a bowl.

Mum ruffles my hair, which makes me happy. 'What lessons have you got today, Nick?'

'Maths, boring.' He eats another spoonful of cereal without looking at her and then takes the bowl to the sink.

'How about you, Gilly? Mrs Curtis says you're really coming on.'

I can hear the strain in Mum's voice, the effort it takes to talk to us – the equivalent to climbing a mountain in high heels.

I now spend all my time writing my diary. Mrs Curtis told me writing was a good way to cope with a death; that when she feels anxious about something her husband often finds scraps of paper with her scribbles all around the house.

Sometimes the only thing I write is that I'm scared because Mum's always buried under the covers in bed. Is she sick? I write that I don't think she wants Nick and me around any more, that she must have loved Megan more than us. I really worry about Mum smoking. The cigarette packets say smoking can kill. I imagine Mum dying of lung cancer because she doesn't read the warnings on the side of the packets. Mum smokes about forty a day. Will she die, just like Megan? Then what? Dad can't look after us.

I wonder if I should ask Mum if she wants me to clean and do the shopping. I worry that we don't have food in the house. I could never *say* this to her, so it helps me to write it down. I sit propped up in bed writing while Nick reads his comics. Dad used to read to us at night, but he said we were getting too old for that now. When Dad's at home he's very tired after a long day in London. He has great big circles under his eyes. He gets up at 6 a.m. and is out of the house until suppertime. The first thing he does when he comes in is open the drinks cupboard to pour himself a gin.

My writing helps me at night, otherwise I go to bed feeling so sad that I can't sleep.

28

It's Friday night and the Olympians have just been for an early evening swim. I tell Gloria that I might go again tomorrow, in fact I might even have some front crawl lessons as it's about time I stopped being overtaken by perky pensioners. 'No offence,' I say, drying my hair in the changing room.

'None taken,' she says, before asking me if I'd like to have some supper with her. She's going to make one of her special vegetable roasts. I ask her if she wants red or white to go with it.

As I chop the herbs for Gloria, she tells me in detail about her week. I'm glad to have her company this evening because I need distraction. All day long I haven't been able to think straight. I sat in the shop dreaming about Jack like some lovesick puppy. I smile to myself, thinking how strategically planned our night was, in that going out on a Thursday meant we didn't have any awkwardness the following day because Jack was going home. I am relieved to have the weekend to recover and also I can enjoy the anticipation of seeing him next week. This Monday to Friday arrangement is wonderful. In fact, every relationship should be Monday to Friday. That way, they might stand a chance.

Gloria has been away so she doesn't even know I've had a date with Jack yet, let alone slept with him. Wait till I tell her! When I woke up this morning, Jack had left for work, but had written a note on his side of the bed. I grabbed it, fearing he was going to say we shouldn't have done that and please could we forget it ever happened?

Gilly, I didn't want to wake you, you were sound asleep – and by the way, you talk in your sleep too. You said something about how great Jack Baker was and how much you'd like to have another date with him next week. PS You mentioned something about putting on your best dress, dancing shoes and no knickers. PPS You're hot for thirty-five.

I'd rolled back over onto my side of the bed, kicked my legs up and down against the mattress and screamed with delight at the wickedness of the man. I was also relieved because last night I'd also been brave enough to tell him my real age. 'Thirty-five. I love an older woman,' he'd said.

'I'm not thirty-five yet,' I'd replied, laughing, 'and I'm not that much older than you.'

I sang 'Who Wants to Be a Millionaire?' from *High Society* at the top of my voice in the shower; I couldn't eat any breakfast and Ruskin and I skipped to the park, my feet barely touching the ground. And then, of course, under the oak tree I reported my evening, slightly censored for some.

'Oh, how I wish I was your age again,' Walter had said, taking my hand and dancing the waltz with me. 'I'd have whisked you off your feet, Gilly.'

Sam pulled me to one side and told me she had a good feeling about Jack Baker.

Brigitte wanted to hear about the restaurant and if I'd enjoyed my sea bass.

Ariel wasn't in the park that day. I know he'll be furious to miss out on the gossip.

Mari inhaled deeply on her menthol cigarette, unusually quiet.

There was just one person I missed. I wanted to tell Guy.

'Chop some garlic too,' says Gloria.

Gloria is an adventurous cook who doesn't need to follow recipes. Like me, she enjoys food, and tonight she's baking me my favourite pudding, lemon meringue pie. I often think of Gloria as the mother I lost when Megan died.

I enjoy my evenings with Gloria. Her sitting room

never fails to have a vase of purple tulips. Paintings and illustrations of Guinness, her cat, are mounted on every wall. Each object has a story. She has pieces she's collected from all over the world: Moroccan rugs and lights that she bought from Marrakesh, linen cushions that she found in a French market. She sleeps on a thin mattress on the floor; she's never enjoyed a soft double bed. Her favourite object in the house is a glass ornament that her old boss gave her, engraved with an image of St Thérèse.

Pictures of her parents, both dead, are displayed in photograph frames. Her mother died of cancer in her fifties; her father died only two years ago, aged eighty-six. Gloria couldn't leave the house for months; his death hit her like a freight train. I used to drag her round the park with Ruskin and me to get some fresh air. I took over meals: hot soups and stews. Sometimes I'd just sit with her on a Sunday evening to make sure she wasn't alone. You see, her father had visited her every Sunday; he'd helped her in the garden, and in the evening they'd go to the pub together. When he died, I was with Ed at the time, and I sometimes wondered if she'd ever be able to pick herself up again. But she did — that's the remark-able thing about the human spirit.

Beneath Gloria's sunny facade, she's carried a lot of burdens. Over the years I discovered that she had lost a brother, Laurie, when she was five years old. Laurie died from cot death. Gloria couldn't eat afterwards, she felt sick all the time, believing it was her fault. She recalled how her mother had to cram porridge into her. After his death she didn't enjoy being an only child. She told me it had made her grow up too quickly and, just like me, she knew what it was like living in an atmosphere of sadness.

With supper plates on our laps, Gloria switches over to some of the digital channels and pauses on a repeat show of *Stargazer*.

'It means the world to me,' the contestant says emotionally. 'I'll be devastated if I don't get through.'

'For pity's sake, she can't be more than fourteen,' Gloria huffs, tucking her chin in, before going on, 'they don't know what devastation means. Devastation is losing a loved one or your house burning down without insurance, or being diagnosed with some awful incurable illness.'

I smile, picturing Jack and me dancing last night. We must have been drunk.

'I don't want to go back to school and be ordinary,' the contestant continues. 'All me life I've wanted to be famous.'

'Fame,' Gloria berates. 'What happened to good old-fashioned work? I tell you, we're losing tradesmen like plumbers, electricians, builders like my dad, school-dinner ladies like my mum, because all children want now are jobs that don't require hard work.'

'Switch over then.'

'No. I love this show. I really want little Hal to win. What about you? Who do you think should win?'

Gloria turns to me, waiting for an opinion, but I'm still thinking about last night. I'd forgotten how lovely it is to feel arms around me, how sexy it is when a man kisses the nape of my neck, how wonderful it is to be touched by someone. I remember him slipping off my nightshirt, kissing my bare shoulders . . .

'What is it with you tonight, Gilly? You've been grinning like a Cheshire cat ever since you arrived. More wine?'

'Ugh. No thanks.'

Gloria turns the television to mute. 'Oh my God, you're not pregnant, are you?'

'No!'

'Well, what is it?'

'I saw this show live last night. I was there. I had a date with Jack.'

Gloria smiles, as if it all makes sense now, especially my keenness to return to the gym tomorrow for more swimming.

I tell her about the evening and she listens as attentively as a child being read a bedtime story. 'One evening with Jack has knocked a whole year off my life,' I tell her. 'He's the kind of person that makes me feel like *anything* is possible. But . . .' I put my head into my hands.

'What's the problem?'

'Everyone knows you shouldn't sleep with a man too soon,' I say.

'It's been a long time since I've seen you this happy,

so you go for it. Tell me more. What's he like apart from being a real dreamboat?'

I smile at the word 'dreamboat'. 'He's charming, makes me laugh . . .' A great kisser, I think to myself. 'I don't know much more about him, Gloria. The strange thing is, whenever I ask him anything personal, he seems a bit uneasy.' When I had asked Jack about going to university at Bath he'd told me he'd meant to say college, repeating that he'd left school after taking his A levels. When I'd asked him what he gets up to at the weekends, he'd changed the subject quickly.

'Well,' she says dismissively, 'that's no bad thing. It takes time to get to know someone.'

'He does make me feel young again,' I sigh happily.

'You make the most of it,' she advises. 'I'm not saying marry the guy, just get to know him, enjoy the sex and if he's not right, see if he has any nice friends. Broaden your horizon, that's what life's all about.'

I nod. 'I'd love to meet someone, but then again if I don't ever marry, if I live a life like yours, I'll be a lucky girl.'

Gloria retired a year ago, and now she travels to see friends, 'does' lunch, goes to the theatre, enjoys art exhibitions, eats out, visits her old aunt in California, holidays with her best friend in Rome; she basically does what she wants and looks wonderful on this diet of 'do as you please' for life.

She shakes her head. 'I'm not saying that a man will

make you happy,' she says. 'Goodness, you marry someone and you're simply trading one set of problems for another. But believe me, I wish I was young again, see how I'd do things differently, Gilly,' she says. 'Let the music play with Jack. See what happens.'

My mobile rings and Susie's name lights up the screen. I excuse myself, telling Gloria that I won't be long.

The children are finally in bed, Susie tells me, and she's sitting with a glass of wine in the kitchen, dying to know how the rest of the evening went, after she'd rushed off last night. She screams down the phone, before trying to compose herself. 'Don't rush into it, Gilly.'

'Bit too late for that.'

'Oh my God, Gilly!'

'You liked him, didn't you?'

They'd only met briefly after the show. 'Yes.'

I'm sensing a 'but'. 'He seemed great. Just be careful,' she says. This is what Anna had hinted at too. 'Take your time, get to know him,' she'd said. Since Ed left me, friends now treat me like a fragile piece of glass, terrified I'll get broken again.

When I hang up, I join Gloria back in the sitting room. 'I just hope I'm not being too head in the clouds about this. I'm thirty-four, – I haven't got time to muck around with the wrong men. I need to make good choices.'

Gloria surveys me, twitches her mouth. 'You're never sure about a damn thing, sweetheart. If you're not dithering you're asleep. Something else is bothering you. What is it?'

I'm thinking about Guy. I tell Gloria about our close friendship and while I fancy my lodger, I have this strange need to be with this other man. 'I can't explain it,' I say.

'You're heading down a dead-end road with him.' She shakes her head wisely. 'Just leave that one be and keep Guy as a friend. Believe me, it's no fun going after men who aren't attainable.'

She's right. Leave it be.

Gloria looks at me. 'Why don't you cut your hair?' she suggests.

My style hasn't changed in years. My hair is long. Self-consciously I flick a hand through it.

'You should have a makeover,' she continues. 'Get some *va va voom* back in your life!'

'Oh Gloria,' I roll my eyes.

'Don't you dare, "oh Gloria" me. You're a beautiful woman, Gilly, don't let the world pass you by. As much as I enjoy having you here you should be out with the likes of Jack Baker having fun. It's time to forget about the past and be happy.'

I confess to Gloria that my friends are overly protective towards me now.

'Maybe you will get hurt, but isn't that better than feeling nothing?'

I think about this. 'What's the most daring thing you've ever done, Gloria?'

She thinks. 'I was seven at the time, shopping in the Portobello market and suddenly had this wild urge to steal something. So, I picked up a potato and a carrot, stuffed them both down my jumper and ran home, but the funny thing was I felt so guilty that I threw them over the neighbour's garden fence.' She smiles. 'I went to confession that week. I was convinced I'd burn in hell.'

I smile. 'When I was about seven too I was sure I'd go to prison for walking onto a station platform without a ticket. How about as an adult though? What's the biggest risk you've taken?'

'I've done lots of things I shouldn't have,' she admits, 'like falling in love with a married man and thinking I'd never get hurt.'

'Oh, Gloria,' I say. 'Do you wish you'd ever met anyone else? You're too special to be alone,' I add.

'But I'm not alone. I chose this.' She strokes Guinness, now on her lap. 'The thing is, ducks, I must be about the only woman who said she didn't want to get married and who actually, deep down, meant it.'

29

'It's time for a makeover,' Gloria had said last night, 'time to get some *va va voom* back in your life!'

It's time to go shopping.

I ring Susie on the offchance she's around today. Maybe Mark can look after Rose and Olly? Damn. Susie's not free. She has to take Rose to a birthday party. I know Anna is spending the weekend with Paul. I try Ariel but get no answer.

There is only one more person to ask.

'Nancy Cooper-Brown speaking.'

'Nancy, it's Gilly.'

'Matilda, darling, there's a good girl. Those are Mummy's organic oats, aren't they? Put them DOWN!' she insists.

Deep breath. While Nancy proceeds to scream at Tilda for tipping up the breakfast cereal I check my emails.

'Sorry, Gilly,' she says finally. 'This is unexpected. What can I do for you?'

'Well, I'm sure you have plans this weekend . . .'

'No plans. Nicholas is upstairs. Working. Why?'

'I have a small favour to ask,' I continue tentatively. 'I need some advice.'

'You want my advice,' Nancy repeats, and I can sense her excitement and surprise.

'Like you said, I'm nearly thirty-five and if I want to meet someone perhaps it is time for a change, a new me and . . .' I am going to have to be brave and risk allowing Nancy into a corner of my life. 'I need your help. I'm going out with a lovely man next week and I want to look *sensational*!'

'Tilda!' she says, 'Auntie Gilly has a date! A date!'

I can't help smiling, holding the phone away from my ear.

'I'd love to help. I've always told Nicholas you could make so much more of yourself. Let's go to Fenwick's!'

'Well, I was thinking . . .'

'I know what you should do straight away! Cut off that mop of hair and . . . oh! I'll call Lydia, see if she can squeeze you in for a facial. New hair, new clothes, a brand new you! I'll pinch Nicholas's credit card and take you shopping; he'll never know.'

'He will if you don't keep your voice down,' I suggest.

'When can we start?'

'Well, how about now?'

'Nicholas! Change of plan!' she cries out in ecstasy. 'You need to look after the kids. Oh, this is so exciting! Who's the lucky man?'

'There's nobody old and ugly in LA, you can't get away with it,' Nancy tells me as we take a black cab to Bond Street. She looks out of the window. 'I mean, why does that young man over there think that jeans halfway down his bottom is a good look? The world has to look at us, so we owe it to people to look decent.'

Nancy feels more at home in Los Angeles than in London. She and Nick lived there for two years when they were first married because my brother had landed a high-profile copyright job in the movie industry. Nancy didn't want to return to the UK. Richmond seemed so drab and suburban by comparison.

As Nancy discusses our itinerary for the day, I find myself switching off and going back to the time when I first met my sister-in-law. I can remember her so clearly saying to Dad and me that she didn't like shopping or fancy things; that she was a simple girl at heart. However, the weeks leading up to their wedding proved otherwise. Nancy, estranged from her mother, didn't want to get married at home. She wanted to marry abroad, in Greece. My father offered to pay for the wedding. He wanted to support them both, especially Nick, but became increasingly concerned when the costs started to spiral out of control. Nancy had arranged various parties including a rehearsal dinner consisting of a five-course menu and the finest wine. For the wedding itself, a vintage car transported the couple to the church and then when the time came for them to leave for their honeymoon, a speedboat whizzed them across the sea. When I hinted to Nick that it was possibly vulgar to be this showy he wouldn't listen to me. He was in love.

Once he married, Nancy changed everything about him that she could. Nick used to have a small gap between his teeth that gave him character, but she took him to a private Harley Street dentist to get it fixed. He also had a small mole on his left cheek, which again made him look individual, but the mole didn't have a hope in hell. It was gouged out by a leading dermatologist, Dr Cream (Nancy didn't laugh at the name), famous for his removal of moles.

There was a moment when I was worried for my twin. On the morning of their wedding, Nancy had lost her engagement ring on the beach. Anyone would have thought she'd lost a child. We sent search parties out, metal detectors were hired, and Nancy was in turmoil, convinced that it was a terrible portent of their marriage. Seeing how much distress she was in, I said reassuringly, 'Don't worry, Nancy, it's just a ring. The main thing is you haven't lost Nick.'

If looks could kill, I'd have been dead on the spot. It was then that I felt a dread that perhaps this wasn't the fairy-tale marriage that I'd imagined.

Fast-forward eight years and Nick and Nancy are still together, but I fear, behind closed doors, there isn't much affection left. I look over to Nancy and try to remember the last time I saw them holding hands or laughing with each other.

As Nancy and I enter Fenwick's I feel as if I am following a sergeant major.

'Gilly, keep up!' she shouts over her shoulder.

'Yes, sir!' I say, struggling along behind her.

Nancy marches round the store, knowing precisely what to pick off the rails for me, without even a glimpse at the price tag. It would appear she's not only sorting out a dress for my date but rebuilding my entire wardrobe.

'Absolutely not!' she says when I glance at a pair of flat shoes. 'Men love women in heels,' she insists. 'They have to be as high as the Empire State Building.'

'Why are you always in trousers?' she demands when I hide a pair of skinny jeans in the changing room. Matilda also tells me I can never be a princess because I don't wear dresses enough.

'What makes you think you suit black, Gilly?' she asks, grabbing the dark tops from me. 'Do you want your date to mistake you for a crow from across the table.'

'You should have your colours done, you've got to be a winter,' she asserts, handing me a selection of deep-blue, emerald, silver and plum-coloured dresses. 'You've got good 'legs, show them off,' she says, thrusting a pink suede miniskirt through the changing-room curtain.

'Those can go straight in the bin,' she says, pointing to my comfortable cotton knickers. And, before I know it, a lingerie manager is measuring my bust. She then proceeds to tell me sternly that I am wearing the wrong-sized bra.

As I am trying on push-up bras and lacy thongs Nancy winces at my pale body. 'Gilly, you have a lovely figure, I'd love to be tall like you, but honestly, dead people look more warmed up than you,' she laughs before telling me a fake tan will take off the edge.

'Where's Jack taking you on this date?' she asks from behind the curtain as I try on what feels like the thousandth dress. 'It's a surprise,' I call out, 'probably some club – he mentioned dancing.'

'Mm. I want to meet him,' she says thoughtfully. 'You must invite him to your birthday dinner.'

As planned, Nancy is organizing my birthday party in five weeks.

'Perhaps, I'll see how it goes, Nancy. Now this is the last one,' I tell her, stepping out of the cubicle in a shimmering emerald-coloured dress that falls just above my knee. The shop assistant tells me that the colour looks striking set against my dark hair. Nancy doesn't utter a word.

'You hate it, don't you?'

'Oh my God! Gilly, you could go to the Oscars in that dress.'

'Really?' I examine myself in the mirror, my cheeks flushing from Nancy's compliment. 'It's not too dressy, is it? Over the top?' I ask, fiddling with one of the straps.

'It's perfect,' she declares. 'You are going to knock Jack Baker's little socks off.'

Nancy and I are waiting for our lowlights to cook, sitting under large hairdryers and reading glossy magazines.

How much longer, I think, looking at myself in the mirror with these ridiculous silver bits of foil sprouting out of my hair like worms. I'm worried about Ruskin. He's been on his own for too long and will need to go out.

'He's just a dog,' Nancy says, reading my mind. 'They have no idea about time. Tell me more about this Monday to Friday man then,' she demands.

'Well, as I've said, he works in TV, lives in Bath . . .'

'Yes, yes, but what's he like?'

'He's fun, generous, he's . . .' I stop, unsure what I want to tell Nancy. 'I think I really like him,' I say, 'but I don't know if he feels the same.'

She nods understandingly. 'Well, I look forward to meeting him. You'll knock him out in that dress. Inviting him to your birthday is the perfect way to test him,' she says.

'Test him?'

'Yes. You can tell him you have a monster sister-in-law,' she turns to me, silver foil flashing in her hair and pulls a scary face, and for the first time I find her endearing, 'so if he says he'll come along then it's serious, Gilly. Men who aren't keen don't want to suffer family parties and photograph albums.'

Good point. I don't want to be too pushy too soon, but maybe I will ask him. Thinking about Jack, I might just call to say hello and thank him for the naughty note he left on the bed. Nancy watches me carefully as I pick up my telephone.

Jack's mobile clicks into voicemail so I decide I'll try him later.

'Never mind,' Nancy says watching me hang up. 'Now it's Sunday tomorrow. I'll book us in for a massage, tan and a makeover.'

'Listen, you've done more than enough, Nancy.' I gesture to the collection of shopping bags at our feet.

'Rubbish. I'll get Lydia to do you because she can work miracles.' I don't know whether to be insulted that I need such a lot of work done or touched that she wants to make me look beautiful for Jack.

'Don't worry about the cost. It's all on Nicholas, remember.'

I prickle, feeling angry on my brother's behalf that she's quite so free with his money. 'No. I won't allow that,' I insist.

'Up to you.'

One of the stylists approaches us, and checks on our highlights. They need to stay on for another five minutes. 'Nancy, do you mind if I ask you something?'

'Go ahead.'

'It would be awful, wouldn't it, if . . .' I pause, trying to work out how to put it. What I would like to say is please don't take Nick for granted. 'What would you do if Nick lost his job?'

She looks horrified.

'He could, in this recession. I know he's worried about it, which is half the reason he works so late,' I add.

'I'd tell him to get another job, and quickly. We want to send the girls to decent schools so there's no way he can afford to be out of work.'

'How about if he wasn't well?'

'Why! Has he said something to you? Is he unwell?' she says, panic in her voice.

'No, he's fine, sorry. It's just . . .'

'What, Gilly?'

'Are you happy, Nancy' – I really want to ask her if she loves Nick, but I don't have the nerve – 'with Nick?'

She purses her lips together. 'Yes. Gilly, my parents were poor. Dad drank himself to death.' She turns to me. 'I've never told you this, but there was never enough food in the house because Dad spent all Mum's dole on alcohol. I used to wear secondhand clothes for God's sake! When I left home I went to elocution lessons, learnt how to speak properly and was determined to do better for myself,' she says. 'I worked hard to get a man like Nicholas.'

I feel uncomfortable hearing this admission from Nancy. Clearly Nick wasn't an object of affection, he was a target.

The hairdresser comes back over to test if the dye has set on Nancy's hair. 'Don't you dare tell your father,' she whispers to me in a threatening tone. 'I'd hate him to know the whole story.'

'Do you still love him?' I burst out. I can't believe I said it. I feel relief because I've wanted to ask her this for so long, but have never had the courage.

'I'm a good wife and an excellent mother.'

I frown, without realizing because she says, 'Gilly! You can't ask me things like that!' She is led to the washing basin to have her hair shampooed. 'I'm happy the way things are. And so is Nicholas,' she says in a definite tone, before the young assistant asks her if she would like conditioner.

On the way home, I decide to try Jack again. The number rings. 'This is Jack Baker, please leave me a message after the tone,' he says. I switch it off, wondering what he's been up to all day.

'Everything off and slip into these,' Lydia says, handing me a pair of plastic flipflops and a bath cap.

I strip right down to my underwear and cover myself quickly with a towel when someone opens the door. It's Nancy, and I try hard to suppress laughter but it doesn't work. She's been sprayed already; it looks as if she's rolled around in a mud bath.

She perches on the side of the couch and fans herself. 'Can't put my clothes on yet. It has to cook for five minutes. Stop laughing, Gilly!'

There's a knock on the door. 'Ready?' Lydia calls for me.

'I'm stark naked, except for my knickers, standing in . . .'

'Oh don't be so modest Gilly. It's only me,' Nancy says, watching as I struggle to peel off my own knickers from underneath my towel, before sticking on a plastic bath cap over my hair. 'D'you think I should go on my date looking like this?' I ask, doing a sexy pose, and for the first time in *years* we both start laughing.

I'm stark naked, except for my plastic thong, standing in a narrow cubicle as Lydia blasts from a machine what feels like air-conditioning over my body. I lift one arm, hold up the other, turn sideways, turn to face the wall, turn back to face her, feeling increasingly like a prison convict. I shut my eyes and think of Jack, and seeing him tomorrow evening. I think about Guy too. I wonder how his work is going? Does he miss me like I miss him? Guy has a habit of creeping into my thoughts.

'I don't want to look too brown,' I say, panic beginning to set in when Lydia asks me if I want one or two layers.

'Trust me, this'll give you a lovely sun-kissed look. People will think you've been to San Tropez.'

Right, but what do I tell them? It's mid-October and I haven't been anywhere except Ravenscourt Park.

Later that evening, plucked, manicured, exfoliated and tanned, Nancy and I make our way back to Richmond. I want to see Tilda and Hannah.

'Ta-dah!' I say as I join Nick bathing the children.

My brother smiles. 'Wow, doesn't Auntie Gilly look lovely?'

Matilda laughs. 'You look funny,' she says. Hannah doesn't say a word.

'I've been to San Tropez,' I tell them, sitting on the edge of the bath. Guilt overwhelms me that Nick has had to look after the children all weekend, but my guilt is misplaced. He tells me he's had a lovely day.

'Haven't we, angels?' he says as he swishes a toy crocodile in the water. 'He's going to eat me up!' Tilda wriggles, splashing water.

'He can't eat you,' Hannah says, deflating her imagination. 'He's plastic.'

'Daddy bought croc for us today, Auntie Gilly!' Tilda says.

I plunge my hands into the water and grab the crocodile, chasing it after the girls. 'Snap!' I shout before I gasp, 'Oh shit!'

Even Hannah breaks into a smile at that. 'I mean,

oh no, I mustn't wet my hands! The tan will wash away!'

'Oh shit,' Tilda copies.

'No, Matilda,' my brother says firmly. 'Now tell Auntie Gilly what else we've done today.'

'We went to the playground,' she says.

'The Princess Diana Memorial one,' fills in Nick.

'Why didn't Mum come with us?' Hannah asks Dad, and from Nick's weary expression, she's clearly been asking him that all day.

'When are you going to get married, Auntie Gilly?' asks Tilda.

'She won't now,' Hannah predicts. 'Her time's run out.'

I look over to Nick, knowing Nancy must have said this to them. 'My time isn't running out, but yours is! If you don't get out of the bath right now you will both turn into prunes!'

When they step out, Matilda particularly excited, I wrap a fluffy towel around her; Hannah is getting to the age where she wants to do everything on her own.

'Nick, is Hannah all right?' I ask him, when we're alone in his study. 'She's very quiet.'

He presses his head into his hands. 'I think she heard us arguing again this morning. Nancy's latest thing is we send her to boarding school, but I think she's too young.'

'Perhaps you should try talking to Hannah, maybe she's feeling insecure or nervous . . .'

'I've tried but . . .'

'You could take her out for an afternoon, just the two of you? Sometimes it's easier to talk out of the house.'

'Anyway . . .' He sighs, turning to me. 'I like your hair shorter. It suits you.' The contrast between his fragile marriage compared to my hair makes me feel ashamed, as if I am in a child's game, far away from the grown-up world.

'Jack's a lucky man,' he says.

'Thanks . . . and thanks again for this weekend. Nancy was pretty amazing,' I have to confess.

'Good. I'm glad she could help.' For a moment I have an overwhelming urge to hug him. 'Anyway, it was a treat to have the girls to myself,' he confides, before whispering, 'no one nagging in my ear. I should be the one thanking you.'

'Oh, Nick,' I say, hitting his arm affectionately.

30

'So come on, where did he take you and the emerald dress?' Sam asks under the oak tree.

'Wow, you look incredible,' Jack had said when the waiter slipped off my coat.

I tell them he took me to Gordon Ramsay's.

'But don't you need to book two months in advance?' asks Brigitte.

'Not if you're Jack,' I claim proudly. He only has to say the word *Stargazer* and everyone treats him like royalty, I think to myself.

Then we went on to a nightclub and danced.

Jack had held his arms around my waist, his hand moved up and down my back against the silk of my dress . . .

'And?' Ariel demands. 'Then what?'

'That's it,' I smile, urging him not to go on because Walter is by my side.

'No it's not!' Ariel shakes his head.

And then we made love, in my room this time, with the bedside light on.

'Did he notice your hair? Your tan?' Sam continues.

'When's Guy back?' asks Mari. 'I don't know why, but I miss Hatman.'

It's Friday morning and I'm at the gym. I have enrolled myself into a new 'fat-busting' gym class. I used to love working out with Ed and it's time to get fit again. I am not scared of bumping into him at the gym any more. If I do happen to see him on the treadmill, it's time to show him I'm over it.

I owe this transformation to Jack. He has entered my life like a whirlwind and by the time the weekend arrives, I need Saturday and Sunday to recover. In the past fortnight my diary has been packed with private screenings of films, nightclubs and restaurants. For the first time in months I have had to cancel my regular supper with my father, and when I told him why, he said he was thrilled that I was dining with a younger man.

Last night Jack flew in through the front door like an aeroplane, scooped me up from the sofa and whisked me into a cab to Soho, where we met a few of his television friends in a trendy wine bar before jumping into another taxi to go to Annabel's nightclub. I'm enjoying meeting new people and Jack's friends are an easygoing, live-for-the-moment crowd. When Ed and I split up, inevitably I lost a chunk of my social life; it has been difficult keeping in touch with his friends. People don't take sides, but of course they gravitate to the person they originally knew.

Annabel's never fails to please me. The cushions are comfortable, the soft lighting intimate, the company last night perfect, and I love the feeling of glamour in the air. With a champagne cocktail in one hand, I could hear Gloria's advice to enjoy myself, and when I'm with Jack I *do* feel happy. When we arrived home I thanked him. 'You make me forget my problems,' I said.

'What problems?' He smiled, before adding, 'You do the same for me, so thank you.'

'No. Thank *you*,' I said, peeling off my top and throwing it seductively over my shoulder.

'No, thank *you*,' he retaliated as he chased me upstairs.

After my gym session and swift walk in the park, Ruskin and I walk down the Pimlico Road. I spot Kay, who works in the florist's, and wave to her. She often gives me leftover flowers on a Friday evening. I then nip into the local coffee shop, before tying Ruskin's lead to one of the chairs outside.

'The usual, Gilly with a G?' Manuel asks me, turning round to the cappuccino machine. Manuel is Italian and has worked in this café for years. He doesn't like change.

He hands me a *grande* cappuccino with one sugar, no chocolate sprinkled on top, and a plain croissant, heated up but not piping hot. 'How's the shop?' he asks, as he always does each morning when he hands me my coffee cup on a cardboard tray. I tell him that Ruskin lifted his leg on a Russian lady's expensive-looking coat. 'I think she was a countess,' I whisper, before saying luckily I don't think she noticed. Manuel laughs, always enjoying the gossip on Mari's customers. 'You have a lovely weekend, Gilly,' he says and I raise my coffee cup to him and wish him the same as I leave.

As I walk on, past all the smart interior design and photo-gallery shops, I think about this coming weekend. I might see if Jack wants to stay. While it is nice to have the weekends to myself, maybe he could just stay tonight? I know it's not the deal: that's probably why Jack hasn't mentioned it. He doesn't pay to stay for the weekend, but strictly speaking, I'm not Jack's Monday to Friday landlady any more, am I? I wonder in fact, if I should charge him for living at No. 21 at all? I feel guilty charging him when he takes me out all the time. No! I have to! His rent helps towards my mortgage . . . but I could offer him the weekends for free.

'I can't, Gilly babes,' he says when I call him from the shop. Normally I don't make too many private calls from work, especially not with Mari's beady eye on me, but she and Basil are on a long weekend break in Cornwall, spending time with her mother.

'Oh, don't worry, it was just a thought.' I twist the telephone cable, wishing I hadn't asked.

'I've got this family thing on and . . .'

'It's fine,' I repeat. 'Really, it was just a thought.'

'Maybe another time, OK?'

'Of course,' I say, hiding my disappointment. While I love our evenings, I want to have some slow time with Jack. No racing to work but breakfast in bed, coffee and a walk in the park, a film and a pizza. I want the opportunity to tell him about my birthday party.

'Got to run. See you Monday.'

I hang up. 'Yep, see you Monday.'

Later on in the afternoon I open the writing book Guy gave me. Since he's been away I've barely picked up my pen. I read his message inside again. *Maybe this is your something*. I can hear him ticking me off, asking me what I've been doing with my time. Why haven't I started? Why am I so scared of failure? I open the book, determined to make some progress when the doorbell tinkles and in he comes, Mr Platter Man. Ruskin barks, but I pull him back onto the sofa. Today the old man's wearing a diamond-checked tanktop over a pair of mustard-coloured trousers and he's carrying a canvas bag with bumblebees on it. 'Oh . . . er . . . hello,' he says, 'I was just . . . er . . . just . . .'

'Yes?'

'Wondering . . . um . . . do you . . . er . . . sell . . . er . . . irons?'

'Onions?' I mishear.

He chuckles. 'No, dear . . . er . . . irons?'

'Oh, I'm sorry, no. We sell antiques, unless you're after an old iron? You might find something in the Portobello.'

He's not sure.

'How about Peter Jones?' I say, showing him to the door and directing him to the department store again. 'Did you find your plates, by the way?'

'Platters? Er . . . no.' He looks confused, loses his balance and staggers back, grabbing hold of the doorknob.

Next thing I know, I'm ushering him back into the shop and offering him a cup of tea and a custard cream, and telling him to come and meet my Ruskin. Over tea (lots of slurps) I discover his name is Dennis. He's seventy-nine and he lives in Victoria. Ruskin attempts to sit on the man's bony lap, 'He wants to give you a kiss,' I tell him. Dennis blushes profusely, gently stroking my boy.

'You're a man, Dennis, I need some advice,' I say, when we're on our second cup of tea.

'Oh . . . I'm not . . . very . . . er . . . qualified.'

'Oh yes you are,' I say, not allowing him to get out of it. I tell him about Jack, more to get it off my chest than expecting Dennis to understand. I find myself confiding that Jack never wants to stay at the weekend. I leave out no detail. 'I have no idea what he gets up to, Dennis. Would you ask him outright if he's got a family or some deep dark secret? What would you do?'

Dennis takes a long time considering this, as he munches his biscuit. He rests a hand against his ear, thinking deeply.

'I don't . . . er . . . know,' he says.

'Don't worry.' I smile, putting him at ease. 'Here, have another biscuit.'

He refuses another, winding himself up to say something more. 'I think . . . er . . . Gilly . . . he sounds like . . . er . . . a bad . . . er . . . egg.'

On Sunday afternoon, curled up on the sofa, *Eastenders* omnibus playing in the background, I call Jack, but his phone goes straight into answer machine mode. I decide against leaving a message. I try to picture what he gets up to at the weekend. Why would I even doubt that he lives in Bath? That he has made up this excuse of having a 'family thing' on?

Later on that evening Mum calls, telling me there's a heatwave in Perth, unusual for this time of year. Then she wants to know my news. I find myself describing Jack to her, though I don't go into all the detail. 'What is it?' she asks. 'Something's worrying you, I can tell.'

If Mum were sitting on the sofa next to me, I'd probably tell her; or if she lived a couple of hours' drive away I might even get into the car, but . . . 'Nothing's worrying me,' I say. 'Really. I'm having a great time.'

31

Susie, Anna and I are out at Susie's local pub, the Owl and the Pussy Cat. It's a lively place, with candles on wooden tables, comfortable leather sofas to sink into and a fireplace where the owner's cat, Pickles, is always found sleeping. Anna is filling us in on how it's going with Paul.

'Love that by the way,' Susie says, gesturing to my turquoise top that I'm wearing with jeans.

'I thought it was new,' Anna smiles, and briefly I tell them about my shopping trip with Nancy.

But back to Paul!

She's still in a dream, Anna says, in that she's hankered after him all this time but never believed it would happen.

'What's he like?' Susie asks. Unlike me, she hasn't met him yet.

'He's creative, ambitious at work,' Anna replies. 'He's quiet too, but not in a boring way,' she's quick to add.

We tell her he needs to be fairly quiet as Anna can talk enough for two.

'He asked me if we should move in together, but I'm not sure. I want to, but his divorce isn't even finalized,' she says.

'Don't rush,' Susie advises her. 'Are you sure you're ready to take on his son?'

'I know it's not going to be easy,' Anna answers, 'and I didn't dream of meeting someone divorced with a child, but that's just the way it is.'

'All I'm saying is don't rush it,' Susie insists now. 'There's so much time for arguing about whose turn it is to put out the bins.'

'I'm thirty-five. There's not *that* much time to . . .' She stops, turns to me. 'Oh God, listen to me. I'm sorry, Gilly.'

'Yes, you've deserted me!' I say, followed by, 'Don't you dare feel sorry for me. I'm happy for you, Anna, really happy. You've waited long enough for Paul and I know it's been hard at times.'

'What about Jack?' they both ask at the same time.

I tell Susie and Anna about my evening with Jack last night, confiding how I can't stop thinking about what Jack's brother, Alexander, had said to me.

We were at an art exhibition, organized by an old family friend of Jack's. I was deep in conversation with one of the guests when a man interrupted me. 'I'm Alexander,' he said. 'I think I saw you arrive with my brother.'

It dawned on me then how little I knew about Jack.

As far as I could recall, Jack hadn't mentioned he had a brother since he'd lived with me.

'Hi. Yes, I'm Gilly,' I said, offering my hand and he shook it. 'Jack's living with me at the moment.'

Alexander was tall like Jack, but had darker hair, and dressed more like my father or Nick, in his suit with cufflinks. He looked me up and down before saying, 'So you're his latest victim.'

'Latest victim?' I'd smiled, trying to make a joke of it, but he didn't smile back.

At that point Jack joined us and Alexander excused himself with a curt nod. I couldn't imagine Jack being related to him; they seemed completely at odds with each other. 'What were you talking about?' Jack asked, and appeared relieved when I said we'd only just had time to introduce ourselves. When I asked Jack to tell me about his brother he said he worked in the civil service. 'Don't you get on?' I asked.

Jack shook his head. 'He's boring. Conservative and always telling me what I should do.'

He had stiffened when I'd told him about the latest victim comment.

'That's typical Alexander,' Jack said, and leaned in towards me. 'Truth is, Gilly, he's jealous that I get all the beautiful girls like you.'

I caught Alexander's eye again.

Now I try to picture his face and hear his tone of voice again.

'Maybe he meant it in a light-hearted way?' Susie suggests.

'He didn't.' I shake my head. 'I just have this feeling . . .'

'Oh no, not one of your feelings,' Anna rolls her eyes.

I think of Dennis, who can't seem to understand that Mari's shop doesn't sell platters, but who can probably see a whole lot more than most people. Ruskin loved Dennis and dogs always know when a person is kind and real; they can sift the good from the bad in an instant. When Jack picks up Rusk, he wriggles and does his best to get away.

'There's something I don't know about Jack. What if he's hiding something?'

'Look, he can't be married or anything like that,' Anna states. 'I wouldn't read too much into it.'

'You're right,' I tell them. 'It probably meant nothing, but . . . I just don't know that much about him, although he doesn't ask me anything either,' I tell them.

'Does he know about Ed?' Susie asks.

'No, not really.' All he knows is that he left me two weeks before the wedding, but he has no idea of how it affected me.

'Men don't ask that many questions,' Anna reasons.

'Yes, but Jack's Gilly's boyfriend,' Susie interrupts. 'Isn't he, Gilly?'

'I think so,' I say, 'from Monday to Friday.'

'Has he asked you about any other relationships?'

'No! You shouldn't talk about your exes anyway,' Anna argues. 'Although it is true to say I'm longing to know more about Paul's ex-wife,' she admits.

'What about your family?' Susie continues. 'He does know about Megan, doesn't he?'

I shake my head. 'Not really.' That means no.

Equally, I haven't asked him about his past or his family. When I'm with Jack it's as if we're both blank pieces of paper, up until today not wanting to blot our problems into the sheets, but I want to know more about him now.

'What you need to do is spend more time with him when the show's over,' Anna advises. 'Once he's moved out, you'll both know if you want to keep the relationship going.'

I nod, realizing Jack will leave by Christmas and that the thought terrifies me. I'm having such a great time with him that I don't want to have these doubts. 'The sex is great too,' I confide.

They laugh. 'Sex? What's that?' asks Susie. 'Mark falls asleep on the sofa these days, it's a miracle if we even *go* to bed together, let alone have sex.'

We smile at that.

'Jack's coming to your birthday, isn't he?' Anna asks. I nod.

'How about Guy? What does he think of Jack?' she asks.

Guy. I miss Guy. 'He hasn't met him,' I tell them. 'Yet.'

32

'Hi,' he says. He was the last person I expected to see at the shop. Ruskin and Basil bark and wag their tails as he approaches me.

'Guy! How are you?'

'Great. I was passing by . . . This is an amazing place,' he says, gingerly making his way through the obstacle course to reach me. Guy didn't really have time to explore the shop when he last visited. 'How do you find anything?' He touches a lamp vase and a layer of dust coats his fingers.

'Is that Hatman?' calls Mari from the basement.

'Yes!' he calls down to her.

'Welcome home!' she shouts back.

I am taken aback by how lovely it is to see his familiar face. 'You look . . .' He analyses me, attempting to work out what it is that has changed. 'Different.'

Self-consciously I touch my hair.

'It suits you,' he says.

Ruskin jumps up against Guy, wagging his tail.

'I've missed your big head and that long snout of yours Rusk,' Guy strokes him before looking up to me and asking if I have time for lunch.

'Go on,' Mari calls. 'I'll hold the fort.'

I pick up my coat. 'Let's go round the corner,' I suggest.

'How did the work go?' I ask Guy as we eat toasted-cheese sandwiches in Manuel's coffee shop.

'Work? Forget about the garden, Gilly. I've discovered far more about their relationship,' he claims.

'What do you mean?'

'OK, so it's like this. To begin with I'm dealing with Mrs Morris. "Call me Sarah," she insists. Sarah's the one who rang me in the first place, wanting me to redesign the garden and put in a new terrace. So I meet Sarah, carry out a basic survey of the site, she really likes my designs and together we think up some ideas. Won't go into them, boring for you. She then tells me that her husband Tim needs to be at the second meeting, just to make sure he's happy to go ahead with the plans. Now, Tim's a lawyer.'

'My father's a lawyer,' I say, before he's rude about them. 'And my brother.'

'Well, I wouldn't like to work for your family. Lawyers are the worst clients! Their favourite word is "clause". So Mr Morris strides into the kitchen wearing shades, pushes little wife out of the way, glances at my plans, doesn't get them and says, "Where's the house?" He then starts firing questions at me, as if we're in court. "What did you do before you designed gardens?" and "What qualifications do you have?" Sarah is dealing with their screaming children, nose massively out of joint because Tim is now taking over and demanding more options.'

I smile, remembering option is another favourite word.

'These lawyers, they don't want to commit to anything,' Guy goes on. 'All Tim's interested in is stuff like, "What if the roots interfere with the drains?" "What if we sell the house?"

'So I say, "Are you going to sell?"'

'"Well, it's an option," he replies.'

I laugh.

'Tim doesn't like the red that Sarah suggested. You know it's pretty basic, if you have a red flower you can incorporate another plant that has a red vein in its stem. Tim is afraid of colour in case it's not commercial when it comes to selling. Instead he wants me to put in cream and neutrals because it's a safer "option".'

'Frustrating,' I sigh.

'Exactly. When Tim's at work the following week and the children are at school, Sarah talks to me while I'm doing the planting, right, and she confesses how much he drives her insane, that her husband's so unimaginative. I tell you, Gilly, her skirt hitched up another inch by the day, and then there was this one time . . . do you remember that really bad storm we had last week?'

'Oh yes! I had to give Ruskin a bath.'

'Well anyway, I went inside to dry off and she . . . she . . . you know . . .' Guy adjusts his hat.

Of course I know. I know, exactly. 'But you didn't . . .'

'She's a lovely woman, but so lonely, Gilly. She's the kind of person who'd call out the boilerman, just to have the company. I'd watch her in the kitchen, staring into space. God that house felt so empty.'

It makes me think of Nick and Nancy, even my own parents.

'What did Sarah do all day?'

'I have no idea.'

'But you didn't, you know, did you?' I find myself asking again.

'No.'

'What happened?'

'It was awful. She fled into the house, I didn't see her for the rest of the week, until I produced my bill.'

And at that point Guy picks up the bill and pays Manuel. I smile, remembering Harvey with his calculator.

'So, how about you?' Guy asks, as we walk back to the shop. 'What have you been up to?'

'Me?' I'm not sure where to start.

'You look well,' Guy continues. 'Thinner. Have you lost weight?'

'I've been going to the gym again.'

'Well, you look great on it – not that you didn't

look good before,' he quickly adds. 'Have you been writing?'

'A little,' I lie.

'And Jack? How was your date?'

I attempt to open the shop door, but find it's locked. Mari must have gone out for something. 'That feels like years ago,' I say, rummaging in my handbag for the keys. Keys are like mobiles. I'm sure they hide on purpose too. Finally I unlock the door.

'I know. I feel like I've been away for ages,' Guy says as I lead him inside. 'Anyway, come on, was it good fun?'

I nod. 'We've been going out,' I tell him.

'Out? What *out* out?'

'Sort of. Yes.'

'Really?'

'Yes, really.' I tell Guy about our recent evenings together.

Guy listens, but can't help mentioning that Gordon Ramsay is a slightly obvious choice. It's no doubt a good restaurant, he says, but he loves this run-down lobster joint in Islington, owned by a French family. He takes off his hat, runs a hand through his hair.

'I've always wanted to go to Gordon Ramsay's though,' I claim, not liking the defensive tone in my voice.

'I'm sure it's good,' Guy says. 'I've never been.'

When I tell him about Annabel's, he's quick to point out that he's relieved his clubbing days are over.

'Oh don't be so old, Guy, and boring!'

'You're right. Mustn't get my pipe and slippers out too soon.'

I make Guy a cup of coffee; he seems in no hurry to leave and I don't want him to. We talk about the dogs; he tells me how much he's missed Trouble. I tell him that I'm having great fun with Jack. I fill him in on our dog-walking circle. Mari was furious because she had been fined for driving at thirty-seven miles per hour along a Cornish lane. Ariel has split up with Gareth again. I tell him that I'm also enjoying working in the shop and just sold a chandelier to Gywneth Paltrow's interior decorator . . .

'Are you serious about Jack?' he asks. 'Or is it just a fling?'

'Have you been listening to a word I've been saying?'

'Yes,' he nods, 'but I want to hear more about Jack.'

'I don't know, Guy. Maybe.' I hesitate whether to tell him about my encounter with Jack's brother last night.

'Do you want it to be more?'

'I don't know.' I smile. 'Why do you care so much?'

'Why do I care?' He looks at me. 'Well, I just want some gossip because my own life is so boring.'

I tell him about Alexander, then immediately wish I hadn't.

'Victim? That's a strong word, isn't it?'

'Oh, Guy, I think it was a jokey thing. I'm having a great time. You haven't shaved since I last saw you.'

'You're changing the subject.'

'I'm not going to worry about it,' I say. 'Alexander did look like a stuffed shirt too. He's nothing like Jack.'

'Perhaps, but just be careful, Gilly.'

'Careful? Only recently you were telling me not to think about things too much, that I over-analyse everything!'

'I know. But I'm not sure about Jack and this brother,' he admits. 'I always thought you should have found out a lot more about him before he moved in.'

33

It's early Friday morning. 'Can't you stay this weekend?' I ask Jack as I lie in bed watching him pack. 'I've hardly seen you all week.' I reach out to grab his arm, pull him towards me and kiss him, one hand stroking the back of his neck. 'Don't go tonight. We could have a lie-in tomorrow,' I say slowly, 'I could make us breakfast, we could stay in bed all day.'

'Oh, Gilly,' he says, in a tone which suggests no, but his lips remain close to mine, and we kiss again. I run a hand through his soft hair and he murmurs in approval.

'We could do nothing but this, Jack, all weekend.'

'I'd love to,' he says, before pulling away, 'but I can't, honey.' I sit up and bring my knees to my chest, watching as Jack opens his wardrobe. He takes out his jeans and a couple of tops, flings them into his leather suitcase.

'Why?' I ask. 'Have you got plans?'

'Yep,' he says, refusing to allow me entry into his life at the weekend.

'What are you up to?' I could kill Alexander . . . and Guy for making me question Jack.

'I've got stuff on, Gilly.'

What the hell does 'stuff' mean? If I'm not careful I shall ruin this relationship, stamp it to death with my suspicion. Is that what I want? I don't like the way Jack makes me feel insecure, when he's always so cool and composed. What's going on behind the mask? He gives nothing away. If only Jack wasn't so mysterious, then I wouldn't have to ask these questions, would I?

'Stuff?' I ask, trying to sound casual as I play with the corner of the duvet cover.

'Just a few things I have to do. I need the weekends to be at home, catch up.'

That is reasonable, I say to myself. Instead I work up to suggesting, 'Why don't I come to Bath on Sunday then, just for the day?'

'No.' He registers he said that too fiercely. 'I mean, no, it's not the best time.'

'We could go out for lunch . . .'

He squashes my ideas with, 'It's the busiest time for the show. I need to keep my head down, and I won't if you're around,' he adds with a smile. 'Right.' He zips up the conversation as well as his suitcase. Ask him about his brother, Gilly. Go on. Ask him.

'Jack, why don't you ever talk about your brother?'

'We don't get on, that's why.'

'Guy says . . .'

He rolls his eyes as if he hasn't got time to hear what Guy says again, before glancing at his watch. 'I need to shoot.' He kisses me on the lips before rushing out of the room with his suitcase. 'Have a great weekend,' he calls.

'You too! Whatever you're up to,' I mutter to myself as I get out of bed and slip on my dressing gown.

He's back again. 'Shit, left my . . .' He grabs his BlackBerry from the bedside table. He must notice my back turned towards him because next thing I know, a pair of arms are wrapped round my waist. I try to pull away but he doesn't let me. 'Aren't you sick of me by the weekend?' he asks, holding me tightly. Then he brushes a strand of hair away from my face and kisses my neck. His touch feels warm.

'No, I like having you around. Just stay tonight,' I say again, turning towards him.

'I wish I could, but I really do have to work, Gilly. I've got to finish a whole script by Monday.'

I nod, reluctantly.

'We're OK?' he asks, lifting my chin.

I nod. 'Go.'

He's off.

'Oh, hang on!' I call him back.

He sticks his head round the door. 'What? Quick!'

'You're coming to my birthday party next week, aren't you?'

If Jack lets me down I'll have to explain this to Nancy and, besides, I want to show him off to my nieces. Hannah and Tilda have been allowed to stay up extra late, just to say Happy Birthday to me, and I know they are longing to meet Auntie Gilly's boyfriend, the handsome Jack.

'I'll be there,' he promises. 'Wouldn't miss it for the world. Now can I go?'

I smile. 'Go.'

'See you Monday!' he calls as he rushes downstairs.

I hear the front door slam and Ruskin bark.

34

Thirty-five today. Happy birthday to me, I sing in the shower.

My birthday morning starts well with a visit from the Interflora man. Quickly I open the small white envelope tucked into the flowers, praying they're not from Aunt Pearl, Dad, Gloria, Nick or Nancy.

They're from Jack, signed,

> With lots of love.
> ps You're hot for thirty-five.

I smile at that part, realizing that I've got to relax about Jack and the weekends. I'm not ready for us to be over, not yet, and especially not as I turn thirty-five. That would be adding insult to the injury.

In the post is a card from my father, enclosing a cheque. There are cards from all my friends, including the Digbys up north and the Heron clan in the Hebrides, and Helen my nursing friend from Middle Wallop in Hampshire, who signs it from all the family including the dogs and the chickens. Hannah and Matilda have both made me cards. Hannah has painted a picture of the sea with colourful fish and inside she has written, 'Have a fishy fun birday'. Matilda has painted a heart and in the middle she's written, 'Happie birfday'.

Mum sends a package from Australia. Inside are book tokens, perfume and some old black-and-white Audrey Hepburn movies, which she knows are my favourites. In her card she asks me to visit her again.

My dog friends and I congregate under the oak tree, wrapped in thick coats, scarves and hats. I open their cards.

'If any of you tell me I'm over the hill, or . . .'

'Losing your marbles,' suggests Walter.

Thankfully none of them do. The cards mostly have dogs on the front, surprise surprise.

'Happy birthday,' says Sam, giving me a small white box. Inside is a chocolate cupcake with creamy icing and one single candle in the middle.

Sam lights the cake with Mari's cigarette lighter and they all sing Happy Birthday, telling me to make a wish.

I wish for everything to go smoothly at Nancy's tonight.

Guy and I part at the zebra crossing. 'You've got the address for this evening?' I call after him.

He nods. 'I'll see you later.'

'Oh, and Guy—'

He turns, walks back to me. 'Why have you got your worry face on?'

I press my lips together. 'I'm not worried, not at all, but . . .'

'Um?'

'You won't mention anything to Jack about his brother, will you?'

'I promise to behave,' he says reassuringly with a salute. 'I'll put on my best hat.'

Great. I smile as I walk to work.

I'm glad Nancy suggested a party. She's right. Nick and I should celebrate, not hide under our duvet covers. I think about everyone meeting Jack this evening.

I'm looking forward to it.

35

Nick opens the door, looking handsome in dark trousers, polished shoes and a soft blue jumper like the ones our father wears. 'Happy birthday, twinnie,' he says, hugging me. Hannah and Matilda race down the hallway in their fluffy pyjamas and slippers. 'Auntie Gilly!' Tilda cries out. I crouch down and she throws her arms around my neck. 'Happy birfday!'

'Remember,' Nick reminds me as I hug the girls, 'I was born twenty minutes before you.'

As I approach the kitchen, the children clinging onto me and demanding I open their presents right now, I hear the sound of corks popping. Nick whispers into my ear that Nancy's tipsy already. When I enter the room she thrusts a glass of champagne into my hand and surveys me in my raspberry-pink suede miniskirt that we bought together on our shopping trip. 'Perfect!' she proclaims before hustling me out and into the sitting room. 'You didn't mind me asking Guy last minute?' I say breath-lessly.

'No! I've cooked an enormous paella, so the more the merrier!'

The sitting room is a shrine to Nick and me, with glittery 35 TODAY! banners hung from the ceiling and delicious-looking canapés on the coffee table. 'No more crisps, Tilda,' Nancy says, swiping the bowl from her. 'Where's Jack, Auntie Gilly?' Tilda asks impatiently.

Anna and Paul are the first to arrive. Nick hasn't asked his friends this evening because he's having a separate party, also organized by his wife – lots of his work colleagues, of course. Besides, there wasn't space around the table to invite everyone. Nick offers drinks and turns on some music. Hannah and Tilda hand round bowls of crisps and olives. Anna hands me a present. Oh! This is such fun, I tell her and Paul, saying I love presents more than food. As I'm about to open my gift, Nancy confiscates it, saying she wants a present-opening session at the end of the evening, after dinner. 'Is everything all right?' I whisper to Nick when she's walked away, noticing he's quiet.

'Just another row,' he whispers. 'She's impossible.'

When Mark and Susie arrive, I hear more champagne corks flying from the kitchen. 'Ugh,' Hannah says when she tries one of the smoked salmon blinis.

Susie joins me by the fireplace. 'You look beautiful,

Gilly.' She kisses me on both cheeks. 'Thirty-five is clearly the new thirty,' she says as we raise our glasses to each other. 'I like the look of Paul,' she adds. 'Guy's coming too, isn't he?' she then asks casually.

'He'd better be, I'm dying to meet Hatman,' Anna says, joining us now.

'What's Hatman?' Tilda asks with excitement, plunging her hand into the bowl of crisps.

'Guy,' I tell them.

'Have you got two boyfriends?' she asks, surprised.

'No, he's my dog-walking friend,' I tell her.

'Do you show them both your boobies,' Tilda asks, jumping up and down in front of me, and everyone laughs. Nancy appears at the sitting-room door, red-faced. 'You two, bed,' she instructs.

'No, Mum! I want to see Jack!' Tilda begs.

'Well, behave then.'

Thankfully the doorbell rings and Nancy leaves the sitting room. 'Jack Baker,' I overhear. 'You must be Nancy.'

'Yes! Come in, come in,' Nancy says, voice rejuvenated.

'Quick update,' Susie insists, and Anna leans in towards me.

'Great,' I whisper.

Nancy leads Jack into the sitting room, a room of beiges and whites, tall vases filled with lilies and cream curtains with tiebacks. The girls are silent. They stare at him, until Jack says, 'Oh! Now you must be—' He turns to me, hoping I'll remind him.

'Hannah and Tilda, this is Jack,' I say cheerily.

Tilda hides behind my skirt, murmuring, 'Hello, Jack.'

When he is introduced to Anna I can tell from her face that she also understands what the fuss is all about now. When you first meet Jack fireworks do explode. I have become more immune to his good looks since picking up his boxer shorts and sweaty running pants off the floor, and scooping his teabags out of the sink and into the bin. However, when I introduce him to all my friends and Nick tonight, I do feel proud. If Jack and I weren't serious, he wouldn't be here, would he?

Jack strokes my arm, before turning to everyone and commanding the room. 'Doesn't the birthday girl look beautiful? And tall,' he gestures down to my heels, before kissing me.

Nancy's mouth twitches as she says, 'Come on everyone, dinner is served. Girls, bedtime now.'

'Hang on, what about Guy?' I say.

'The famous dog walker,' Jack adds.

The doorbell rings and in he comes, dressed to my surprise in smart trousers and a shirt. But he's still wearing a hat. His navy hat, the one that I love. The girls giggle at his hat, before being whisked off to bed.

★

'This is delicious paella, Nancy,' Jack says. I reach for his hand under the table, to signal well done, as I'd told him that she loves compliments about her cooking.

Everyone murmurs their approval around the table, especially Jack and me. When Nancy goes to this much trouble I feel guilty that I don't give her enough credit. My sister-in-law and I are wired in completely different ways, but perhaps I need to understand her, just as people need to understand me.

'I've never had it with chorizo before,' Jack continues, squeezing my hand now and I hold back from laughing.

'It's just one of my secret little ingredients, Jack,' Nancy enthuses. 'So, come on, Gilly. What do you wish for this year?'

I look at Guy. 'Well, I'd love to write a novel.'

'Have you read any of her children's stories?' asks Anna loyally.

'What else?' Nancy asks.

'I don't know.' To meet someone, I want to say and to be happy. 'What about you Nick?'

'Be happy,' he says, reading my own thoughts, 'that's all.'

'Well, I'm so glad Gilly didn't move to the country,' Nancy states.

'Me too,' Jack says, clutching my hand territorially, 'otherwise I wouldn't have met this fabulous girl,' he claims, addressing all of us now.

Guy looks over to us. 'I'd jump at the chance to move.'

'Would you?' Anna asks in disbelief. 'I always think of the country as a place to retire.'

'No no. When we retire,' Nancy emphasizes, 'we're not going to plant ourselves in some half-dead village where the highlight of the month is a bric-a-brac morning, are we, Nicholas? We'll go back to Los Angeles,' she declares.

'I love LA,' agrees Jack, and I catch them exchanging smiles again. Going well, I think with relief. A good lively debate is what it's all about.

'I much prefer London. We used to live in LA,' Nick says, turning to Guy, 'for the first few years of our marriage, but I'm glad I'm home.'

'Right. So you want to live somewhere where it rains all the time,' Nancy says, 'and where no one smiles.' She starts to clear the plates; Jack jumps up to help her. I watch him resting a hand against her back, asking what he can do. 'No, no,' she giggles, 'you sit down.'

'Where do you live, Jack?' Nick asks, when he returns to the table.

'Bath.'

'Just out of interest, why don't you live here?' Guy asks.

'Gilly thinks I'm secretly married.' Jack smiles, leaning back into his seat, hands held behind his head.

'Oh Jack, I only said that as a joke because you can never stay the weekend,' I say. 'He's with me during the week but then disappears into a cloud of smoke on Friday.

Puff!' I clap my hands. 'He's gone! No one can get hold of him, his phone is switched off . . .'

'Gilly.' Jack frowns.

'And then as if by magic he comes back on Monday.' Everyone laughs, I notice, except Jack.

'So come on, what *do* you get up to at the weekend?' Nick asks.

At that point Jack's telephone rings. Again. 'Don't take it,' I urge. Is anyone that important going to call him tonight?

'Sorry,' he mutters, leaving the table with his BlackBerry.

When he returns Nancy asks him who it was. 'Just my wife,' he replies, winking at her, and I notice Nancy smiling back at him. She looks as if she wants to tear his hand off mine and eat him with lashings of whipped cream.

'What do you do?' Nancy asks Guy, after quizzing Jack on his career and marvelling at his success at such a young age. She's already established that Jack's thirty, Guy thirty-seven. I wonder if she would find Jack so attractive if he were a traffic warden? Would I, for that matter? Jack grabs the bottle of wine, waiting for Guy's response.

'I'm a landscape gardener.'

'A gardener!' Nancy repeats.

Oh God. She's getting drunk. Does she realize how rude she sounds?

Guy nods, detecting her tone.

'How much can you earn doing that?' Jack asks. 'What?' he says to me, when I kick him under the table. 'It's a reasonable question!'

Nick glances his way.

'Guy, just ignore him,' I say with false merriment. Not going so well now, I think.

'I admit I don't earn a fortune,' Guy says to Jack, without raising his voice.

'Money isn't everything,' interrupts Nick.

'Yeah, but it helps,' Jack argues, gesturing to the lavish table decorated with candles and confetti, and the food in front of him.

'Will you come and look at our tiny garden?' Susie asks Guy, trying to steer the conversation somewhere else. 'Mark and I are both useless and never have enough time, do we?'

'Never,' Mark agrees.

'Of course,' Guy nods, 'I'd love to.'

'Gardening,' Nancy says again, 'you're really just a gardener?'

'Nancy!' we all shout at her. I can see Paul's face expressing panic that these are the kind of people Anna hangs out with. I want to reassure him that we're not all like Nancy. I turn to Jack, who's gazing at her, almost in awe.

'Well, I used to work in advertising, Nancy, but I stopped when I realized that I didn't want to say at the end of my life that all I'd ever done was advertise tooth-paste.'

I notice Nick and Paul smiling with Guy now.

'At least I go to bed at night knowing I've earned a good honest day's wage,' Guy continues, 'I'm not diddling anyone out of money, I'm not some dodgy bloke trying to convince you that you need life insurance at the age of twelve and I'm not some politician ripping off the taxpayer.'

'Noble,' Jack sums up.

'At least I don't make my money exploiting people,' Guy says.

'Sorry, what was that?' Jack leans forward with great exaggeration.

'More wine anyone?' I ask, jittery.

'I wouldn't like to earn a living making a fool out of people.'

'Oh, don't be so moralistic, it's entertainment,' Jack says.

'I love *Stargazer*,' says Nancy, reaching across to touch his hand.

Next thing I know we descend into an argument for and against reality television.

'Are you one of the judges?' Mark asks Jack.

'He's a top producer!' Nancy puts him straight.

'Yeah, but I do judge too. Before all the singers are in front of the panel for the live show, I've heard them sing in the audition suite,' Jack informs us. He stares at Guy. 'So if you can't sing a note and think you're the re-incarnation of Elvis, I'll put you through.'

'And you don't feel guilty?' Guy asks.

'Shall we change the subject?' I ask chirpily.

'Not at all.' He stares back at Guy. 'It makes good TV.'

Guy excuses himself, asking Nancy where the loo is.

'Down the corridor on the right,' she directs, waving a hand dismissively at him.

I jump up to show him, giving Nancy a stern look on the way out.

As I lead Guy to the bathroom, I pull him to one side. 'I'm sorry about Nancy. She's had too much to drink and . . . you're not enjoying this, are you?'

Pause. 'Gilly?' he says, searching my face.

'What?' I whisper.

'Gilly!' I hear Nancy now calling.

He looks at me, as if he wants to confess something important, but . . . 'You'd better go,' he says.

Nancy stands up, loses her balance and grips the edge of the table. I can see Paul is looking at Anna, his expression saying, 'Are your friends like this all the time?'

'Gilly, may I just say,' she announces, 'your time will come, sweetheart. Your time will come and when it does, I'll be right by your side!'

Oh my God! I want to kill her. Very soon there's going to be a death in the kitchen with the candlestick.

I notice Jack isn't saying a word. Instead he reaches for the bottle of wine, knocking over a glass of water in the process. 'Whoopsie,' he says, followed by a hiccup. His telephone rings again, and he staggers out of the room.

'He needs some black coffee,' Mark suggests, but the only thing I can think about is who is calling him all the time. 'Cheer up, Gilly. All I'm saying is your time will come,' Nancy reaffirms.

Guy taps his spoon against his wine glass. 'Time for what, Nancy?' he asks, silencing everyone round the table. 'Maybe Gilly's time has come already.' I catch both Susie and Anna smiling.

Nancy claps her hands. 'Enough of this! Present time!' She dashes out of the room and it's some time before she returns with Jack, swaying on his arm. 'Sorry,' Jack whispers to me, 'was dying for a fag.'

Nancy's forgotten the presents. She stumbles out of the room again, and returns with a bag of gifts.

Soon I'm ripping off paper and ribbons and opening boxes of body cream, bubble bath, soap . . . 'Do I smell?' I laugh. Nick is opening his presents too, mainly clothes and aftershave from Nancy. I gave him some silver elephant cufflinks. Nick loved the elephants in London Zoo. I open Jack's present. It's an expensive-looking perfume, which I open excitedly and test against my wrist. I nearly choke, the scent is so overpowering. 'I love it,' I tell him. I catch Nancy turning to Guy disapprovingly.

'I didn't have time . . .' he says. 'I've been away and . . .'

'Don't worry, Guy,' I tell him reassuringly.

'You haven't even got her a card?' Nancy tuts.

Nick sighs. 'Oh, Nancy, give it a rest. Sorry, Guy.'

Guy takes off his navy hat, leans across and puts it on me. He knows it's one of my favourites. 'Happy birthday, Gilly,' he says.

Nancy places a chocolate cake in front of Nick and me, iced with the words, 'THIRTY-FIVE TODAY!' Everyone sings Happy Birthday to the twins.

'Delicious,' Jack says appreciatively, tucking in.

'It's lovely, Nancy. I must use this company,' Guy says.

'Excuse me?' She stares at him and a silence descends across the table.

Guy looks up and over to me for reassurance. 'The Gourmet Company? The boxes . . .' His voice trails off.

Nancy's face crumbles.

'I'm so sorry,' Guy says, realizing his blunder now.

'Please leave,' she orders.

Guy gets up, and I can't help but notice Jack grin as he watches him leave the room. 'Nancy, it was an innocent mistake,' both Nick and I assure her, but it's said in vain. She looks distraught, before emitting one giant moan and bursting into tears.

I look over to the door, wanting to rush after Guy, but then Jack's mobile rings yet again. 'They can leave a message,' I insist, gesturing to Nancy, but when he looks at the number on the screen he takes the call and walks briskly out of the room.

'I'll be back in a second,' I promise Nick and Nancy, determined to catch up with Guy. I open the front door; it's pouring with rain. I race down the slippery wet steps and towards a white van. 'Wait!' I call out to him. 'Don't go!'

36

I wake the following morning, disorientated. Slowly recollections from the night before come back to me. I reach over to my bedside table and pick up my mobile. No message from Guy. I'd asked him to text me when he arrived home.

Last night, I'd caught up with him just as he was unlocking his white van outside Nancy's house. I wasn't sure how much Guy had had to drink. 'I'm sorry,' I told him breathlessly.

'I had no idea, I wasn't thinking,' he explained, opening the passenger door, and quickly I stepped inside and sat down next to him.

The heavy rain slashed against the windscreen, my hair was damp. 'I know,' I told him, 'you don't have to go. Are you OK to drive?'

'Fine. I'm not over the limit,' he assured me.

'I'm sorry about the way Jack and Nancy spoke to you about your job. She loves to tell me I'm just a shop girl.' I'd smiled, hoping he wasn't hurt.

We both sat quietly for a minute or so, listening to the rain. I rubbed my arms to keep warm.

'Go back inside,' Guy said eventually when the rain had settled. He gestured to a panel of buttons in his van. 'You must be cold, the heater doesn't work.' He raised an eyebrow at my very short skirt.

'I'm sorry,' I apologized again.

'Gilly, please don't worry.' He smiled that endearing smile. 'Us gardeners,' he said, 'we don't get out much. I had a great time.'

I hear the sound of water coming from the bathroom. Now, as for Jack, we slept in separate rooms last night. Jack was too drunk even to notice. His head thumped against the pillow the moment he sat down on his bed, so I left him to it. Until he apologizes for behaving like a twat last night I'm not going to speak to him. When the cab had dropped us home last night and I was carrying my bag of presents inside, Jack picked up Guy's hat and said, 'When are you going to wear that thing? Out on your bike selling onions?'

He enters my bedroom with a cheerful 'Morning!' as he towel-dries his hair and virtuously tells me that he's already been out for a run, which has shifted his hangover. He didn't wake me because when he stuck his head round the door, I was sound asleep.

I sit up and pull the duvet closely around me, watching Jack get dressed.

'Nancy would be wonderful on TV,' he says, perched on the end of my bed, putting on his shoes, unable to sense the atmosphere and smiling about something. 'I love the fact she's been pretending to cook all this time,' he says. 'I think it's hilarious, rather charming too.' His telephone rings. 'Sorry,' he mouths, taking the call outside on the bedroom landing. I lie back in bed, cross. Who's he talking to so early in the morning?

'Who was it?' I ask, when he comes back into the room. I'm sure I heard him say Vanessa.

'Just work.'

'It's quite early to call, isn't it? It's only seven o'clock.'

'Are you checking up on me again?' He smiles, but I don't let him get away with it this time.

'Yes,' I say. 'Your phone kept on ringing last night too. Who were you talking to?'

His eyes darken. 'Don't ruin it, Gilly.'

'Ruin what?'

He ignores me. 'I'll see you later.'

I rush to follow him.

'Don't ruin what?' I repeat. 'What exactly have we got going on here?' I ask him at the top of the stairs.

He looks up at me. 'We're having a fun time together,' he says, as if talking to a moron.

'Fun? Is that what this is? I thought I meant a bit more to you than that.'

'I'm not listening to this.'

'Wait! Don't you dare go!' I join him at the front door. 'If this is leading nowhere, tell me now.' Ed was always 'live for the day rather than worry about tomorrow' and I'm not wasting my time going down that dead-end road again.

'Gilly, what's got into you?'

'I know nothing about you,' I burst out.

'I'm a private person, Gilly, always have been.'

'So private I don't know who you are.'

'I have to go.'

'That's right. Avoid my questions.'

'You ask too many.'

'I didn't like the way you talked to Guy either,' I say now.

'He can talk!' he shouts back, before slamming the door in my face.

I'm fuming in the shower. What is Jack hiding? I'm not going to be made a fool of again. This relationship, if that's what you can call it, it's all on Jack's terms.

Walking round the park later that morning, still cross, my mind wanders from Jack to Guy, Guy to Jack, Nancy to Guy, me to Jack and then to Ed.

So much has changed since my last birthday. My life is going backwards. This time last year Ed and I were engaged. I always thought he would propose in the conventional way, over a candlelit supper, or on a gondola during a weekend trip to Venice, or on my birthday he would save the smallest present until last. For each occasion I would prepare my acceptance speech, just as an actress prepares her speech for the Oscars. Dad used to call me repeatedly, saying, 'Any news?'

Ed's proposal happened in a crowded lift at Covent Garden station late one night. He'd taken me to see *Così fan tutte*. I remember being squashed up against a couple arguing like fishwives and I'd whispered to Ed, 'God, can you imagine if this lift got jammed and we were stuck with these two all night?'

'I wouldn't mind being stuck. I'd have you,' he said. He clutched my hand. 'Will you marry me, Gilly?'

'Shush!' I said. This had not been my rehearsed reaction at all. For months now I'd imagined flinging my arms around him and saying, 'Yes! Oh yes!'

The first person I called was my father. He couldn't bring himself to say 'congratulations'. That's not his style. Instead he said, 'About time,' but I could hear the happiness in his voice. He approved of Ed. I called Susie and Anna, who both wanted to know exactly how he had proposed; I wasn't allowed to skimp on any of the detail.

When we emerged from the lift and passengers threaded off in different directions, Ed asked me why I was being so quiet.

I took his hand, telling him that his proposal had taken

me by surprise, that's all. It was the last thing I'd been expecting him to ask in a crowded lift.

'I only said it to shut the fishwives up,' he said, before adding, 'I'm sorry, I should have asked you a long time ago.'

I should have asked you . . . Well, why didn't he? For the first time I find myself feeling differently about Ed. No longer do I have that deep heartache that we didn't marry. I wanted that security, but did we love one another? Would we have married for the right reason?

Oh Guy, why haven't you called? I don't know why, but I'm nervous. Did you get home OK? My phone rings and I pick it up, without thinking. 'Guy?'

'Sorry to disappoint you.'

It's Jack. 'About this morning,' he starts. 'I'm sorry. And I'm sorry also if I was rude to your friend. It's just I felt he was judging me, and I'm sick of the way people do that, and I know I had too much to drink.'

'Look, it doesn't matter,' I say, no energy to argue.

'But listen, I've booked us into this five-star hotel in Somerset in December, the weekend after *Stargazer* ends.'

'Lovely,' I say vaguely, still scanning the park for him. He crashed on his way home. He's in hospital. I can hear ambulance sirens.

'Gilly?'

'Um?

'You're going to love this hotel. I'll send you the details.'

When Jack hangs up, I try him again. No answer.

When my telephone rings I rush to answer it, but can't ignore my disappointment when it's Anna, ringing from the office, asking me how I'm feeling this morning.

37

It's nearly one o'clock and Mari's out, buying us both some lunch. The shop's been quiet this morning so I've finally started some writing, and I'm enjoying it. It's also been a good distraction because Guy still hasn't called me back. I look at my mobile. No messages. Mari didn't see him earlier in the park either. 'Why am I worrying about him?' I ask Ruskin.

On my own, with only the sound of Ruskin and Basil's heavy breathing coming from the sofa, I glance at the Venetian vase, poking out from under the table and decide it could easily be knocked if somebody isn't paying attention. Carefully I pick it up and glance at the two-thousand-pound price tag. I survey the room to see if there is any space on one of the tables. Ah, it could just squeeze onto the middle shelf.

I fetch the ladder from the basement, and Ruskin and Basil stir from all the activity, watching me as I climb it.

Clutching the vase, boldly I take each step, but when I hear the tinkle of a bell and a customer entering the shop my balance falters and next thing I know I'm watching the vase fly through the air. Then I hear the terrible sound of shattering china.

'What am I going to do?' I say in despair, wrapping the broken pieces in newspaper. 'Mari's going to kill me! It's your fault you know.'

'My fault?'

'Yes, your fault! Everything's your fault, Guy,' I add when he hands me some flowers. 'A belated birthday present,' he says.

Any moment now Trouble is going to break another precious piece of glass with her wagging tail. After I've put the deep red dahlias picked from Guy's garden into a vase, we decide to let the dogs out into the back garden.

'You weren't in the park this morning,' I say, as we continue to clear up the mess.

'The park's like an office,' he remarks. 'If you're not there, you're off sick.'

'I was worried.'

'Worried?'

'You didn't text me. I still feel bad, about last night.'

When Guy was more or less kicked out of the house last night, Nancy had turned to me and said, 'You are not to bring that man into my home again, do you understand?'

Later, during coffee, when she'd calmed down, she said, 'Jack, on the other hand, is welcome any time. Now *he's* a gentleman.' Jack had smiled at that.

'Oh God, last night was a disaster,' I admit now to Guy, laughing nervously as I finish wrapping the broken pieces in newspaper and hiding the damage in a black bin bag. 'I think you're banned from the house,' I tell him.

'Am I?' Guy is smiling too.

We both sit down on the sofa.

'It was a fucking disaster,' I repeat. 'You're kicked out of the house and I'm some sad old spinster waiting for her time to come.'

'Well, I'm just a gardener!'

'I'm just a shop girl!'

'I'm thirty-seven!'

'I'm thirty-five!'

When I see Mari walking outside the shop window with our lunch and coffees, towards the front door, I stop laughing immediately. 'How am I going to tell her about the vase?' I say.

'Blame it on me,' Guy whispers. The doorbell tinkles, Mari says hello to Hatman, before asking if he'd like to have some lunch with us. She's bought some Greek salads, hummus, crisps and crusty brown rolls. 'There's plenty to go round,' she reassures him. 'What is it? What's going on?' she asks, when neither of us says a word.

I confess.

'The Venetian one?' she asks, pain in her voice. I promise Mari I will pay her back. Quite what with, who knows, but I don't tell her that. I tell her again how sorry I am when she asks to see the broken pieces.

As we're finishing lunch, Guy walks over to the bust of a Dutchman, kneels down and looks him in the eye. 'This man seems important,' he suggests. 'Someone to be reckoned with.'

'He's got a great nose, hasn't he?' I say.

'If you look closely at the detail on his coat too,' Mari adds, 'you can see he's someone rich and powerful. Oh, and this is fascinating. See this.' She crouches down next to Guy and points to the hole on the left side of the bust, where his left arm should have been.

'It's broken,' Guy says.

'You're just like Gilly,' she tuts. 'Of course it's broken, but this is where his wife should have been, by his side. She's been hacked off.'

'I wonder where she's gone,' I say.

'Where did your wife go?' Guy asks the bust directly. 'Are you lonely without her?'

'Maybe she went on a cruise around the world,' I put forward.

'Or maybe he proposed and then she took off? Things just didn't work out,' Guy replies. Mari and I exchange secret looks. Guy gets up, brushes the dust off his knees. 'I've never been downstairs. Can I take a look?' he asks.

'Gilly, show him. I'll clear up,' Mari says. I can sense she's still thinking about the vase.

'You've got a great boss,' Guy smiles at Mari, trying to cheer her up. 'It's no wonder you don't want to leave, Gilly.'

I lead Guy down the treacherous steps, showing him on the way the crumbling ceiling. 'Look at this,' I whisper, touching it, and the plaster flakes off. Mari's shop is a tumble-down ruin, but at the same time there is something magical about it. It could be the kind of place where I could set up a small table, light some candles and eat a romantic meal, surrounded by beautiful objects. I wonder if Jack would appreciate this. I don't think so. 'Mari keeps on saying she'll get it seen to, repaint it, but she never does,' I say quietly. 'Careful here, Guy.' We manoeuvre our way through the dark room. I know this room so intimately now that I can sense exactly where to place one foot after the other. Guy on the other hand is trying hard not to stumble over everything.

'Over here,' I tell him. 'I want to show you something.' I find myself offering him my hand to help him through the obstacle course. He takes it. It feels warm in mine.

I let his hand go when we reach a large circular silver light. 'I've learned so much from Mari,' I explain, able now to describe this light, which was made in the twenties, the design taken I think from the old eighteenth-century circular peasant lights that were mounted against walls and lit by a single candle.

I gesture to one of the old chandeliers, explaining how easy it is to work out if it's modern because modern glass reflects blue and green. 'This glass here,' I say, 'is foggy, stained by cigar and cigarette smoke. Modern chandeliers don't have half the character, do they?' Guy smiles as I talk.

'Now you can see this is old glass too,' I say, returning to the silver circular light.

Guy nods. 'I like it.'

'I thought you would. I feel terrible about Mari,' I whisper, his face so close to mine, 'that vase was one of her favourites.'

'Accidents happen,' he insists. 'It was my fault too.'

As I guide Guy back upstairs, we overhear Mari talking to Bob Chamerette, her glass and metal man. He's finished restoring some of the items Mari bought at the last fair she attended in France. 'Look, Gilly!' she says, in a brighter mood when we reach the ground floor, 'you remember that old lantern, don't you? Look what Bob's done to it!'

Bob is small and stout with a round face and bright eyes. Whatever the weather, he always wears loose, slightly grubby T-shirts over old jeans. When Mari compliments his work, he rocks back and forth on his feet, his eyes glowing with pride. 'I'm so glad you like it, Mrs Gordon.'

'Oh, Bob, call me Mari for heaven's sake! We've worked together for how long now?' she laughs, adding, 'It must be at least twelve years.'

Guy gathers his coat, saying he'd better be going. I lead him to the door and step outside with him.

'Thanks for lunch,' he says. 'And I'm sorry if you were worrying about me this morning, I should have called but I had some things to think about.'

'Is everything all right?'

He nods, but I detect he wants to say something more. 'About Jack . . .' he says, clearing his throat.

'Yes?'

'I'm not sure about him.'

'Well, I know you hate his job and . . .'

'It's not that. It's more that I . . .' Guy glances down to the pavement. 'How do I put this?' He looks at me directly now. 'There's something about him I don't trust.'

'You don't trust?'

'I don't want you to get hurt again.'

'I'm a big girl, Guy, you said it yourself.'

He looks confused.

'I overheard you say it to Mari in the park the other day,' I explain. 'Listen, I know he behaved like an idiot last night, but there is a lovely side to him.'

'I'm not sure he's right for you though.'

'You've only met him once,' I say defensively. 'Jack's helped me through so much, Guy. Honestly, before he moved in I was depressed, I was lonely. You didn't know me all those months ago, when Ed left. I was a wreck and my friends had to pick up the pieces. Since Jack's moved in I've been happier, so much better.'

'Well, maybe . . . but . . .'

'I like his friends, I enjoy his company, he makes me laugh.'

'He's not good enough for you!'

I catch Mari watching us from inside. Quickly she looks away and continues to talk to Bob.

'Guy, you don't know him,' I say, lowering my voice as some people steer their way past us.

'I know men like him though. Young guys, they lead women on and . . .'

'That's not fair. You know nothing about Jack and he is not leading me on!' I tell him that Jack's taking me away before Christmas to a five-star hotel with a luxury spa. I hate myself for sounding so superficial but equally I hate Guy for pouring doom and gloom on my relationship. It's between Jack and me.

'Five stars,' he says, but he's not impressed.

'I think Mari's right. You're jealous,' I say, my heart beating fast.

'Jealous?' he splutters. 'I'm not jealous!'

Mari looks over at us again, knowing something is going on.

'Finally I've met someone,' I say, lowering my voice, 'and I'm changing my life, I'm doing new things, and you can't handle it, can you?'

Guy grabs my arm and pulls me away from the shop. We walk briskly down the street. 'Of course I can, it's just I can't see you two . . .'

'What about you?' I rise angrily. 'Is your relationship going anywhere?'

'I'm sorry?'

'Here you are, criticizing Jack and me, but look at Flora and you! What's right about her taking off the moment you propose?'

'That's not the same!' But I can tell from his wounded expression that I've hit a nerve. 'It's none of your business, Gilly.'

'Exactly. I don't interfere in your relationship, do I, so what right have you got to interfere with mine?'

I turn and run back towards the shop.

'Gilly?'

'I need to go back to work! Leave me alone!' I push past Bob, who is heading out, and retreat back inside.

Guy returns only minutes later. Mari senses the awkward atmosphere between us when Guy asks her if he can have a word with me in private.

'Can we start again?' He proposes calmly, taking me to one side of the room. 'Besides, I left Trouble in the garden. Oh, and Mari, I have a confession. It was my fault. I broke the vase,' Guy says.

'No he didn't,' I tell Mari. 'It was me. He's lying.'

'It was me, Mari, I distracted Gilly.'

'No you didn't!' I tell him. 'I take full responsibility Mari. I lost my balance on the ladder and . . .'

'Yes, but you wouldn't have done if . . .'

'Quiet!' Mari shouts at us.

Shocked, we all take a deep breath. Mari shakes her head. 'Take the afternoon off, Gilly.' She stares at both of us. 'Whatever's going on between you two, sort it out,' she finishes.

Guy and I walk the dogs along Pimlico Road, heading for the tube, both of us quiet. My mobile rings, breaking the silence.

'Can you talk?' Jack asks down the line.

'Go on.'

On the telephone Jack insists that this party tonight will be fun. 'Oh God, I'm quite tired . . . after last night,' I offer as an excuse.

Guy glances my way.

'I feel like a night in,' I say, realizing I haven't had one in weeks. 'Listen, you go.'

Jack doesn't like that idea.

'I've got nothing to wear,' I go on.

'That's perfect,' Jack says. 'Look, how about we ask Nancy too, it might be nicer for you to turn up with a friend?'

I frown. 'It's too last-minute for Nancy . . .'

'She can.'

'What? You've asked her already? How come you had her number?'

'You gave it to me,' he says, not liking my tone. 'Last night, in case I was running late or got lost,' he reminds me. 'Look, I tried to call you first but you were engaged, so I rang to thank her for last night, then thought she might like to come along too . . . it was a spur of the moment thing. In a way I felt sorry for her, after what that idiot did and I thought she might need cheering up.'

I glance over to Guy. 'Why didn't you mention the party this morning?'

'We were too busy arguing. Think about it,' he beseeches. 'Last night was pretty intense. I think we need to let our hair down, don't you?' he suggests.

I look at my watch. It's three in the afternoon. Nancy said yes. I don't know why it irritates me so much that she's going. I guess I have time to find an outfit. I think about the glossy magazine I was reading the other day, telling its readers how important it is to try out new things, that routines can be the death of us. 'OK,' I say determinedly. 'Where is it?'

When my telephone call has finished, I tell Guy that Jack has asked me to this party.

'Sounds fun.' He waits for me to say more.

'The theme's Playboy mansion,' I mutter.

'Sorry? It's what?'

Do something that surprises those around you, the article advises. 'He's asked me to a Playboy party,' I declare as we stop at a pedestrian crossing.

Guy breaks into a smile.

'What's so funny?' I challenge him.

'Nothing.'

I laugh. 'I don't want to go.' I come clean now.

'Yes you do.'

'I don't.' We cross the road. 'I'm not sure about anything any more,' I say, against the noise of the traffic and running on ahead.

'Go, Gilly, you'll enjoy it.' He catches me up, slows me down and puts an arm around my shoulder as we approach the tube station. 'Wait!' he says, as I walk on ahead. 'I'm sorry about earlier, the things I said about Jack.'

'It's OK. I'm sorry about what I said to you too, about Flora.'

'Don't worry about it. Why don't I help you?'

'Help me?'

'Well, what are you going to wear tonight?'

Practically nothing, Jack had said. I laugh. 'I have no idea! God, I wish Jack had told me about this party earlier. I hate not having time to prepare! I'm no good at doing things spontaneously, Guy. I can't even post a letter without checking it a million times before I shove it into the box,' I say, standing in the middle of the pavement, Ruskin and I getting in everyone's way. Guy takes me to one side.

'You've lost me,' he smiles.

'I'm not going.'

'Yes you are.'

'I haven't got anything to wear.'

'Well, as it happens, I know just the place,' Guy says in a tone that suggests he's my new fairy godmother. 'Come on, let's go. This will be fun.'

Guy has brought me to a smart fancy-dress shop in west London and I'm in the dressing room which is lavishly decorated with a rich velvet curtain, fur-lined stool and fancy mirror with cupids all over it. I squeeze myself into a minuscule scarlet halter-neck dress, pull up white fishnet stockings and slip on matching killer heels. Looking at myself in the mirror, I smile, wondering how Guy knows about this hidden place. I try to walk. Oh my God! How do people move in these? I love heels, but these are in another league.

'I can't come out.' I call through the changing-room cubicle. 'I look like a tart!'

'That's the whole idea,' Guy says, Trouble perched on his lap, Ruskin at his feet. 'Come on. The dogs and I are here to give you an honest opinion.'

I open the curtain and tentatively reveal myself. Guy surveys me. 'Six out of ten,' he states.

I look in the mirror. 'Is that all?'

He nods. 'You need to own the outfit, not just be in it,' he advises. 'You look in pain.'

'Right, Guy. I'm going to find something that blows you away.'

'I look forward to it.'

Soon I am trying on every single outfit in the shop. I greet Guy in a classic French maid outfit with sexy white suspenders and my modest cleavage bursting out of the tight black corset. I can hardly breathe as I pose provocatively in front of him. 'Bonjour, monsieur.' He laughs as I tickle him under the cheek with my pink feather duster. I tickle Ruskin too and he tries to eat it.

Next I'm putting on a baby-pink fairy outfit. One of the assistants helps me with the wings.

'Getting hotter,' Guy says, as I blow a fairy kiss at him. 'Seven out of ten.'

'I bet you're enjoying this, aren't you?' I call out, on the next costume.

'Haven't had so much fun in years,' is his reply, as I rush out shaking Playboy cheerleader pom-poms. 'I didn't tell you. Nancy's coming tonight.'

'Nancy? Oh God. Why?'

'Jack thought it'd be less frightening if I had someone to turn up with.'

'You're braver than I thought.'

'How did you know Nancy hadn't made the cake,' I ask, poking my head round the curtain.

'You know when I went to the loo?'

'You were ages.'

'I went out for a cigarette,' he admits, 'and saw the Gourmet Company boxes hidden in the garden. The paella wasn't homemade either.' I confess to Guy how Nancy's always prided herself on her cooking. I wonder if

Nicholas has known about the Gourmet Company all this time too. As I replay the cake episode in my head, I find myself smiling.

'She's always seemed so perfect, but there's a chink in her armour,' I conclude as I face him dressed in a satin waistcoat, bow tie, white satin gloves and a magician's hat.

'I'd say there were several chinks,' Guy says as I put the hat on him and he shakes it off with a laugh. 'I loved the hat you gave me, by the way,' I add.

'I'll have to go back to Prague, buy myself another. But it suits you more than me,' he concludes.

I smile, wishing I understood why I am so drawn to Guy.

'Breathe in,' the assistant is urging me as I try on the last outfit.

'I am!' I giggle. This is ridiculous. I can't pass myself off as a playgirl.

'Fabulous,' she says, 'just don't eat or drink anything. Or sit down. Or breathe.'

'Come on,' Guy demands. 'I'm waiting.'

'Patience!' I shout.

Finally I parade out in a silver dress with a fake fur trim. 'Oh, you've forgotten these,' says the assistant, placing a silver and white fur bunny headband over my blonde wig. She also hands me some feather things. 'What are these for?' I ask.

'Tickle ties,' she says simply. 'You drape them around your prey.'

According to the assistant, I am a platinum bunny. For once Guy is lost for words. 'Well this is it, there's nothing more to try on,' I say, exhausted and irritable as I hold these bloody tickle ties. 'This will have to do.'

Guy pretends to listen to what Ruskin is saying. 'He says you look hot. Cute.'

'And what do you think?'

'Ten out of ten,' he votes, approval in his eyes.

38

As I get ready for the evening I wonder why is it so difficult to change. Despite Guy's reassurance that I will enjoy tonight, the truth is that I'm not sure at all. I smile, remembering Dad being dragged off to salsa classes when all he wanted to do was lie in a deep bath with a cigar.

Now that I'm thirty-five I do need to rethink my life because I haven't changed my habits, big or small, in years. For example, like clockwork I always put my gym kit in the same changing-room locker, number ninety-nine. The one time that I did put my clothes in a different place, I was convinced they'd been stolen and alerted staff, furious since I'd just bought an expensive new anti-chlorine shampoo. Eventually it dawned on me that this time I had been forced to choose another locker because number ninety-nine had been in use.

I always use the same hairdryer in the gym too, the one on the left-hand side of the first table in the downstairs area. It has to be on the left-hand side. When it comes to habits, look at the way our dog-walking circle meet under the oak tree so faithfully every morning. Why do we meet there, in a spot that blocks out all the sun? However, we are not the only people to be slaves to our routine. Guy and I have noticed Rita, the ex-mayor of Hammersmith, always feeding the squirrels in the park from her scooter, which is positioned, without fail, in exactly the same spot near the Polish memorial statue at the same time every day. Perhaps it's true. We don't think to change our routine, even when it comes down to when and where we are going to feed the squirrels.

As I add the final touches to my outfit and slip on my bunny heels, I decide that it is time to change and I am going to start by enjoying tonight. Maybe Jack is exactly the kind of person I need in my life. I need to be spontaneous again, embrace being young and alive, and not be scared of the future. Jack's right. Sometimes I question everything to such a degree that I often miss out on half the fun.

Susie calls me, wanting to talk about the dramas of last night. 'You're doing what?' she asks, when I know she heard me loud and clear.

'Don't laugh,' I beg. 'Give me some tips to get through the humiliation.'

'OK, I'd buy the host a large present, not in cost but in size, and cover yourself up in it.'

I smile. 'What do you think of Jack by the way?' I can't help asking, since Susie hasn't offered any commentary.

'I like him,' she says diffidently, 'he's very good-looking but . . .'

'But what?'

'I don't know. Listen, he seems fine,' she repeats.

'He's booked us a weekend away next month.'

'Great. Where?'

'And Guy? What did you think of him?'

'Oh, now he's interesting,' she remarks, her voice stronger. 'Mark and I were talking about him. I thought he was lovely, nothing like what I'd expected but . . .'

I wait.

'We liked the way he challenged Nancy. He's a good person to have on your side.' She pauses. 'I'm sorry but we couldn't help laughing about the cake incident,' she concludes, a smile in her voice.

Nancy joins me in the taxi wearing a fabulous red diamanté corset with a flaming red wig. She looks amazing, like a femme fatale.

During the journey I apologize for Guy's blunder, re-inforcing the fact that he truly hadn't intended to show her up, but all Nancy is concerned about is making sure I believe her when she says that my birthday cake and the paella dish have been the one and only ready-made meal that she's ever bought in her entire lifetime. So I pretend to believe her.

'I can't think what you have in common with him,' Nancy says, as she reapplies her red lipstick and then shrieks at the taxi driver for going over a ramp too fast because her lipstick is now smudged.

She then goes on to tell me that Nick didn't mind not being invited by Jack tonight. He was happy to babysit.

'He doesn't know what he's missing out on,' she goes on. 'You'd think he'd jump at the chance of seeing women in PVC corsets. He's no fun any more.'

Our taxi pulls up alongside a smart private house in South Kensington. We are ushered inside, into a wide hallway with a chequered floor, sparkling chandelier (modern) and paintings of important-looking though somewhat lugubrious aristocrats on either side of the walls. Nancy shows no sign of inhibition as she flings off her coat and hands it to the cloakroom attendant without as much as a thank you. I, on the other hand, peel my coat off self-consciously and thank him for the two of us.

We hand over our invitations and a gentleman in black tie stamps a Playboy bunny print onto the back of our hands. I follow the noise downstairs. My knees are trembling and ironically I am pleased Nancy is right behind me, wafting perfume. 'How's it going with Jack?' she shouts above the noise.

'Great!' I shout back.

We walk into a crowded space packed with women in suspenders, corsets and fishnet stockings. I brush past a woman wearing just a thong with glitter wings on her back.

'The trick is,' Nancy whispers, as if she were a pro, 'to keep on moving, then no one can latch onto you.' Across the room stands a woman with blonde hair extensions, being photographed dressed in nothing but tassels on her bosoms, and I stand in awe at her self-confidence, unable to take my eyes away from her.

'Cheap Euro trash.' Nancy dismisses her, after scrutinizing her from head to toe. 'Men don't like that. They like *class*.'

Jack stands behind Nancy and me. 'That's an example of where less is not always more,' he whispers to us. 'Both of you, on the other hand,' he says, looking at our outfits, 'look incredible.'

Nancy laughs flirtatiously as he leads us to the bar.

Jack plies Nancy and me with drinks all evening, and when he's out of earshot, I attempt subtly to ask some of his friends about Jack, his place in Bath and whether they know his family well. His colleagues mention how easy he is to work with, but that's about as far as I get. I feel stupid digging around for dirt that isn't there. I reach over to touch his arm and Nancy seems put out that I've interrupted their conversation. 'Just off to the Ladies,' I tell them both. I wrap my arms around Jack's neck, Nancy irritably moves to the side. 'When I come back, I want you to dance with me. Don't move.'

'Promise,' he says and blows me a kiss.

I enter the Ladies and see a couple of women surreptitiously approaching a cubicle.

When I'm on the loo I hear the unmistakable sounds of snorting coming from next door. The first time I took cocaine was when I was at Manchester with Anna. It was three in the afternoon on a rainy Sunday and I can remember Anna chopping up this white chalky mess with one of her debit cards. When I tried it, it felt like nothing more than a strong cup of coffee, but I do remember feeling conspiratorial with Anna, as if we were doing something forbidden on a wet sleepy Sunday afternoon. Although it's not my thing, nearly everyone in the media seems to do coke, though to my surprise I don't think Jack does.

Jack isn't in the bar. There's no sign of him anywhere. Where's Nancy? I stagger down the dark stairs and into the musty basement, where everyone is dancing. I lurch through the sweaty throng, the room is spinning, my feet are trampled on, a woman crashes into me, drunk. People are kissing, pressed up against each other. I've had enough of this now and want to go home. Where are they? I scan the room frantically. I look at my watch. It's past midnight. Maybe Nancy's gone home, but how odd that she didn't tell me? It's too hot in here and I desperately need some fresh air. I make my way across the room, music booming in my ears. Someone or something latches onto my leg. I turn to see a man who looks like an Italian footballer, thighs like nutcrackers, behind me, his legs locked into mine, gyrating against me. Oh good grief! I try to detach myself, then gasp when a woman with blonde wig and an enormous cleavage hurls herself to the floor, right in front of me, and starts doing, let's just say, acts of a highly sexual nature which encourage men to jump on top of her, including Mr Nutcracker Thighs. I'm pushed against two people groping each other like rampant teenagers. Rapidly I edge away and run upstairs, determined to retrieve my coat from the cloakroom and just go. I'm cross. I shouldn't have come, and Nancy shouldn't have left without me. As I hand my ticket to the curly-haired cloakroom assistant I hear muffled voices coming from the corridor.

'I have this feeling she thinks it's more serious than I do,' he says. 'I get the strong sense she wants to settle down . . . I mean, she is thirty-five . . .'

'Her clock is ticking, Jack.'

'Oh God, I can't handle that. I seriously can't handle that. There's no way I'm settling down. I'm going to have to talk to her.'

'I think you should.'

'She's always banging on and on about the weekends too, doesn't understand I need my own space. Also I have to work.'

'Of course you have to work, darling. You're very successful. She should understand that.'

'Yeah, but she doesn't have a career, does she?' He laughs. 'She's only a shop girl!'

'Exactly. Honestly, Jack, you mustn't feel guilty about ending it,' Nancy advises, 'and I think you need to do it now.'

'Excuse me?' says the cloakroom attendant, staring at me. 'Is this your coat?'

'How do I tell her?' Jack goes on. 'I always said that it was only a bit of fun . . .'

'It's not your fault, darling. Come on, we'd better find her.'

'Hang on, Nance. Just one more kiss.'

Nancy giggles. 'I'm married.'

'So?'

'You're a naughty, naughty man, Jack Baker.'

When I hear them leave, I grab my coat and run.

In the taxi, I take out my powder compact and look at myself in the mirror. My eyes are bloodshot, my cheeks flushed. I snatch off my wig, vigorously wipe the red muck from my lips and scrub the caked foundation off my cheeks. Shivering, I pull my coat closely around me, cold with the memory of Jack and Nancy together. Nancy and Jack are disgusting, pathetic excuses for people. I should have trusted my instincts. I knew it. Who was I fooling? Myself, that's all.

I've always tried to see Nancy's point. OK, she isn't my type, but I respected the fact that she was married to Nick and the mother of Hannah and Tilda. How could she have done this? Why would she want to humiliate me?

Then there's Jack. Nancy! He likes Nancy! He kissed her! I snap shut my powder compact. I hate myself for falling for a man like him. I should have known better. Look at me! Guy was right. I don't fit into his life and I never will. He wasn't ever serious about me; he was just out for a good time. He's a liar. All those secret phone calls. I bet he *is* married! He goes back to his wife at the weekend. I don't trust anything he's said any more. I feel so upset and stupid. My mobile rings and his name lights up the screen. I don't wait for him to say 'hello'. 'I heard you Jack. I saw you.'

'Saw what? Where are you?'

'Going home, and don't you dare follow me. I want you out of my house.' I switch my phone off.

'Everything all right?' the driver asks, looking at me with concern through his front mirror.

'I'm fine, thank you,' I tell him, my chin wobbling.

'Men,' he says. 'We're not worth crying over, love.'

The driver pulls up outside No. 21 and I pay him with a tip before rushing to Gloria's door, knocking frantically. No answer. I look up to her bedroom window and then vaguely remember she's in Ireland, going to a friend's birthday party. I need to see Gloria! I can't be on my own tonight! I can't see Jack. What if he's on his way back now, determined to talk to me? I don't want to be in the same room as him ever again.

I rush across to No. 21 and unlock the front door.

I strip off, tossing my stupid platinum bunny costume

to the floor and pull on jeans, a jumper and slip on some trainers. With Ruskin in my arms and an overnight bag slung over my shoulder, I hail another cab.

Guy opens the door, hatless and in his dressing gown and when he sees my crumpled face he pulls me inside.

'I'm sorry for just turning up . . . I tried Gloria . . .' He leads me down the hallway, guides me into a small sitting room. I watch him manically tidying the sofa to make some space for us to sit down. He appears nervous as to why I have turned up on his doorstep in the early hours of the morning, and excuses the mess. Sprawled across the floor are garden-design books and pencilled drawings. 'What's happened?' he asks me.

'You were right,' I blurt out. 'Jack and I, it's all over. I caught him with her . . .'

'Her? Who?' he says gently.

He sits next to me, an arm around my shoulder, and waits for me to say something. 'You were right,' finally I admit. 'How stupid of me to think I had anything in common with him! I was just so lonely after Ed and . . .' I tell Guy about the evening, how one moment we were drinking at the bar . . . the next moment . . .

'Jack and Nancy,' he repeats in disbelief. I don't think even Guy can comprehend it. I'm waiting for him to say, 'I told you so', but . . .

'Oh, Gilly,' he says, pulling me into his arms, 'I'm so sorry.'

*

Guy and I drink tea and talk. I'm relieved Jack can't find me here. 'You were right not to trust him, Guy,' I say more calmly. 'They deserve each other.'

'Well, one thing's for sure – Jack doesn't deserve you.'

I lean in closer towards him, resting my head against his shoulder.

'He doesn't, Gilly. I don't think you realize how lovely you are. You have no idea, do you?'

'Guy, stop it,' I say, though inside my heart melts at his words. 'Tonight, it's all my fault, I should have known . . .'

'No. Jack is deaf, dumb and blind if he doesn't realize how special you are.' He hugs me more tightly, 'And unlike all the other girls I know.'

'I wasn't his type,' I console myself.

'You don't need to change, Gilly. None of this is your fault. He's the idiot, not you, and I think it's just as well you went to this Playboy party tonight.'

I sit up. 'Why?'

'It's better to find out now rather than later,' Guy says.

We sit quietly for a while, Ruskin and Trouble lying by the fireplace, keeping an eye on us. 'Can I stay here tonight? On the sofa?'

'Of course you can,' he says, kissing the top of my head tenderly.

I turn to him abruptly, aware of a major piece in this puzzle that I am forgetting. 'Oh my God. What am I going to tell Nick?'

'You tell him the truth,' Guy insists. 'He needs to know.'

'Nancy, she'll make out I'm lying, she'll . . .'

'When it comes to trusting you or Nancy.' Guy shrugs his shoulders. 'Come on, Nick knows you love him, he's your twin. I'd trust you with my life.'

'You would?'

'You can't tell a lie, Gilly. You'll always do the right thing.' He takes a strand of my hair, sweeps it away from my face. 'That's what's so wonderful about you.'

39

I wake up the following morning on Guy's sofa bed, Ruskin lying by my side. When I stroke him he moves away and resettles himself, reminding me he's not a morning dog. My head pounds and slowly the realization of last night comes back to haunt me: Gilly Brown, single again, humiliated, soon to be without a lodger (how am I going to pay for all my bills *plus* my mortgage now?) and soon to be a messenger to Nick, bearing bad news.

Guy enters the room. 'Fancy some breakfast?' he asks, handing me a dressing gown.

I nod, stretching out my arms before following him into the kitchen. It's a small open-plan space, and on one wall is a pinboard mounted with black-and-white photographs of family members. I smile at the picture of Guy standing next to his sister Rachel, dressed in his wedding suit and electric-blue shirt. 'You kept your hat off.' I sigh proudly.

'All day long.'

'That tie looks great on you.'

There's a lovely black-and-white picture of Guy and Flora together in New York, when Guy pressed the confirm button. Flora's long hair is swept across her face and she's laughing as she clings onto his arm. 'It was really windy that day,' Guy smiles. Flora is tall, slender and bohemian in style. She's in her early thirties but has a young face and a serene, graceful quality about her. I can picture her trekking in a foreign country with her camera equipment slung onto her shoulder, exploring places and capturing moments.

'How are you feeling?' he asks, as I move away from the photographs and pull up a stool. He opens the fridge, takes out a bottle of milk and scans the shelf for butter. I'm aware, after feeling so close to him last night, that he hasn't fully looked me in the eye, preferring to keep busy. 'No nasty Nancy dreams I hope?' he continues.

I smile. 'I'm sorry, Guy, for offloading all of this on you, for coming round so late.'

Guy flicks on the television, offers to make me some scrambled eggs and bacon. 'You don't ever need to be sorry for needing a friend in the night,' he tells me, finally looking my way.

We swap sections of the newspaper, I pour him some more coffee, Guy feeds the dogs scraps of toast under the table. 'What are you up to this weekend?' he asks.

'Jumping off a cliff,' I suggest.

We both find ourselves smiling. I tell Guy about the arguments Jack and I had had about the weekends, his elusiveness, how he'd keep on using his work as an excuse. I tell him I wish I'd had the time to talk to his brother, Alexander, that night. I might have found out more about the real Jack, if he hadn't interrupted us.

'I don't know, Gilly. He probably does need to work. These shows are full on. I'm not defending him,' he quickly adds.

'Or maybe I just have terrible taste in men.'

'No you don't,' he says, gesturing to himself.

My telephone rings. I turned it back on this morning. Talk of the devil. 'It's Jack,' I mime to Guy, who encourages me to take the call. Heart racing, I go into the other room.

'Whatever you saw, Gilly, it's not what you think,' Jack begins. 'Nancy was upset, things aren't going too well for her, and I happened to . . .'

I cut him off. 'I might be naïve, but I'm not stupid,' I tell him. 'I meant what I said last night. I want you to pack your bags and go.'

'Gilly, please! Come on. I like you, you know I do.'

'Really. You like me? So why are you kissing my sister-in-law?'

'It's just I can't make the commitment you want. I sense you want more from me than I can give. Things are complicated . . . if only you knew . . .'

'That's fine. Just leave. I don't want anything from you any more, except for you to go.'

There's a hesitant pause before he says, 'Where am I going to go?'

I laugh. 'That's not my problem.'

'Gilly, I need my room, the show's not over. I've paid rent. You can't do this.'

'I can do whatever I like.'

'It says on the site it's polite to give tenants notice.'

'Well, if the site knew that you'd kissed Nancy, I'm sure they'd make an exception.'

Jack, for once, is silent. Until he says, 'Gilly, please. Can't we talk about this?'

'No. Why don't you ask Nancy if you can sleep with her?'

'Now you're being childish. Look, I want us to stay friends . . .'

'Stay friends?'

'Stay friends and remain civil. I'll be gone by Christmas.'

'Fuck off, Jack.'

I hang up.

I return to the kitchen. 'He tried to make out nothing happened, that I'd got the wrong impression.' I sit down. 'He wanted us to remain friends! The stupid thing is we were never good friends in the first place, not like . . .'

'Not like me and you?'

I bite my lip. 'I told him to pack up his stuff tonight and get lost.'

'Good. Time to move on.'

Our attention turns to the television, another gruesome attack in London.

'Oh, Guy, I feel blue.' I push aside my breakfast. 'I hate Jack, I really do, I hate him . . .'

'But?'

'He made me feel young again. I know it sounds shallow, but . . .'

'Right,' Guy says, as if he's plotting an idea. 'There's not just one Jack Baker in town. I'm taking you out.'

'Where?'

'It's a surprise.'

'Tell me. Go on.'

'No questions, Gilly. Just put something warm on,' he adds.

Guy clutches my hand as we skate across the ice rink, the Natural History Museum lit up by the Christmas lights twinkling in the trees. I wobble and stumble, laughing as I nearly fall over. I rush to the safety of the rails when a little girl in a bright-blue bobble hat and cream outfit pirouettes in front of me like a professional. 'I just need to catch my breath,' I tell him.

Guy raises an eyebrow. 'We've only just started.'

I look at the other skaters, a whirl of vivid colours, fur hats and scarves, gliding round the ice rink, some more effortlessly than others. 'I'm terrified I'm going to fall and someone will skate over my hands,' I confide to him, 'and chop my fingers off.' I pull a scary face.

'Don't be such a wimp. You can do it.' He grabs my hand and off we go. I shriek when he pulls me towards him, forcing me to go faster. Guy is a natural on the ice, but as for me . . .

'Come on!' he bosses me.

'Slow down!'

As I gain confidence and momentum, I begin to enjoy myself, letting go of Guy's hand and telling him I want to skate on my own. He moves on, then turns and watches me. A surge of adrenalin rushes through my body as the cold air blasts my face and I skate a full circle on my own, and then another . . . and another. This time round I try to catch him up.

'Come and get me,' he calls.

A group of children sweep past me, one knocks into my back and I'm on my bottom. I reach for Guy's hand and he pulls me up. I brush myself down and start again. 'How come you're so good?' I ask.

'Used to skate on the farm,' he calls over his shoulder, 'when the lake froze over. I loved it.'

Determined to catch him, I race forward and in my excitement lose my balance again, but this time manage to stay upright. I can't stop laughing as I grab his arm as if playing tag in the playground. 'Got you!' I say.

He takes my hand and we skate round the rink once

more, together. I don't want to let him go. 'Thank you,' I say. 'Oh Guy, this feels amazing. I feel ten again.'

For the rest of the day, we walk the dogs in the park and drink too much coffee. Late in the afternoon we drive in Guy's clapped-out van to his favourite nursery just outside London because he needs to buy some flowers for a new job. Guy is a changed man when he wanders around pointing out to me the plants he particularly loves. 'The names aren't that important, Gilly, it's what they look like,' he says when I ask him what each one is. He tells me that he used to work in a nursery in his teenage years, loading up trolleys with geraniums and lupins, and that's how his love for flowers started. 'This client of mine, she's into tapestry planting, so I need to find lots of different types and interweave them – it's fun,' he says.

On the way home Guy glances over at me, saying I'm quiet. He asks me what I'm thinking about.

'How foolish I've been,' I admit. 'I thought something didn't add up with Jack, but I kept on telling myself I was worrying too much, that I should just enjoy it, go with the flow. Even Dennis got it right,' I murmur.

'Dennis?'

'Just someone,' I say.

'Right. Not going to even ask.' He smiles, before adding, 'You should always follow your gut instinct, it's normally right.'

I nod. 'I didn't expect him to kiss Nancy.' I stop, shaking

300

my head, realizing how ridiculous it sounds. 'But if I'm honest, I think I knew it wouldn't work out between us. He was too closed off, too secretive, there was something wrong about him.' Guy looks deep in thought. 'What?' I prompt.

'Why don't we follow Jack home tonight?'

'Follow him? Why?'

'You said it yourself. He was so shifty when you tried to talk to him about his private life and he never invited you to his place, so maybe he doesn't live in Bath at all. Maybe he's married and leads a double life.'

'He's not married.'

'Let's follow him,' Guy continues, 'find out for sure.'

'No!'

'What are you doing tonight?'

'I'm having a night in. I'm not going to start stalking the man, Guy.'

'Oh, come on, Gilly. Don't you want to know if he really is who he says he is? It doesn't matter if we discover there's nothing weird about him, but at least we'll know and then you don't have to think about him ever again.'

'I'm not sure I even care now.'

He's not listening. 'We should definitely do this.'

'No, we can't! This is crazy,' I say. 'Anyway, what if he sees us?'

Parked on the street outside my house, Guy and I watch Jack enter No. 21. Part of me thinks I should go in and face him. Maybe I'm a coward for not confronting him face to face. However, I said all I'd wanted to on the phone. I told him again that if I came home to find any of his belongings, I'd fling them out on the street. I've always longed to hurl a suitcase out of the window in a fury and see clothes scattering across the pavement. I didn't get my chance with Ed.

Nancy is the one I'm more furious with. I want to kill her for betraying Nick and her children.

'Shh, he's coming,' Guy says, hunched low in his seat like me. We see Jack leaving the house with his bag of laundry and suitcase. He zaps a button to unlock his convertible, tosses the luggage into the boot and revs the engine. Guy and I turn to one another conspiratorially. I nod. 'OK, Agent Brown,' he says, turning the key in the ignition.

Guy's dilapidated white van struggles to keep up with Jack's fast BMW. I continue to tell him this is an insane idea, that we are no doubt heading for Bath and all we'll see is Jack entering his flat and then we'll have to drive all the way home again and what a waste of petrol! Besides, I question whether his old van will make it both ways.

'Looks are deceptive. This baby can go quite fast when she wants to.'

'We'll see.'

'You need to have more faith,' Guy says, before asking me to open the packet of snack-a-jacks and ramming his foot on the accelerator.

★

As we're driving down the M4, with only one car between Jack's and ours, I tell Guy that I've had a lovely day. 'Thank you for looking after me.'

'Any time,' he replies.

'The thing is,' I start apprehensively, 'when Flora comes back we won't be able to do this. I won't be able to turn up at your door like some mad woman in the middle of the night.' I smile. 'I'll have to find someone else.' Right now I can't stop thinking about how much I value being with Guy, alone, and how I can talk to him in a way that I could never talk to Jack, and not even Ed.

'I know,' he says quietly, as if he's been thinking about it too.

'Are you looking forward to seeing Flora?' I ask, dreading the answer.

'Yes,' he says in a tone that encourages me to say, 'But?'

'Well, just between us, there's this part of me that's also loved being on my own. I can order takeaways and watch episode after episode of *The Wire* with a curry on my lap. I can do exactly what I want at weekends, I'm not being dragged to some wedding where I don't even know the bride. I even enjoy the park now.'

'I love the park.'

'I love Trouble. In the past few months, she's become . . . well she's become *my* dog. I won't like Flora taking over again, being her mistress.' Guy glances over to me. 'And then there's you.'

'Me?' I shiver as I pull my cardigan sleeve over my hand.

'What you said earlier . . . you're right. We won't be able to do this.' He looks ahead, runs a hand through his hair. 'I'll miss it. I'll miss you.' He hits the steering wheel. 'What is it about cars? They're always a good place to chat, to tell people our secrets, aren't they? Stick two people in a car and send them off to Scotland and they're going to know each other pretty well by the end of the journey. Is it because there's no escape? You've got a captive audience?'

I nod. 'Partly, but I think cars are good places to talk because you're looking at the road. You're avoiding eye contact. It's the same with dog walking.'

'Dog walking?'

'Yes. Think about it. You can say whatever you like, true or false, and the person walking by your side will never know the difference because you're always looking ahead.' I turn away. 'Because the truth is in our eyes.'

'You don't talk much about Ed,' Guy says, as I unpack the sandwiches and glance at the map. We have one more junction to go.

'There's nothing to say.'

'Does it still hurt?'

'Yes, but if I'm honest, I think it was more the way he did it.' I reflect. 'It was a shock. It's hard to start over again, after a long relationship, but I know I'm not the only one. Maybe it was brave of him to pull out,' I say. 'Susie and Anna . . .'

'I really liked them by the way,' he cuts in.

'Good. Anyway, they said he was a coward, but it takes guts, just as it takes guts to walk out on a marriage. To leave behind children must be heartbreaking.' I look out of the window, thinking about Mum and how she could have done it to us. 'Sometimes the easy thing is to do nothing, like I did with Ed.' I confide to Guy that I think Ed and I became too comfortable, that perhaps our relationship had run its course. 'We went on holiday,' I tell him, 'and all Ed wanted to do was sleep by the pool and read his book.' We lost something, I know that now, I just didn't want to acknowledge it was over. When I think about it, Ed had to deal with the wrath of my family and friends for months. He'll always be blamed because he was the one that ended it, but Ed must have believed that we wouldn't make each other happy in the long run. Now I think he was right, and I am to blame too. I only wish both of us had figured it out sooner.

'Do you think it's just as easy to fall out of love with someone as it is to fall in love with them?' I ask Guy.

'Possibly. Love is a weird thing. It has no rules, no logic or reason. You can't explain it.'

'So back to the dating game,' I say with false cheer. 'Tell me your worst date.'

'My worst date . . . Christ, I've had quite a few. Oh,

I remember! It was with this woman who was pushy and overbearing, to put it mildly.' Guy indicates to move into the fast lane, only one hand on the steering wheel, the other holding his cold beef sandwich.

'Careful! Car . . .' I squeal.

'I know. I can see it.' He gestures to his rear-view mirror.

'OK. Sorry.'

Guy successfully manoeuvres his van into the fast lane.

'Watch your speed. Camera coming up.'

'I've got to keep up with him, Gilly.'

'Sorry. Back to your date.'

'She dragged me round all these nightclubs until finally I said I needed to get home. I had to pretend I had an early breakfast meeting, and do you know what she said?'

'Go on, tell me.'

'What time shall I set the alarm clock for?'

I laugh.

'Talk about presumptuous. I jumped into a cab and escaped. How about yours?' he asks me.

I slam a foot onto an imaginary brake and Guy looks at me crossly.

'Sorry.'

I tell Guy how I'd once gone out with a man who had talked about nothing but his Porsche. 'When I went to the loo I had this idea. As interested as I was on the subject of Porsches, I opened the window, climbed through and never went back into the restaurant.'

'Gilly, the poor man! You probably scarred him for life.'

'I doubt it.'

'What was Ed like by the way?'

'Nothing like you,' I reveal.

'What do you mean?'

'Quick!' I suddenly shout. 'He's going left. This is our junction!'

We follow Jack off the M4.

We turn left, swing right, sweep around another corner. 'GO!' I screech, and we fly through a red light. I'm impressed. I didn't think the old van had it in her.

We're at a junction, right behind Jack's car. I cower in my seat, convinced he's going to see us. 'Will you act cool?' Guy snaps.

'I've never acted cool in my entire life, Guy, so I'm hardly going to start now.'

'We're not doing anything wrong, you know,' he states.

'Yeah, right,' I say dismissively. 'We're just out on an evening drive.'

Jack's BMW ploughs up a steep hill and then finally parks outside a line of terraced houses.

Casually we drive past Jack's car and take the first right into a dead-end road. 'What now?' I whisper.

'We count to ten, go back and park on the opposite side.'

As we turn back into Jack's street, Jack is closing the boot to his car. We park on the opposite side and I daren't look over to him, just in case . . . Guy shakes my shoulder and I turn to see Jack standing with a woman in her sixties. She's fair like Jack, slender in build, wearing a striped apron. She hugs him. 'What's she saying?' I ask Guy.

'He lives at home,' Guy murmurs. 'He lives at home with his mum.'

I shake my head. 'He can't. He doesn't.' Jack had told me she lived in Eastbourne.

Carefully Guy winds down the window. 'Your dinner's in the oven,' we overhear her say. 'I've made your favourite shepherd's pie. How was your journey, dear?'

'No wonder he didn't want me to go home with him,' I say in shock.

'I always knew something was odd,' whispers Guy.

'But why would he still live at home? It doesn't make sense. He told me he . . .'

'Shush!'

We watch as a little girl in spotty pyjamas and pink slippers runs towards Jack. 'Daddy!' she cries out and he lifts her into his arms, strokes her hair and smothers her in kisses.

Guy and I turn to one another, and for the first time neither of us knows what to say.

Guy turns on the engine and Jack, sensing the noise, glances around the street, before stopping at our van. He stands on the edge of the pavement, looking at us, unsure at first, until we lock eyes. I stare at him and immediately he turns away. Jack's mother takes his suitcase and Jack carries his daughter back inside without as much as a brief glance over his shoulder.

Driving home, Guy and I attempt to work out the mystery behind Jack's daughter. Guy suspects Jack kept her a secret because he wanted to be Jack Baker in London, a producer, single and out to have a good time. However, at home in Bath, he was living with his mother and was either a single father or his daughter came to stay at weekends. Guy thinks Jack wanted to be black and white about the situation; there was no need for one life to overlap the other, no need to confuse the two, especially when he was only going to be living in London until Christmas. I was a distraction, a very pretty one, but after our few months together he would have brutally cut me out of his life and moved on to the next opportunity that arose.

'I think he manipulated last night,' I say, thinking out loud. 'He reckoned I was becoming too much of a nuisance butting into his private life, so he made sure to invite me to this awful party that he knew I'd hate and, just to make sure I got the message, he'd kiss Nancy too. That would get rid of me and my questions.'

Guy tells me I'm probably right.

We talk about the mother of his child. Where is she?

'Maybe this has something to do with what the brother said?' Guy suggests.

'All those lies he told me,' I say in disbelief, 'making out he was single and carefree and how he found the whole family thing boring. I don't understand. Why didn't Jack just tell me he had a daughter? Why keep her a secret?'

'Would you have fancied him quite as much if you had known that he'd lived at home, with his mother cooking him shepherd's pie, and that he had a child?'

I weigh this up. 'Probably. If he'd been honest right from the start.'

'Yeah, but would you have jumped into bed with him quite so quickly?'

'No. Oh, I don't know. I don't think we know the full story. He could still be married or separated . . .'

'He wanted to be Jack with no baggage . . .'

'We all have baggage.'

'Some worse than others.'

'If Jack had just told me,' I say again. 'I wonder why he didn't. The older we get, the more likely we are to meet people who've maybe been married or have children. So Jack has a child. So what! I still can't believe he lied about her. I admire people who raise children on their own. My father did.'

I go on to tell Guy about how my mother had walked out on our family when we were thirteen. Dad raised us and I have more respect and love for him than for any other man. He never remarried, but I think deep down he had loved our mother; I saw that love when Megan was born.

I tell Guy that I understand now that Mum had a breakdown. I believe her when she said she couldn't be our mother, that she had stopped functioning. She was like a car that had lost its engine. Nick hated her, couldn't forgive what she'd done, but with hindsight sometimes I wonder if Dad could have helped her more in those months following Megan's death. Instead he became increasingly irritated by her lack of direction. Dad wasn't able to give Mum reassurance, give her love and unconditional support, or help her seek medical help when she needed it most. Guy listens patiently.

'We did see Mum occasionally, but Dad sent us to boarding school at sixteen – it was easier for him to manage his work if we were away – then I went to university, so I hardly saw her. Each time I did, I found it harder and harder to talk to her. Then she moved to Australia when Nick's first child was born, over seven years ago.' A well of sadness overcomes me. 'I didn't tell Jack any of this,' I reflect. 'We never talked about anything, not properly anyway.'

'Of course you didn't. That would have been his goal, keep things light and simple. Easier to walk away from that.'

'I almost feel sorry for him,' I find myself saying. 'I know he behaved like an idiot, but having a daughter? It can't be easy for him.'

Guy parks outside No. 21. He turns off the engine and I unbuckle my belt.

'Let's face it, Gilly, he was just out to have a good time, wanted some freedom, time out from his domestic situation at home. I don't blame him either, though he should have told you the truth.' Guy turns to me. 'I just wish,' he takes my hand, 'that of all people he hadn't hurt you.'

I nod.

'Are you all right?'

I shrug.

'Come here,' he says, pulling me towards him. He holds me in his arms, and strokes my hair tenderly. When we part, I look into his eyes and before I have a chance to thank him for being my friend again today, he takes my face in both his hands and kisses me. I kiss him back, no questions running through my mind about whether it's right or wrong.

'Gilly,' he murmurs, 'I've wanted to do this for so long.'

Nothing tells me to stop . . . until Guy's mobile telephone rings.

I withdraw first, and reluctantly he answers it, without taking his eyes away from mine, a small smile surfacing on his lips. My heart is beating fast. I want to feel his arms around me again, his touch against my skin.

'Flora, hi! Right . . .'

I turn away, reality hitting me.

'Tomorrow?' Pause. 'No, of course I'm pleased.' He listens. 'No, that's good. I'm surprised, that's all.' I reach for the lock, open the passenger door. 'I'll be there,' he says, trying to wind up the call. 'We'll talk about it when you're home.'

'Good news?' I ask, opening the boot to let Ruskin out. I reach for my overnight bag.

'She's coming home, flies in tomorrow night.' He follows me to my front door. I struggle to unlock it, my hand shaking.

'Tomorrow?' I repeat. Inside No. 21 I drop my overnight bag on the chair, before numbly picking up my junk mail and flicking through it.

'Gilly?'

'That didn't happen. I won't say anything.'

'We need to talk.'

'You must be excited.'

'Gilly . . .'

'What did she say?'

'Um . . .'

'Tell me.'

'She said she wanted to hug Trouble and . . .' he pauses . . . 'marry me.'

The thud of disappointment and humiliation I felt when I saw Jack and Nancy together, followed by the revelation that Jack had a child, is nothing compared to what I am feeling now.

I was never in love with Jack; my feelings for him

barely scratched the surface. Guy is getting married. What's the fucking point? I want to scream.

'Right, I see.' I make myself busy by drawing the sitting-room curtains and turning on some lights, aware that Guy is watching my every move. I pick up my Playboy costume, strewn across the floor, throw it towards the banisters.

'Gilly, stop. Look at me.'

I can't look at him.

'Gilly . . .'

Guy follows me into the kitchen. I talk to Ruskin, let him out.

'Please. We need to talk.'

'Oh, Guy,' I burst out. 'We don't! What's the point? You're getting married!' I turn on the kettle, even though I don't want a drink. I open a few cupboards aimlessly.

He pushes his way in front of me. He stands so close to me, looks into my eyes again. 'I know we shouldn't,' he says calmly, 'but we need to talk about what just happened.'

I long to kiss him again, but . . . I push him away from me.

'We can't pretend that there's nothing going on between us,' he claims.

'We have to,' I say, my voice trembling. I compose myself. 'We had a moment, Guy. Flora's coming home, and you still love her, don't you?'

He's quiet. 'I don't know. Maybe . . .'

'You see. We have to forget it.'

'I can't. It wasn't just a kiss, it was more and you know it.'

I turn to face him now. 'You still love her and she's coming home. Where does that leave me?'

'All I know is I have feelings for you. Strong feelings.'

'It leaves me nowhere, Guy.' I move away from him, but he follows me.

'Look at me,' he's saying, grabbing my hand. 'Gilly, look at me!' Next he's holding me in his arms again, I let him, but . . . 'I can't get hurt again,' I say, pulling away. 'I can't, Guy!'

'Gilly, I'd never hurt you.'

I press my head into my hands. 'I think you should go.'

'I don't want to.'

'Guy.' I raise my voice. 'I can't do this. I can't. You need to leave me alone.'

'Gilly . . .'

'Please go!' I cry out now.

In the hallway, alone and in the darkness, I hear him drive off into the night.

He's gone. Tears run down my face.

I don't want to be upstairs in bed alone tonight. Instead I curl up on the sofa and Ruskin joins me, but it's hopeless. I can't sleep. I pick up the phone and call Mum. Please pick up, I plead, desperately needing to hear her voice. The dialling tone clicks into the answer machine. It's Patrick's voice saying, 'Elizabeth and Patrick can't get to the phone right now.' I slam the receiver back on its stand, without leaving a message. I daren't call Nick because Nancy will pick up first. I want to talk to Mum. I can see her cradling me in her arms, rocking me to sleep like a child when Ed left me. I don't think children ever grow out of needing their mums. I try her again, but still no answer.

'Gilly,' Gloria says, tying her dressing-gown cord around her as she lets Ruskin and me in. 'What is it? What's happened?' Thank God she's back.

I tell her about Jack first. Ruskin takes his usual spot by the fireplace.

'What a lying, bleeding scoundrel,' she says, handing me a second glass of brandy. 'I'm so sorry, Gilly. It's my fault. I encouraged you to see him, I was the one that . . .'

I glance at some estate agency brochures on her coffee table. 'You're not moving, are you?' I say, cutting her off.

'Gilly, I was only getting a valuation, I was curious to see what my house might sell for now.' She moves from her armchair to sit next to me, sensing my sadness.

'Gloria, don't go . . .'

'Gilly,' she says, 'if this is about Jack, he's not worth it, my darling.'

'I don't care about him.' I start to cry. 'You're all I've got,' I say, clinging onto her like a child.

'That's not true, you've got so many friends.'

'I miss my mum . . .' I swallow hard, thinking of Guy. I can't even begin to tell Gloria about Guy. Soon he'll be gone. Married and gone. 'You can't go,' I say, unable to let her go.

'This perky pensioner is not going anywhere,' she promises, stroking my hair, just as Mum used to do when I was little, until finally my sobbing subsides.

I feel a warm blanket being laid across me, and a glass of water is placed on my bedside table.

'You'll never get rid of me, Gilly,' I hear Gloria whisper as she kisses me goodnight on the cheek. 'Never.'

40

1990

Nick and I return home, tennis racket bags slung on our shoulders. We're thirteen now and it's half term. Mum enrolled us on a week's tennis course; Nick says it's to get us out of the house.

Dad is at the table, reading something, a frown on his face. I open the fridge to help myself to some orange juice. Nick reaches for crisps in the cupboard. 'Where's Mum?' he asks. I expect Dad to say she's upstairs resting. She spends most of her time asleep, or if she's not asleep she's smoking.

'Dad?' I sit down at the table. 'What's wrong?' I peer over his shoulder and see the letter is in Mum's handwriting. He shields the piece of paper from me.

'Dad?' I say.

'I'm so sorry,' he murmurs, looking up at me with

tears in his eyes. I know it's bad because Dad hardly ever cries. Mum accuses him of having a heart of stone. 'She's gone,' he says.

Dread overcomes me.

'Gone? Gone where?' Nick asks.

'She's left us.'

When Mum walks out on us, I cry myself to sleep. Dad doesn't show any emotion, nor does Nick, which makes me feel like the odd one out in the family. When I'm crying in bed Dad attempts to comfort me. He says we have to be strong, learn to live without her.

'Will she come back?' I sniffle.

'I don't know.' He takes my hand, rubs it. 'As you grow older, Gilly, you begin to realize that life doesn't always work out . . .' He stops, looks up to my book-shelf, 'as it does in fairy tales. I'm afraid people let you down. It's a hard truth, but they do.' Dad goes on to tell me never to doubt Mum's love for Nick or me; she didn't leave because she didn't care about us any more. No, she left because she couldn't be our mother.

'You won't leave us, will you Dad?'

'Never.' He hugs me. 'You're stuck with me forever.'

Over the next eighteen months we find our feet and slot into a routine. Nick and I take the bus to school, we return, make ourselves something to eat and do our home-work at the kitchen table. Dad returns at six o'clock, opens the drinks cabinet and pours himself a gin. Later he cooks us supper. Mum always used to cook, so we laugh watching him study the recipes with his black-rimmed glasses perched on the end of his big nose. I help chop and wash up. Nick is always on 'laying the table' duty. Sometimes we talk about Megan and Mum and how Mum used to love cooking fish pies with her classical music playing in the background. As I'd walk into the room, Megan would say, 'Hello, Gilly,' without even hearing my voice. She couldn't turn because she had no control in her neck, but she knew from the pattern of my footsteps. I remember Mum handing Megan some parsley, which she'd clutch with both podgy hands, pulling at it, rubbing it between her palms.

When Dad's in a good mood he allows Nick and me to stay up late to watch television, as long as we don't tell anyone at school. At the weekends we make ourselves a cooked breakfast with fried bread and poached eggs. That's my favourite meal.

Mum sends us postcards from different places around the world. She signs the cards with her love, but she doesn't say when she's coming home. Nick throws his cards in the bin. I keep mine, slotting them into my schoolbooks.

One evening, when Nick is laying the table for supper, and I am making us all a butterscotch Angel Delight pudding, I get the strangest feeling that Mum is about to come back. I can't explain it, but sometimes I see things unfolding before me. I know when the wind is about to change. When I tell Nick this he slams the cutlery against the table. 'She's more stupid than she thinks if she reckons she can just turn up and be our mum again,' he says.

'What are you arguing about now?' Dad calls.

'Nothing.' Nick stares at me with those dark, unforgiving eyes.

Dad turns to me, unconvinced. 'Come on,' he urges. 'If you're in trouble at school, I need to know. You can talk to me.'

The doorbell rings.

41

I keep my finger on the door buzzer until I hear an, 'All right! I'm coming!'

Finally Nancy lets me in.

'Are the children here?' I ask, storming into the hallway without taking my shoes off.

For the first time, Nancy doesn't make a point of it either. 'Look, Gilly,' she starts, catching me up, her tone as sweet as honey. 'I'm glad you're here, we need to talk.'

'The children?' I demand.

'They're out with friends. They've gone to . . .'

'Right now I don't care what they're doing, just as long as they're not here.'

Nancy follows me into the kitchen adorned with Christmas decorations and twinkling lights that mask their unhappy household. The television is on, advertising the quarterfinals of *Stargazer*.

'Coffee? Tea?' she asks, quickly turning the programme off.

My stare says I want neither, that I'm not here for a cosy chat. 'I know what you're going to say,' she prompts.

'No you don't. You have no idea.'

She touches my shoulder and I pull away. 'Gilly, it was only a little kiss,' she whispers. 'It meant nothing.'

'Oh! Well, that's all right then. Silly old me for getting upset!'

'Keep your voice down.' Nancy shuts the door. 'Nicholas will be home any minute.'

'Why did you do it?'

'I didn't mean to, it just happened.'

'Things don't just happen.' I sit down. 'Why did you do it? I don't understand.'

'Gilly, he's a player . . .'

'That's not the point . . .'

'He wasn't right for you, he's not the settling-down type at all.'

'Oh right, so now I should be *thanking* you?'

'Well, yes.' Nancy tucks a strand of hair behind an ear. She looks proud that she's managed to turn the argument upside down. 'He wasn't right for you,' she affirms.

'It's not about whether Jack is right or wrong for me, it's about being loyal. What about Nick?'

'Don't you dare mention it to him – he doesn't need to know.'

'Really? I think he needs to know you're unhappy because I know *he* is,' I say.

'Gilly don't, please don't . . .'

'Did you know Jack has a child?'

'What?'

'He has a little girl.'

Nancy opens her mouth, but nothing comes out.

'And he lives at home with his mum,' I continue.

Nancy swallows hard.

'Looks like he fooled us all, didn't he?'

'Gilly, please don't tell Nicholas,' she begs now.

'Why did you do it, Nancy?'

'I don't know. I was bored . . .'

'Bored?'

'I liked his attention . . .'

'I heard you that night, talking to Jack. You laughed at me.'

'I didn't, I . . .'

'Do you have any idea how it felt?'

'I didn't mean to hurt you.'

'If you had to throw yourself at some man, why Jack?' I protest.

'I didn't throw myself at him! It was the other way round! I'm sorry, Gilly, I know I shouldn't have kissed him . . . but . . . but I'm lonely!'

Nick enters the room. We didn't even hear him come in. 'Kissed who?' he asks.

★

'Nick, I'm so sorry. I didn't want you to find out, not like this,' I say.

'You kissed Jack?' he asks Nancy in shock.

She clutches his hand, guides him to the table. They sit down and he doesn't shake her hand away. How can he let her touch him? 'Darling, we all got a bit the worse for wear, it meant nothing,' she promises.

Nick shakes his head numbly.

Is that it? Is Nancy forgiven?

I cannot hang around listening to this. I'm off. However, just as I'm reaching the front door something inside me explodes and I find myself back in the kitchen facing them. 'Nick, I was so nervous about you finding out because I didn't want you of all people to get hurt, but come on!'

'Gilly,' Nancy says, 'that's enough. We're all upset, you're emotional and . . .'

'Fuck off!' I scream.

She steps away from me, startled.

'Nick!' I confront him. 'Are you not a tiny bit angry that your wife has kissed another man? And what about me? He was my boyfriend!'

I feel a hand against my back. Nancy is pushing me out of the kitchen.

'You are married to a dreadful cow! She doesn't care who she hurts to get her own way,' I yell as I'm being propelled out of the kitchen.

'That's not true! How dare you!' she shouts back.

I swing round. 'Believe me, I've wanted to say a lot worse for a long time. There isn't a single nice bone in your body, Nancy Cooper! You're cruel and selfish and Nick deserves better than you . . .'

'Get out!' She turns to Nick. 'I will not have her under my roof insulting me. You are never to . . .'

'Stop it!' Nick finally shouts at Nancy. 'How dare you speak to Gilly like that, after what you've done?'

Nancy turns from the door and bolts upstairs.

'I'm trapped,' Nick says quietly in the kitchen, when I ask him why he stays in a loveless marriage.

'No you're not,' I reply.

'Gilly, I have my girls,' he says. 'I can't walk out. I can't lose them.'

'But it's OK that they grow up with you two shouting at one another, both of you unhappy? They're only little now, but the longer this goes on . . . Children aren't stupid – we of all people know that.'

'Gilly, I have thought about leaving, but the alternative . . .'

'We have a choice in life.'

'Yeah, Mum chose to leave us. I don't want to make a bad choice.'

'It wasn't all bad, we got by.'

'It was terrible!' he says, tears in his eyes now. 'Gilly, you know it was.'

'It wasn't,' I say weakly. 'We were happy before Megan, before she . . .'

'I know, but afterwards? It was awful the way we had to creep around Dad, we couldn't talk about it. I never forgave Mum for doing it to us. I can't even think about leaving them. I have to protect them.'

'I know, but you're not happy,' I say again.

'I can't just get up and walk out on my children!' he says, raising his voice.

I understand. 'But it's not the same,' I say gently. 'I just feel the longer you stay with Nancy, the more I'm losing you.'

'You're not losing me. You could never lose me.' We clutch hands.

'I'm not asking you to choose between Nancy and me,' I continue, 'and I know the girls need you, but . . .'

'Gilly,' Nick cautions me, hearing the front door open.

The children run into the kitchen, both clutching a bag of crisps. 'Hi, Auntie Gilly!' Matilda says. 'Are you staying for tea?'

I shake my head and briefly kiss them goodbye.

'Daddy? What's wrong with Auntie Gilly?' Hannah asks perceptively, as she watches me leave.

'Nothing, poppet,' I hear him say, 'everything's fine.'

42

1990

Dad opens the front door and the colour in his face vanishes.

'Beth?' My father stands back.

Mum forces her way inside. 'Can I come in? Let me explain,' she says.

Nick catches her eye, runs upstairs to his bedroom, shuts his door and turns on his music loudly. I stare at Mum in shock. She reaches out to touch me, but I shudder and move away, sticking close to Dad's side. He takes my hand.

Mum looks better. Her eyes are no longer bloodshot; she's put on weight, her face is less gaunt, she's not dressed in a blue dressing gown and she doesn't smell of smoke.

'I don't expect you to have me back,' she starts.

Dad nods, careful what he says in front of me.

'I know I have no right to walk back into your lives, I let you down . . .'

'You let your children down,' Dad says sharply.

'Will! You have to understand.'

'Oh, I understand,' he vouches, his words fuelled by anger. 'You left us when the going got tough, you couldn't cope.'

'But . . . I need Gilly and Nick to understand.' Mum looks at me desperately. Dad then remembers I'm by his side. He releases my hand, tells me to go to my room. He needs to talk to my mother alone.

I walk upstairs, thinking I must be imagining this scene in my head. Mum can't be back, but when I glance over my shoulder there she is, standing in the doorway. Unlike Nick, I don't slam my bedroom door. Instead, I tiptoe out onto the landing and creep down the stairs. I listen to every word thrashed between them from behind the kitchen door.

'You could have got help,' Dad says reproachfully. 'We would have supported you.'

'You wouldn't talk to me about it! You acted as if nothing had happened.'

'Forget about me. What about Gilly and Nick? They were only *thirteen*,' he impresses upon her. 'You had two children who needed you.'

'Well I'm back now,' she says, her voice shaking, 'and I want to be in their lives.'

'You can't just walk away and then come back when you feel like it. Eighteen months you've been gone, without any clue as to when you were coming back.'

'I know, but . . .'

'You can't undo the past, Beth.'

'I can make up for it. I'm here now. I'm better.'

'I can't forgive and forget, I just can't.'

'Will, I had a breakdown.'

'I know,' Dad says with some understanding, 'but . . .'

'I was grieving. She was my little girl, my baby,' Mum can't help saying, taking more claim in the grief stakes.

'We were all grieving. This didn't just happen to you.'

Later that evening Dad talks gently to Nick and me. He hands us a piece of paper with Mum's temporary address and telephone number on it. He makes sure we understand that he has no wish for us not to see her. She's our mother. He will find her a new home, and this is where we have a choice. We can either live with him or with our mother, and he will support whichever road we choose.

Before I go to bed I knock on Nick's door. He's wearing his black and red leather boxing gloves that Dad gave him last Christmas and he's punishing his punchbag, sweat glistening on his forehead. 'Can I have a go?' I ask.

He stops, breathless, takes off the gloves and hands

330

them to me, but it's too late. I've already hit it. Again and again, and it's Nicholas now standing back in shock.

I wake up the following morning, my heart sore and my knuckles bruised and red.

43

'Oh, Gilly,' says Tanya, the receptionist at the gym, beckoning me to the desk. She's noticed I've been to the gym every day this week and we've struck up a warm friendship as she's swiped my membership card into her machine. 'There's a new course starting up at the weekends,' she informs me.

'Oh right? What is it?' I ask.

'Hi, Gilly,' he says. I turn round and there is Ed, standing by my side in his tracksuit. 'Can we talk?'

Tanya watches with interest, before asking if we can step aside to let a member get past.

Ed and I go upstairs to the small café. I recognize his familiar aftershave, and notice that his hair needs a cut. He never used to let it grow too long. When he hands me my glass of orange juice, he appears as nervous as I am.

'Congratulations,' I say. 'I hear you got married.'

'I handled it badly, didn't I?'

I nod.

'I didn't mean to hurt you,' he says.

He stirs a neat spoonful of sugar into his black coffee. 'And I'm sorry, so sorry. The thing is, Gilly . . .'

I wait.

'I had to stop it. I loved you,' he says quietly, aware of people listening, and I know what he is going to say next because I know the truth now too. 'But I don't think we were in love any more,' he finishes.

'Kick-boxing,' Tanya says, when I ask her again at the reception desk what the new course is. She hands me a leaflet with a timetable.

I smile. Me boxing? I don't think so. But then I think of Nancy and pop the leaflet in my gym bag, telling Tanya I'll think about it.

44

'Morning,' says Sam when I approach our doggy circle under the oak tree. Mari is easy to spot today because she's wearing a red coat with a peacock feather pinned into her dark hair. She looks like an exotic bird.

'Where have you been?' I don't confess that I'm nervous about bumping into Guy, which is why I haven't been to the park for three days. Instead I've been going to the gym and walking Ruskin at different times.

'Hatman's not here,' Mari says when she sees me scan the park briefly. I haven't seen Guy since Flora returned home.

'You look tired,' Sam observes. 'Are you sure you're OK?'

With relief I reveal the Jack story, piece by piece, and they cluster closely around me.

'Hang on, hang on. He kissed Nancy?' Mari gasps.

'The cheating rat,' declares Walter.

'Wait a minute, he has a daughter!' proclaims Sam.

'Stop! Don't go on without me!' says Ariel, racing over to our circle. Breathlessly he tips Pugsy out of the basket attached to his bicycle. 'What are you talking about?' he asks, terrified he's missed out on the gossip.

Briefly I tell Ariel the story, ending with the news that Jack lives with his mum.

'I don't fucking well believe it. I'm so sorry,' he says, hugging me. 'The bastard. All men are bastards,' he adds, 'that's why we have dogs. Pugsy will give you a kiss, come here Pugsy! You need to cheer up your Auntie Gilly.'

Ariel guides me to the bench and scoops up the oblivious Pugsy, who proceeds to snuffle and breathe heavily over me.

Mari lights a cigarette and pours herself some coffee from her silver flask, then offers some to me.

'Got anything stronger to go in that?' Ariel suggests to Mari, and I let out a snort of laughter. Soon we're all laughing. 'Oh God!' I sigh. 'Why is life so difficult!'

'A bit of brandy would be good,' says Walter, one step behind.

I rest my head against Ariel's shoulder. 'It's going to be all right, Gillykins,' he says, stroking my hair. 'You're a strong girl. How did you catch the bugger out?'

I tell them about Guy and how I'd spent the night with him following the Nancy and Jack kiss; that he was a shoulder for me to cry on. I tell them it was Guy who was determined to find out the truth about Jack. I describe how we'd watched his daughter running into his arms. When they repeat how awful Jack is, I find myself defending him in that he clearly loves his child and she loves her dad too. I know he did a terrible thing in concealing her from me, but I won't condemn him as an evil person.

'You're too nice, Gilly,' Mari ticks me off. 'Guy always told us he didn't quite trust him,' she adds.

'I think what Guy meant was that he wasn't good enough for you,' Ariel says.

'Thinking of Guy,' Walter starts, 'he was looking for you the other day, Gilly. I met Fiona too.'

'Flora,' Mari corrects him, tutting.

'That's right,' he nods. 'She told me they were planning to get married before Christmas. She wants a winter wedding.'

They all stare at Walter now.

Sam looks at me. 'Gilly?' she prompts, 'something else is wrong, isn't it? It's about Guy, right?'

Tears fill my eyes. Walter offers me a handkerchief from his rucksack.

'I'm fine, absolutely fine.'

Somehow I can't face telling them what happened. I'm ashamed that I kissed someone who is about to get married. I'm no better than Nancy, am I? I'm a terrible person.

'You're not fine. Tell us,' Ariel insists.

'Oh look, there he is,' Walter says, gesturing to Guy, at the far end of the field. He's walking towards us. I glance at my watch and hurriedly tell them I have to go. 'Wait!' Mari calls, gathering her things. 'I'll come with you. Wait, Gilly!'

45

I race to the tube station with Ruskin. 'What's the rush?' says Mari, struggling to keep up with me. Together we jump on the train and I breathe deeply when I take my seat, avoiding eye contact with Mari, who sits three seats down from me. I know I'm going to have to face him soon, but I'm not ready to hear about Flora and their winter wedding. Not yet. I can't imagine looking Flora in the eye either and not showing my guilt. Guy is right. I can't lie. I will meet Flora one of these days, so I need to be prepared. 'What's going on?' Mari mouths crossly, over passengers reading their morning papers. 'Not now,' I mouth back.

Along the Pimlico Road I grab my cappuccino and heated-up croissant from Manuel, and Mari and I make our way to the shop. 'I wish you'd just spit it out,' Mari says, unable to let it go.

★

Later on in the day, Mari's kneeling down on the floor, spectacles perched on her nose, examining some of the handwritten labels on our vases.

She glances my way, telling me we need to reprice some of the stock because she needs to shift this lot before going on a buying trip early next year. I agree. 'I could make a Christmas sale sign in the window too,' I tell her, thankful that I'm going to be kept busy today.

As I'm about to mount my beautiful 'For Sale' sign in the front window I see him. I drop the board and stagger back down onto the shop floor. 'I'm not here!' I say, squeezing past Mari and all the vases, heading for the stairs. 'Tell him I'm not here!'

'Why? Who is it?' Mari stares at me. 'Oh, it's not Guy, is it?' she says now, swinging round. 'This is ridiculous!'

'Just tell him,' I beseech, before crashing down the stairs.

'Mari, hi. How are you?' he asks, but before she answers he says, 'Is Gilly here?'

Ruskin barks.

'Hey, Ruskin! Gilly? Is she here?'

'Um. Sorry, Guy you've just missed her,' Mari replies.

'Oh. Really?'

I hear the rustle of paper.

'They're lovely. Beautiful flowers.'

'Mari, can I stay here until she gets back? I really need to talk to her.'

'I'm afraid she left for the day. She wasn't feeling great this morning.'

Well done, Mari, you're doing well.

'Left?' he persists.

'She went home.'

'Why didn't she take Ruskin then?'

'Did I say home?' She laughs falsely.

'Mari, you're talking rubbish. She just doesn't want to talk to me, does she?'

Silence. I hesitate. Come on, I tell myself. Talk to him. Get up and go upstairs. Talk to him. What do you think you're doing?

'I don't know what's going on between you two,' Mari finally says, 'but she doesn't want to see you right now, Hatman.'

'Fine. Fine,' he repeats impatiently. 'Tell Gilly that when she's ready to talk I'm around.'

I hear the tinkle of the door.

'I'm never going to do that for you again,' Mari berates me when I join her upstairs. 'I won't pay you until you tell me what's going on.'

'That's blackmail,' I smile ashamedly, knowing I shouldn't have made Mari lie for me.

'Call it what you like, nada money until you tell me.'

'Mari, can I take a week off?'

'Gilly, you're worrying me. Are you in trouble?'

'No. I just need to get away.' And then I tell her.

★

Later that night, I meet Anna and Susie for drinks. They both insist I need to talk to Guy, echoing Mari's advice too.

'OK, he's engaged,' Anna says carefully, 'but I always think you should tell people how you feel. I told Paul, and in the end he worked it out for himself. At least tell Guy how you feel. How do you feel?' she adds.

'Confused,' I say.

Susie tells me she's taking the children to Aldeburgh in Suffolk for five days to see her parents. She's sure they'd love to see me too. The house will be cold, she warns me, but there are some lovely fish-and-chip pubs and the sea air is always good for the mind and soul. 'Would you like to come with us?' she asks.

'Go,' Anna encourages me. 'Get out of London.'

46

Susie, the children, Ruskin and I go on long coastal walks, I read to my goddaughter, Rose, before bedtime and play cards with Susie's parents, Tom and Diane. They are an interesting, glamorous couple. Over supper they tell me about their old life in New York, and how Tom had set up a jewellery company on Manhattan Avenue. 'It was always my dream to live in America,' Tom said.

When both the children and the parents are in bed, Susie and I stay up chatting and drinking red wine until the early hours of the morning. I soak up her company; being with her is like basking in the sunshine. I also have some time to write. During the day I find a quiet space in the house and plot my novel in my head and make notes on each character. This is exactly what I needed, I tell Susie, thanking her for inviting me. Susie agrees with my sentiments and says, 'I love Mark, but it's good for me to get away too.'

The best thing about Aldeburgh, however, is that there is no reception, nor do Susie's parents own a television. So for a week my mobile is dead and I don't have to talk to anyone. Nor am I reminded of the approaching final of *Stargazer*, with all the accompanying adverts. Instead I have time to think. At night my thoughts are dark. I lie in bed and imagine being old and sitting in a rocking chair that overlooks the sea, reflecting on my life. I know I'd have regrets. I'd feel sorry that I didn't have a closer relationship with my mother. Nick and I chose to live with our father, we made a pact that we twins would always stay together, and Nick was determined not to forgive Mum, so my choice was made. I think about Guy and how I feel about him. I replay our kiss over and over in my mind. I know now I was never in love with Jack. Or Ed.

In the morning I'm brighter. I think about the more practical things, for example the list of things I need to do when I return home, starting with looking for another Monday to Friday man and the second, more important thing: writing. No excuses any more, Gilly. Susie's father followed his dream and lived in America. I need to do the same.

The third is to forget about Guy and our kiss because, as Gloria once said, there is no point wasting my time on someone engaged. But I will talk to him.

For a whole week I escape from London: the tubes, the crowds, even Ravenscourt Park, and enjoy the peace of the sea, the fresh air and the company.

It's only when I get back into my car and begin the long journey back to London that my mobile wakes up, telling me I have ten new messages. I'll deal with them when I get home, I promise myself.

My restful holiday abruptly comes to an end when I see him standing outside my front door.

'Where have you been?' he asks, helping me unload the car.

'Away.' I look at him, confused. I can't remember the last time he visited No. 21.

'Nick? What's wrong?'

'I needed to see you.'

'Come in. Are you all right?'

He follows Ruskin and me inside. 'I've had enough. I've left her,' he says.

As I make us a late-night snack of toast and peanut butter, Nick tells me how stupid he's been, how seduced he was by Nancy when they first met. 'She was so glamorous and I was flattered by her attention, but I don't think we ever really loved each other,' he says, hurt in his voice. 'Gilly, when I found out she'd kissed Jack, do you know what I felt?'

I shake my head.

'Nothing. I felt numb. I didn't care. I couldn't even focus on what she'd done to you. It was then that I knew I couldn't continue living a lie because that's what I'm doing, isn't it? I'm living a lie. I care that she's the mother of my children, I care so much that the children don't get hurt, but . . .' He shakes his head sadly. 'I'm scared to leave her, but if I don't . . .' He pauses. 'You were right . . . I deserve more, don't I?'

'Yes.'

'I'm going to need your support,' he declares, vulnerability in his eyes. 'I think I left a long time ago. I'm there, in the house . . . but . . .'

'You're not there? In the way Mum left us the moment Megan died.' I take his hand.

'I am doing the right thing, aren't I?'

I think about this. 'I don't think it's right being this unhappy.'

'I worry about leaving the children, what it's going to do to them. I'm abandoning them,' he says, tormented.

'No, you aren't. You're a wonderful dad,' I stress. 'Wonderful, and they won't lose you. You can't compare your situation to what happened to us. It's not the same, Nick.'

He curls his hand into a fist. 'I won't let them down, Gilly, I can't,' he swears to himself. 'I love them so much. I'm going to be there for them no matter what, just like Dad was there for us.'

'I know you will. I know you will. And Nancy?' I ask, dreading the answer. 'How is she taking it?'

He tells me that they've agreed to part amicably. To his surprise she's been quite gracious, admitting too that she hasn't been happy for some time. For all her faults and despite her loathing of Richmond, they've both agreed to stay in the neighbourhood to cause as little disruption for the children as possible.

'I'm sorry about Jack too,' Nick now says. 'Really sorry. Look at us,' he reflects.

I smile. 'What a pair we are.'

'But maybe, with Jack, it's good . . .'

'Good? What do you mean?'

'Good you found out sooner rather than later,' he explains. 'Being with the wrong person is even more lonely than being on your own.'

47

It's 6 December, Megan's anniversary. She would have been twenty-eight today.

I suffer déjà vu as I re-enter my spare-room details with a photograph of my sitting room, hoping to get a quick response. Over the past three months I've become used to having some extra rent money that helps not only towards my mortgage but occasionally allows me to buy new dresses too. I would still recommend anyone to rent out their spare room from Monday to Friday, not even the likes of Jack Baker has put me off. I press the REGISTER NOW button. As I log off, I smile, remembering the panic it had caused that very first time.

'Oh, Megan, let's hope I find a lovely straightforward person to live with me,' I say, picking up the small framed photograph of her on my writing desk. She's sitting in her special chair wearing a deep-red velvet pinafore dress with matching shoes. A chocolate cake is in front of her, lit with two candles, and her pretty brown hair is pinned back with two pale-pink clips. She was so beautiful.

The telephone rings. It's Anna, to say she's thinking of me today. She has to hang up abruptly because she's just seen a fox in her tiny garden.

Anna's wonderful the way she remembers Megan's anniversary, without fail, every year. I'm lucky to have such a good friend.

I smile, remembering Anna and I rushing home from school, deciding what we were going to sing to Megan that night.

'She loves our ballet stuff,' Anna said breathlessly, her satchel strap flung over her shoulder. 'We could do the wedding dance again!' For my tenth birthday Mum had taken us all to the ballet *Giselle*, and Megan had loved the costumes. During one act girls in pearl-white wedding dresses lit up the whole stage. They looked like sparkling jewels set against the deep-blue night sky. Even Nick held his breath.

'Or we could do the Bonny Tyler song, she likes that,' I said.

I think it was Bonny Tyler, I can't really remember now, but it was a terrible song anyway.

'Hi, Mum!' I called out as we dumped our lunch boxes and satchels in the hallway. We found Mum in the kitchen drinking tea, some spreadsheets in front of her and what looked like airline tickets. She whipped them away as she said hello to us. I crouched down next to Megan and took hold of her plump hand and she smiled at me, that lovely smile. 'Hello, Gilly,' she beamed. 'Look at my tights!' She was wearing navy tights with embroidered daisies. Megan always loved to choose her own clothes, indignant if Mum didn't match her tights with her dress. Anna bent down to join us, taking hold of the other hand, telling Megan she loved her outfit. When my school friends asked me if I wanted to go to their house to play with their new toys I'd always say no. I had Megan, with her long eyelashes that curled like half-moons, her plump cheeks that I loved to kiss and her large blue eyes that shone the moment I walked into the room.

Anna and I drew the curtains and dimmed the lights of the sitting room. Megan was in position, her chair close to the kitchen door. Through the narrow crack of the door I saw Mum at the table again, deep in concentration. 'Ready?' Anna said, standing poised by the music machine after a number of false starts. She pressed 'play'. Megan's laugh filled the room.

I smile at my desk, singing the song, 'Total Eclipse of the Heart', picturing Anna and I cavorting across the sitting room with hairbrushes as microphones, belting out the words. Sometimes Megan would sing and hum along to the tune, especially if it was one she knew well. If we were brave, Anna and I would attempt a descant. At the end of our song Mum would call out from the kitchen, 'Very good!' Sometimes she'd even clap.

*

Later that day Dad, Nick and I walk up Primrose Hill. We visit Megan's church in the evening and we all light a candle for her. I think about Guy, remembering him doing this for her too, and feel a deep ache for him. I hate myself for missing him. I've thought about returning his calls, but each time I picture him with Flora, busy organizing their wedding plans, I shut down and decide to ring him the next day.

Over supper, I ask them both if they think about Megan, as I do. Dad nods and smiles when I tell him how I remember her, but he doesn't give away his own memories. Nick says it's strange how I can remember everything so clearly; it's all a blur to him, but perhaps that's because he chose to forget our past.

I find myself telling them about Guy.

'I really liked him,' says Nick, 'a lot more than Jack.'

I tell them that while I was away in Suffolk I found myself thinking about him, but it's hopeless, isn't it?

'I don't know,' says Nicholas. 'Is it? Is he really going to marry Flora?'

Yes, of course he is. While I know he has strong feelings for me, he can't switch his love off for Flora as easily as you turn a tap on and off. Guy can't leave Flora and I will not be the person who breaks up a happy relationship, only for Guy to realize months later that he's made a mistake and resents me. I have accepted those months with him as a gift, a period that can never be repeated. We stretched our time to the limit, to the very last hour, and I won't forget his friendship. But right now I think it's best to keep my distance for all our sakes: for me, Flora and Guy. 'Dad? I'm doing the right thing, aren't I?' He's not with me. I'm not sure he's even listened.

'Dad?'

He looks at me. 'I'm sorry, it's just today,' he says.

'What?'

'Talk to us,' Nick urges.

'You know I'm useless at talking, always have been. I don't know what's wrong with me.' He knocks his heart, as if it's made of metal. 'There's nothing in here. It was twenty-five years ago she died, twenty-five years and you'd think it would get easier, wouldn't you! I don't know, I just don't feel anything any more.' Nicholas and I look at one another as Dad presses his head into his hands. 'On a day like today I can't even cry. I rattle around in this house, alone, and I know I've been a bad father to you both, and . . .'

Nick pushes his plate aside. 'No you haven't. You've always stood by us, Dad.'

I reach for his hand and he grips mine tightly. He reaches across to take Nick's too. 'It's why your mother walked out on us.'

'No it's not,' I say, though I know this is partly true.

'It's my fault.'

'Shush,' I beg. 'Just let it out, Dad. Please.'

'I loved her. It's my fault,' he cries into my shoulder.

48

After the weekend of Megan's anniversary, I walk to
Ravenscourt Park, ready to meet Guy this time. I look
across the field, to my circle of dog-walking friends. I
see Basil running furiously for his ball and Spike trying
to mount Hardy, Walter pulling him away in disgust.
Sam's on her mobile, probably talking to her husband
. . . Ariel is wearing what looks like a new pair of skinny
jeans and drinking a cup of coffee, Pugsy by his side. But
Guy? He's not there. 'Where have you been?' Ariel asks,
as if I should have sought his permission to leave the park
and London.

'Aldeburgh.'

Sam and Ariel tell me Guy's been in the park every
morning asking where I was.

'I will talk to him,' I promise. I then go on to ask Mari
if I can continue working in her shop next year. I want
to carry on writing my novel, something I should have

done a long time ago. I need a job, which gives me time to follow my dream.

'I'd love you to stay on,' Mari smiles.

I tell them I'm also looking for another Monday to Friday lodger to supplement my income so I can write.

'Good on you, girl,' Ariel says. 'Looks like you've got it all worked out.'

I also break the news that Nick is divorcing Nancy, which sends ripples of shock around the group.

'Those poor children,' Mari reflects, but I reassure them both parents are working hard to protect them.

'Well, they do say 50 per cent of couples get divorced these days, or is it 75 per cent now?' Walter muses, always knowing how to lift our spirits.

Later that evening, I turn on my computer to see if I've had any responses on the Monday to Friday site. As my laptop whirrs into action, someone knocks at the door.

'Any responses yet?' Nick asks me. He's come over for supper. I'm going to cook us my famous spaghetti bolognese. At the moment he's living in a hotel, attempting to sort out a generous maintenance settlement for Nancy. Gloria is also going to join us tonight, once she's finished waxing her legs and slapping a face mask on.

'Just one,' I reply.

'Yes?'

'It was weird.'

'Weird?'

'He said, "I like the sound of No. 21. Whoever lives there, I want to meet her." '

Nick smiles. 'Who's it from?'

'Mr Cox. I'm going to ignore it.'

'Why? It's rather nice!'

'Oh come on! It's weird. What's wrong with a simple, 'I would like to view your spare room, please?'

'God, Gilly, you can be so conservative sometimes. Just like our father,' he adds.

Over supper I notice Nick's smile surfacing again. No one talks over him or puts him down at the kitchen table. Instead, Gloria listens attentively as he talks about his work and his family. The children don't fully understand about the divorce – they are too young to realize why their parents no longer live together. Nick knows he is going to have to deal with the 'Why don't you come home?' questions each time he picks them up at the weekends. He dreads seeing the disappointment in their eyes when he leaves them at the front door with Nancy.

When Nick and Gloria have left, I play with Ruskin, then just before going to bed glance at my computer in the hopes that I've had some further responses to No. 21. Gloria agreed with me that Mr Cox did indeed sound a bit strange. 'You don't want to put all your apples in one basket,' she'd laughed.

No more enquiries.

Reluctantly, wanting to prove to my brother that I am not conservative, I write back to Mr Cox, telling him that he can view the spare room tomorrow evening.

49

When I return from work the following day, I turn on my computer in the vain hope that I have had some further Monday to Friday enquiries. As my screen lights up, the telephone rings. No doubt that's Mr Cox telling me he's either cancelling or running late.

'Hello?' Pause. 'Oh, Mum, hi!' Mum tells me she's spoken to our father about Nick's divorce and that she's planning a trip home, and I am surprised by how happy that makes me feel.

As we talk on the telephone, my computer makes encouraging noises.

Your house in Hammersmith has had 12 VISITORS and 1 ENQUIRY.

I click on the enquiry box. To my amazement, it's from Jack.

Anxious to read his message, I ask Mum if I can call her back after my Monday to Friday viewing.

Jack tells me his little girl is called Vanessa. She means the world to him, 'But I wasn't ready to settle down again,' he writes.

That's arrogant, I think to myself, him presuming that I wanted to 'settle down' with him. I was only asking him to stay the odd weekend.

'I've made so many mistakes in the past, Gilly,' he continues, 'like getting married too young and having a kid. I love Nessa but I can't even begin to think about committing myself until I've sorted out my own situation, and what with you being thirty-five . . .'

I knew my age was a problem! Bloody Jack Baker . . .

'I understand your time is running out, so it wouldn't have been fair to pretend or lead you on as I'm sure you'd agree. I live temporarily at home with my parents because my ex lives in our old apartment near Bristol. I see my daughter pretty much every weekend, which is why I need to get my act together and buy my own place. I need to work hard, not think about diving into another serious relationship.'

All you need to do is say sorry for lying, Jack, I think, as I read on reluctantly. Just say sorry for being an idiot.

'We had great fun, Gilly. I loved being with you, but if you're honest with yourself, you didn't love me.'

I pay more attention now, scrolling quickly down the page. 'I saw the way you looked at him at your birthday party. He looked at you in the same way. I'm not just saying that to excuse my behaviour, I shouldn't have kissed Nancy (though to be fair she came onto me first).'

Oh, the arrogance of this man!

Ruskin nudges my foot, reminding me it's his supper-time. I glance at my watch. Shit! It's 6.45 and I arranged the viewing with Mr Cox for seven and I haven't even tidied up the spare room! I bolt upstairs, check that every-thing is in order, run a brush through my hair, wonder whether to put some make-up on, but then decide not to as I can't really be bothered. I want to finish reading Jack's email.

I scoop Ruskin's meat into his bowl, along with his dried biscuit, and place his meal on the floor by the tele-vision as he likes TV suppers. I then rush back to my computer.

'I'm sorry for being a jerk,' Jack apologizes finally, 'but I hope that maybe, one of these days, I can take you out dancing again. Good luck, Gilly. Love Jack.'

There's a loud knock on the door that makes me jump. Ruskin barks so furiously that anyone would think he was a Rottweiler.

I look through the peephole to make sure that the person has shut the gate. I can't make out what Mr Cox looks like as his back is turned. 'Can you shut the gate?' I call out. 'Dog here!'

I hear the clang of the iron and the latch locking.

Then I open the door.

★

'Can I come in?' he asks.

'No, I mean, it's not a good time. I'm waiting for someone. My Monday to Friday man.'

'Mr Cox?'

'Yes, Mr Cox,' I repeat tentatively, wondering how he knows.

He stands on the doorstep staring at me.

'Can I come in?' he asks again.

'It's really not a good time. Listen, I promise to call you . . .'

'I am Mr Cox!'

'No you're not,' I say helplessly. 'You're Guy. Why are you pretending to be Mr Cox?'

'Gilly. I'm Guy Cox. Mr Cox. I'm your Monday to Friday man.'

'No you're not. You don't need a spare room.'

Guy pushes his way inside. 'I'm going mad,' he says.

'That's not my fault.'

'Yes it is. You won't see me, won't answer my calls, and I know you were at work the other day when I met Mari. You were hiding downstairs, weren't you?'

I nearly smile at that. 'We need some time apart. You can't blame me for that.'

'We don't need time apart, that's just stupid.'

'Why are you here, Guy? Does Flora know?'

'We need to talk.'

'OK,' I agree finally. 'Talk.'

He's standing so close to me that I take a couple of

steps backwards. 'Gilly, I had to see you,' he explains. 'I knew if I'd called again, you'd have either ignored my message or told me we couldn't meet. This was the only way. I was on the computer, just happened to look at the Monday to Friday site because I was thinking of you and . . . Oh God, I haven't been able to stop thinking about you . . . not since that night.'

'I'm sorry for avoiding you,' I say, 'but I've had a lot to think about too.'

'And?' he asks hopefully.

'I've missed you, really missed you. But the thing about you and me Guy is we can't be friends, it's not going to work. It's just not going to work. I think it's best we leave it, for now anyway.'

'Leave it?'

'Yes. I think that's best.'

'But what if I can't leave it?'

'You have to.'

'So you're not going to listen to what I have to say?'

'What's the point, Guy?'

He heads for the front door. 'I'm sick of this. You know what, I've done everything I can to show you how I feel, but you've done everything you can to run away from me! I came here to tell you something important, but if you're not even prepared to listen. You're right – what's the fucking point? Fine. Let's leave it.' He opens the door, is about to go . . .

I swing round to face him. 'Guy . . . wait!'

One hand on the door handle he stops and turns to me expectantly.

'It's complicated,' I say.

'No, it's not. You're just scared to say how you feel so you're hiding from me. You're running away.'

'I'm not running away!' I retort. 'I'm protecting myself! In case you hadn't realized, you're getting married, and I should never have kissed you!'

He grabs my hand. His firmness takes me by surprise. He guides me back to the sofa. Ruskin jumps onto my lap territorially, watching Guy's every move.

'Just listen to me, OK?' he demands.

This time I nod, obediently.

'What I've been trying to tell you all this time is that it's over. When Flora came home I knew it was wrong, all wrong. I should have been happier, not thinking about someone else. We'd been together for all these years,' he continues, 'and I'd slipped into proposing, thinking it was the right thing to do after so much time, but when I picked her up from the airport . . . when she was home . . . all I could think about was you . . . and that kiss . . . and . . . I need to know, do you love me? Gilly?'

I see Guy giving me my writing book, he and I walking circuit after circuit in the park with Ruskin and Trouble, sharing coffees and parting at the zebra crossing, Guy turning left, me turning right . . .

'Gilly?' he pushes again. 'If you don't feel the same way, I'll leave right now.'

I think of the way he'd talked to Megan in our church; how he gave me his precious hat for my birthday; our shopping trip for his wedding suit; laughing in the Playboy shop; going for long evening drives.

'I know you do,' he says, 'but you're scared of losing another person you love, aren't you? Well, I won't leave you. I'm here to stay.'

I remember Guy telling me he loves my honesty and that I am unlike any other girl he knows. I love the way his eyes light up when he talks about his work, the way he listened to me crying on his doorstep late at night and stood up for me at Nancy's. His hand reaching down to pull me up from the ice . . .

'Gilly, please say something,' he begs. 'I need to know how you . . .'

'Mr Cox, will you just shut up,' I say, wrapping my arms around him, 'and kiss me.'

Guy and I are curled up on the sofa together. 'Flora and I, we both pulled out. We felt exactly the same way. I should have guessed by her initial reaction. I mean, who runs off the moment their boyfriend proposes?' He smiles sadly.

I stroke his arm, he clutches my hand again, kisses it.

'We're determined to be friends. I still care about her. We just realized deep down we had grown apart. We didn't want to make the mistake of marrying because we felt we should.'

'I'm sorry I didn't give you the chance to say any of this, that you had to pretend to be a Monday to Friday man.'

'I know. It was either this or climbing that tree in the park, ready to jump down when you and Ruskin arrived . . . but I hate heights.'

I smile. 'Sometimes, when things turn out badly in your life Guy, you don't have the faith that anything's going to change, but . . .'

'But?'

'I should have had more faith in you.'

'Do you want to hear the line I rehearsed as I walked over to yours?'

I nod.

'I don't want to be your Monday to Friday man. I want to be your every day of the week man.'

I turn to him and hit his chest gently. 'That's terrible,' I say. 'Shocking. Worrying, in fact. But I still love you.'

50

A year later

'Here it is,' I say to Guy, as we drive into a small square in Beaminster. Guy and I have decided finally that we want to move out of London. He can work in the country and I can continue to write from home. I told Guy I wanted to move to the West Country, and after months of researching the countryside and house-hunting, he agreed that he also loved the ruggedness of Dorset and we have just put in an offer for a small house in Cattistock. Cattistock is a larger village than most, with a lot more going on than just a post office and a church. The countryside is stunning and, if our offer is accepted, I will have a view from the kitchen of rolling hills, horses, sheep and, from here, not another house in sight. When Guy and I had lunch in the local pub the landlord mentioned it was a young place with families and children and many divorced and singletons here too, reinventing their lives. 'We're just as social as London,' he'd claimed proudly. 'And what's more, Tesco's deliver here.' He asked us what we young folk did and I was proud to say I was a writer.

My novel was accepted by a literary agent who secured a two-book deal with a top UK publisher. My father and Nick, along with my mother, who had flown in from Australia to be with us for three weeks, took me to the Ritz for tea. A year ago I wouldn't have dreamt I'd be in this position. I thought I'd be on the scrap heap. More importantly, as Mum, Dad, Nick and I talked over tea I had to pinch myself – I never believed we could sit around a table again, as a family, and celebrate.

It took a while for me to believe in myself, and to start writing, but I did. This last year, I have felt so happy working in Mari's shop and writing in the evenings, or during my lunch hours. 'When you feel stuck in a rut, you need to change one thing,' Richard had said. 'Life can be like a padlock refusing to open. One little change in the combination can finally open the door.'

I'm glad I met Richard again. It was lucky that Dad knew his father. It was the best advice he could have given me – to stay in London and advertise for a lodger. I have no regrets about Jack Baker, despite what happened. He did do me a favour in that he brought me out of my shell back into life, and, besides, if I hadn't met him, I wouldn't have rushed to Guy's that night he kissed Nancy;

we wouldn't have followed him back home; we wouldn't have kissed. I wouldn't be here now.

I look over at Guy. I think I fell in love with him the moment he gave me the leather book, I was just too stupid to see it. 'Maybe this is your something,' he'd written, giving me a chance to change my life.

Guy parks and I tell him there are no meters or traffic wardens.

We enter the estate agents, now called Butler & Sampson. Today it's busier, with many clients sitting at desks being shown houses on flash computer screens. The office has been modernized, with a plush carpet, fancy lighting and updated furniture. A plump blonde receptionist with spectacles perched on her nose asks if she can help us. I tell her I'm looking for Richard Hunter.

'Richard left well over a year ago.' She tells me she's sure someone else could look after us. Why don't we take a seat? She offers us both a cappuccino, which makes me smile.

I ask her if she has Richard's contact details. 'Do you know where he works now?'

'We don't normally hand out addresses I'm afraid,' she states.

'I know, but it's really important I see him.'

She looks at me curiously.

'He's a very old family friend, but we've slightly lost touch,' I improvise. 'My father's his godfather, and . . . look, I've driven all the way from London to see him.'

She taps her keyboard and scribbles his address onto a card.

Guy and I drive down one small winding road after another until we find ourselves in a village called Cerne Abbas. There's no parking space on the main road, so Guy drops me off outside a delicatessen.

When I open the door a bell tinkles and I breathe in the smell of warm fresh bread, Tuscan salami, pâtés and roasted peppers soaked in olive oil. There are small tables covered in bright red tablecloths.

'Hello, what can I get for you?' he asks. He's wearing a navy-checked apron and I notice that he's lost weight. He looks happier and healthier.

'Richard,' I say, 'it's Gilly.'

He looks at me, a flicker of recognition in his eyes.

I give him a clue. 'Gilly with a G.'

He smiles, slapping his thigh in recognition. 'Gilly Brown! Of course it's you! How did you find me here?'

'I went back to your old office. I see you left?'

He nods. 'As you wisely noticed, I wasn't a very good estate agent.'

'Terrible.'

'Jaded,' he corrects me. 'You made me see that. I needed a change.' He shakes his head. 'I can't believe you're here. I've often thought about you.'

'Me too. You should come to London, visit Dad,' I suggest. 'He'd love to see you.'

'I'd like that. So, what's your news?'

'Well, I've put in an offer for a house in Cattistock and you can't put me off this time.'

'I wouldn't dream of it.'

'And you?' I gesture to the shop. 'This is great.'

He smiles proudly. It looks as if Richard found his something too.

'I wanted to thank you,' I go on to say.

'Thank me? Why?'

'You were right about me not moving out of London back then. I took your advice and started living again.'

'Great. You see, I'm not totally useless,' he adds.

'I found a lodger.'

'How did it go?'

'It was good . . .' I pause, 'on the whole. Interesting.'

Though I'd thought about Jack very occasionally, at times when I was watching *The Tudors* or the radio had played one of the songs we'd sung during our drunken karaoke night, I hadn't heard from him since Guy and I saw him that night at his mother's house. Yet, out of the blue, just last week, he sent me some *Stargazer* tickets. 'Take Guy,' he'd written, with a picture of a happy face, 'as I know how much he loves the show.'

'He was Monday to Friday,' I say, smiling at the note.

'Monday to Friday? What's that all about?' Richard asks as the doorbell tinkles.

'Well that's an excellent question.'

'Hang on,' he mimes, returning to his post behind the counter.

'Oh, don't worry about them, they're with me. 'You remember Ruskin?'

'Thanks for introducing the dog before me,' Guy says.

I laugh as Richard whips round from behind the counter to greet Ruskin. 'I don't really allow dogs in the shop,' he says, 'but seeing as this one's yours . . .'

Richard glances over to the man by my side.

I introduce them. Guy tells Richard we met dog walking.

'I'm her every day of the week man,' he says. Guy was threatening to say that all morning in the car. 'You were lucky enough to get away with it once, don't say it again,' I'd said.

Richard looks bemused.

I hold out my left hand. 'Guy's my fiancé,' I say proudly.

51

Our offer for the house in Cattistock is accepted. Guy and I are finally moving into the depths of the country-side tomorrow. We are frantically finishing packing, organizing delivery vans, sending out change-of-address cards and tying up loose ends in London. I have said tearful goodbyes to Nick, who's now dating a woman called Amanda, who also has two children, to Matilda and Hannah, my father, to dear Gloria, and of course to Susie and Anna. I even said goodbye to Nancy, who, to my amazement is working now, discovering that being a shop girl isn't quite so bad after all. There is just one final goodbye I need to say.

'You take care of her, Hatman,' demands Mari, followed by a piercing, '*Basil!* Over here now! Say goodbye to Ruskin!'

'Come back and see us every now and then, won't you?' Walter says to both Guy and me. 'Especially you, Gilly. No offence, Guy,' he adds plainly, 'but I've known this girl for five years.'

'It won't be the same without you both,' Sam says, before turning to me. 'Don't forget us.'

'Never mind about Gilly, we'll miss Ruskin,' Ariel finishes, before giving me a huge hug.

'Come and stay any time,' I tell them. 'Promise me. Bring the dogs.'

'Take her away Guy, before she gets too emotional,' orders Mari, her own voice weakening. She reaches into her handbag to find her cigarettes.

'It's been fun,' says Guy to our friends. 'Thank you so much for allowing me into your circle.'

Guy guides me away but quickly I run back, hugging them in turn tightly. 'I'll miss you,' I say.

As Guy and I walk home with Ruskin, I confide that I doubt very much they will come and stay with us. That's the strange thing about dog-walking friendships. However strong they are, they exist only under the shade of the oak tree.

'Except for us,' Guy points out.

'Except for us,' I say.

Someone else will come along soon enough though, with his or her puppy, and take my place within the circle. That doesn't mean I will forget them. I shall always treasure my mornings in Ravenscourt Park.

Guy and I reach the zebra crossing.

We both turn right.

52

Two years later

'If you could sign here,' I overhear our postman Nigel saying to Guy, before he asks if it's my birthday. Ruskin is barking furiously at Nigel, as he does every day when he pushes open our front gate, carrying his bright red mailbag over one broad shoulder. Guy ticks off Ruskin, before shouting 'Gilly! It's here!'

'Coming!' I call from the bathroom, staring at the results. We've been trying for so long, so long. I turn on the tap, pour myself a drink of water, hand trembling, and take a deep breath before heading downstairs.

'Gilly!' Guy says impatiently again.

But I can't help it. I rush back to the bathroom and look at it again, just to make sure.

Downstairs, I thank Nigel as he leaves. 'No bills today, Mrs C,' he says, heading towards the gate. 'Don't those raspberries look wonderful,' he adds, gesturing to our fruit cage.

Guy lifts the big brown box into the hallway. 'Where?' he demands.

'Kitchen! Quick!'

Guy passes me the scissors and a small knife, like an assistant at an operating table I cut through the brown tape and rip open the box. I lift out one of the books.

It's perfect. I hold it in my arms like a child. *Mickey the Magic Monkey*. The cover is an illustration of Mickey flying on his magic carpet, a young girl sitting by his side. This is my second book, but it's just as exciting seeing it in print as my first. In many ways this book is more special.

I open the first page, dedicated to Megan Florence Brown. There is a small photograph of her sitting in her chair, dressed in her red velvet pinafore. Her memory will live on in this book.

'What have you been doing?' Guy asks again curiously. 'I was calling you for ages.'

I start to cry. Silly really, but I can't stop.

'Gilly?' he prompts. 'What is it? The book looks great! What's wrong?'

I turn to him, clutching his hand. 'I've just done a test.'

'Oh.' His grip tightens.

'I've just done a test,' I repeat with a smile, nodding encouragingly.

'Oh,' he says, and it's a very different sounding 'oh' this time.

He looks at me, tears now in his eyes, but still he hardly dares ask the question.

So I answer it for him.

Acknowledgements

Firstly, I'd like to thank Jane Wood and Jenny Ellis at Quercus. I have greatly valued your editorial input and enthusiasm, and look forward very much to continuing working with you.

Thanks also to Diana Beaumont. Diana was the first person to read *Monday to Friday Man* in its early stages and she really helped me shape the script. Thank you, D, for all your hard work and the support you have given me.

There are a few friends I'd like to thank for helping me with the research: Rebecca, for her insight into the television world, and Kim Whatmore for describing her landscape gardening work. Anna Callaghan: like Gloria in the novel, Anna is the best neighbour in town. Janet and her son Adam Cartlidge, whom I met in France, in Lourdes; Adam is a lovely writer and he sent me a poem largely based on my short story, 'Mickey the Magic

Monkey'. I shall always remember meeting you, Adam, keep well and carry on writing.

To Bernice Crockford, for being so open about losing her daughter, Alice. Bernice is an old family friend, and one of the most golden people I know. Bernice and her husband, Zek, are an example of how the toughest of times can bring people even closer together. I admire and love you both very much.

Thanks to Judy Niner, the managing director at www.mondaytofriday.com – a business that allows home-owners to advertise renting their spare rooms during the working week. 'Monday to Friday' is a great scheme, which has provided the inspiration for my novel and the title. May I just add that in the past I have rented my spare room out from Monday to Friday, but my lodgers have been professional and very straightforward – nothing like Jack Baker in this novel! I'm not sure whether I'm happy or sad about this . . .

To my dog-walking friends! To Nella, for her stories about the antiques world. To Tim, for inspiring Guy's dress sense, particularly the hats. To John, for being John. To all my dog-walking friends, old and new: Caroline, Ashley, Connor, Duncan, Emma, Gareth, Janine, Tamar, Dons, Kaethe and Susan . . . thank you for our many lovely walks with coffees in Ravenscourt Park. But most of all to my handsome Darcy, my Lucas Terrier, who gave me the idea to write about park life in the first place.

To Mum and Dad, for always being there, and for all the love and support you give me.

Finally, I'd like to thank Charlotte Robertson, my agent at Aitken Alexander Associates. I find writing tough and lonely at times, but Charlotte has renewed my confidence in my work and in myself. Thank you, Charlotte, so much, for falling in love with *Monday to Friday Man*, and for never lacking the faith that we'd see it in print. I couldn't have done it without you.